Tombstoning

All Things are Connected—Tread Carefully

P G Robertson

Contents

My little sister Julene's love of the Northern Rivers coast was intense. It seems fitting to dedicate this book to her memory.

Prologue

It is surprising how clearly sound travels across water, especially when the sound is that of a woman screaming, even more so when those screams, travelling across water as they were, happened in the early hours of the morning.

This wailing, desperate and chilling, rudely interrupted the slumbering coastal village, yet another depressing discord following the cruel and damaging weather of the past twenty-four hours. Countryfolk at heart, curious nearby residents tumbled from their homes, lights popping on as they rubbed their sleep-laden eyes, hastily struggling to pull on jackets still wet from the disgusting day just passed.

There were no busybodies or stickybeaks in this macabre procession. They were a close-knit community and someone needed help. It was obviously a woman, the screamer, at least going by the pitch of the spine-tingling howls. Something momentous was happening, and the small community rallied in support. This was no case of a missing family pet. This was bad.

There was little they could do, in reality. A most dreadful scene greeted the impromptu gathering, probably the worst sight that anyone would ever recall. Someone called 000, asking for the police; 'there's an emergency over at the marina—looks like Dave Fletcher has committed suicide'. On reflection, this call was an exercise in futility. There was nothing that the police could ever do to restore equilibrium, certainly not for the woman screaming her mournful siren of tragedy.

There, strung off the rigging, a man dangled in the shadowy light amongst some fishing nets, as if sending a message about the source of his torment. Nobody ever forgets coming face-to-face with their first dead person.

As in most situations on this complicated planet, there would be winners and losers. The fish would be among the winners for sure, free to swim around in their ocean a while longer. Perhaps some environmental warriors would be secretly pleased that their precious planet was a little safer, for a few weeks at least. Recreational anglers might consider this a win, believing that commercial pirates were the source of their own consistent failures.

Weekend tourists, on the other hand, would be losers, forced to forgo their taste of the ocean after a happy day at the beach. They would be disappointed, perhaps even angry, to find their visit to paradise less than perfection. After all, few things were more important than seaside fish and chips' convenience.

Friends and family would wonder how this tragic loss could have happened. Were they themselves to blame? What could they have done? That's what happens in small communities. Everyone suffers. There would be much sorrow, as well as gnashing of teeth; no doubt recriminations would follow. It would change things, that was for certain, but this soul-searching would not bring back the dead man. Death was like that—permanent.

Chief amongst losers was the wailing woman. She would come to realise, in that part of her heart that wasn't grieving, that something stunk about this situation, and the smell wasn't being caused by dead fish.

Chapter 1

Ange

One Thursday, whilst Detective Ange Watson was stuck in a rut, caught in the mid-afternoon doldrums of administration, her boss, Sergeant Jim Grady, came by her desk.

'Ange. A missing person case has come our way. I'm not sure exactly why it has ended up here, but there seems to be a fair amount of fuss over it,' commented Grady.

'Don't we have a special department based in Sydney to handle missing persons?' asked Ange.

'We do, but it seems like someone knows someone important, which is where you come in.'

'Why me?' asked Ange, thinking to herself that this would be another low-level case to add to the growing pile of trivial tasks on her desk.

'It involves a young male surfer who was last seen at Namba Heads, just down the highway. Seeing as you're a surfer, I figured this job is right up your alley.'

'OK, sounds interesting. Send me what you have and I'll get on with it. There's nothing else particularly pressing on my plate right now.'

'He may have been missing for some time, which makes it hard. I understand Sydney has accessed his mobile phone records, and his phone hasn't been used to make any calls for over three weeks. It's all in the report that I'll email you shortly. He'll probably turn up soon enough, but I've been told to prioritise it. I'd appreciate you getting straight onto it.'

Ange was the only detective at the station and, while not everyone was happy with being outranked by a young female detective, her boss was amazing. Jim Grady was one of the key reasons Ange loved working in Byron Bay so much, one of those rare bosses who recognised talent and how to develop it. He had pushed her to undertake some additional study and become a detective, and Ange considered him as her mentor, a confidant who she could bounce her ideas off, someone to push her forward when she needed support, yet pull her in to line when she was off track.

Somewhere in his mid-fifties, Grady was neither tall nor short, not handsome nor hideous, more grey hair than not, and carrying a tad extra weight than both his GP and his wife, Barbara, would prefer. Whatever he lacked in physical presence, he more than made up for in intellect and acumen. He was also good company, with a wry sense of the ironic showing through from time to time. Ange had observed how Grady never sought the limelight and always accredited his staff for the station's achievements, a sound scaffold around which to build trust.

Happily married going on thirty years, the Gradys' had three children, all in their twenties and having flown the coop, leaving an empty nest. Undoubtedly influenced by his own family experiences, Ange had become almost his adopted eldest daughter. This would normally be a tricky dynamic, but Ange delicately trod that thin line between her work and personal life, careful never to abuse the privileges of the Grady's friendship and support.

She had secretly nicknamed him Bosley—of Charlie's Angels' fame. After the obligatory fight over who would play who, Ange and her young girlfriends used to while away hours and hours on the school holidays, fighting imagined master criminals. Ange had always insisted on playing Sabrina and the trio kept the holidays safe. That the real Charlie's Angels didn't include a red cattle dog was something they ignored, and Ange's dog Buddy was a much-loved addition to the troupe. In hindsight, these childish games undoubtedly had more impact on her than she had realised at the time.

Jim Grady had seen it all, posted to Byron Bay long before it became a mecca for the rich and famous. Back then, Byron was a backwater for those escaping mainstream life and exuded an almost seedy undertone, a haven for hippies and surfers. Byron was an authentic surfing mecca, the actual sauce behind its appeal as one of the coolest places in the county to live.

Securing the posting to Byron Bay had been her lucky break and she loved her job as a detective. She had applied for the job in Byron Bay the moment she'd seen it listed, some four-odd years back. It had been good to get out of Sydney and the rat race. When people thought of Sydney, they immediately conjured up Bondi

Beach, the Opera House, or Sydney Harbour and its iconic bridge, resplendent in its New Year's Eve fireworks extravaganza. However, only an elite few could afford to live around the harbour or the equally spectacular coastline. There is a lot of west in Sydney, and a whole lot of suburbia needed to house its large multicultural and diverse population. Being a Sydney policewoman was a tough and demanding job.

The police service was still very much a man's world, but things were changing. She didn't care about the gossip that her promotion was simply because she was a woman. 'Winners are grinners,' she'd thought, staring down the envious looks around the office as her boss announced her promotion.

She was good at staring people down. Ever since she'd successfully stared down the kids who tried to nickname her 'Watto' at school, everyone called her Ange. She figured 'Watto' was her dad's nickname, a farmer from around Tamworth. Ange was nothing like her dad. She kept herself fit and maintained a healthy diet, her only vice being a glass or two of wine when the occasion warranted. Now on the wrong side of mid-thirties, Ange considered she was 'not unattractive' when she applied some effort towards her appearance.

Her wide-brimmed Akubra hat, the one made from rabbit hide and favoured by countryfolk, had made an immediate return to active duty the minute Ange had made detective and could dispense with her uniform. As the saying goes, you can take the girl out of the country, but not the country out of the girl. It had been a present from her father when she'd started work in Sydney, and Ange's Akubra sat comfortably, a constant companion and front-line defence against the relentless Australian sun. Unless she was staring them down, she was also comfortable with people. Her relaxed and easy manner helped Ange connect with those from all walks of life, an excellent trait for a promising young detective.

Ange's life in Byron Bay was not all beer and skittles, as the saying goes. Gaining the rank of detective hadn't changed things as radically as she had hoped. She reasoned that this was part of the territory, living in a smallish regional centre, insulated from the big, sophisticated crimes of the city. Her work still involved small-town issues like breaking and entering, possession of narcotics, the occasional embezzlement or theft where money or people had gone missing. She was yet to become embroiled in a serious or complicated case, one that would test her skills and push her limits. If only she could latch onto a major case, Ange was sure that she could show everyone how good she was. Unfortunately, chasing a missing surfer up and down the coast was hardly a career defining opportunity.

Before the surfing culture had swept into Byron and taken a permanent hold, the town had served as a whaling station, now a dark period in its history. Ange had heard stories about the massive great white sharks that had patrolled the sea back then, scavenging offal and any remnants left from the whale carcasses. Even now, Byron Bay and the surrounding coastline remained stubbornly overrepresented in statistics concerning shark attacks. With a lifespan exceeding sixty years, there was a school of thought that there were still great whites patrolling the seas who remembered the time of the whalers—if not them, then their progeny. It sometimes seemed as if surfers had replaced whales as the preferred food source for these massive predators. There were lots of theories swirling amongst the surfing community concerning shark attacks.

These nightmarish thoughts hadn't stopped Ange from getting involved in the sport, and learning to surf was an early priority after she moved to Byron. Tagging along with some English tourists, she'd taken surfing lessons during her first summer. Loving the entire experience, she had soon purchased a longboard from the local pawnshop, cast off by some passing backpacker who had secured enough selfies to impress their friends back home. Whenever time and work permitted, Ange became a regular early-morning worshipper of the surfing gods.

She could still remember the first time she'd stood on water and properly ridden a clean unbroken wave as if it was yesterday. The water had been beyond clear on that crisp spring morning. Recalling the memory of that feeling still made her smile, merging to become one with the wave, making her first proper take-off and standing up, that life-changing moment shared with nature—a hi-res full-colour memory, recalled in an instant.

Ange would sometimes lie awake at night and picture the perfect sea of this memory: pale green glass, smoothed by a light offshore breeze, light mists of sea spray feathering off the breaking waves as if somehow alight. She remembered being surprised by how much you could see while riding a wave: the fish, the seaweed, the intricate mottled shadows etched on the sandy bottom; a lazy stingray disturbed, looking like an implausible kite caught in a mugshot until it flew away in a cloud of sand. It was spectacular. In that moment, as she made that first tentative wobbly turn and zipped across the clean wave face, she was hooked.

The water around Byron can be cool, and Ange thought she looked pretty good in her wetsuit, all that training having paid off. She always enjoyed the appreciative looks as she paddled out. Mostly she caught the older guys looking, those on the way to their next wife—they were everywhere in Byron. Thankfully, she could still steal the occasional glance from one of the younger surfers. She always smiled back, but inwardly thought, 'Probably an arsehole,' as she cynically recalled her past failures in that regard.

Byron Bay had certainly proved a nice shift of pace, although it was changing rapidly. Once a sleepy hippie village, Byron had been 'discovered' by the international glamour set a decade or more back. Now the town boasted a bevy of movie and sporting stars, attracting ever more wealthy retirees, seachangers, and plenty of hangers-on and wannabes. The vegan cafes still existed amongst the flashy restaurants, with their open-air dining where one could be seen, but now they dished up thirty- or even forty-dollar plates. As often seems to be the case, the wealthy blow-ins, drawn to the cruisy surfer/hippie lifestyle, were creating a new Byron Bay, inexorably pricing out those who had created the famed Byron lifestyle in the first place.

The local council was super green, pushing back on Brisbane and Sydney property developers who were hoping to cash in on the Byron brand and the stunning lifestyle imagery that they could leverage. There was also plenty of green activism amongst some of the older locals, the lucky few who had already secured their slice of paradise years ago before prices had skyrocketed.

A scratch beneath the sparkly surface exposed plenty of work to keep Ange busy.

Chapter 2

Missing

Ange spent the balance of Thursday afternoon clearing up some odds and ends. She had one complaint that had been languishing on her desk all week. An elderly woman, a long-time resident, insisted that one of the local youths had vandalised her lawn. According to the woman, the word 'BITCH' had been etched into her front lawn with weedkiller, a permanent reminder of her alleged nature. The woman was quite certain who the culprit was. There was 'history' between them. It was hardly life-threatening stuff, almost amusing in a twisted sort of way.

Ange took great delight in wandering over and casually flipping the report onto Gerry Walton's desk. 'Gerry, the boss needs me to head out of town and jump onto a case. Can you look into this matter for me while I'm gone? It should be interesting.' Walton's eyes briefly lit until he scanned the substance of the matter. He threw Ange a dark scowl. She had a devil of a time keeping a straight face.

She had 'history' with Senior Constable Walton and his kindred-spirit colleague, Ernie Lynch. She had overheard the two Neanderthals chatting around the coffee machine, speaking shit as usual. 'Bloody affirmative action. What hope do we have?'

Their disgust at her good fortune hadn't stopped both from trying to hit on her on separate occasions. Ange would never be that desperate. Not that her track record with dating was any stellar achievement. 'Male fails', she called her sequence of unfortunate choices. 'Go figure—I can solve a crime but can't even discern an arsehole when I'm on a date,' Ange often joked to her girlfriends. If she were honest, Ange had imagined that she would have kids by now. Highly organised, Ange figured she would make an excellent mother. However, time waits for no man (or woman), so she had thrown herself into her career, which proved stimulating and rewarding, especially now that she had made detective.

She thought a lot about people and what motivated them, why they made certain choices and behaved in certain ways, and the influence this had on their pathway in life. This deep reflectiveness made Ange a promising detective, often seeing things that her colleagues missed. She doubted those skills would come into play chasing the wandering young surfer. Of course, there were lots of more sinister outcomes that she needed to consider, but at least she might catch some waves.

The next morning, she saw that the missing person's report had come through to her inbox and opened the document, which showed a frustrating lack of detail. Jake Thompson, an eighteen-year-old male from Coffs Harbour. Apparently, Jake was a promising surfer who was turning pro. 'Aren't they all at that age?' she thought. Ange skimmed through the phone numbers logged in the report and noted that Jake wasn't someone who lived in constant contact, unlike most people his age. The report contained a mobile phone number for the boy's mother, Joy Thompson, a number heavily represented in the phone logs. She seemed the obvious place to start.

'Hello?'

'Mrs Thompson? My name is Detective Angela Watson from the Byron Bay police station. I understand that you have some concerns over the whereabouts of your son Jake,' asked Ange.

'It's about time. It's almost three weeks since I lodged my concerns with the missing persons hotline. They seemed to lose interest the moment that I mentioned Jake was a young surfer. I gather my boss has been on the case?'

'What do you mean, your boss is on the case?' asked Ange at this surprising choice of words, alert to a potential police jurisdiction issue.

'My job is driving dump trucks at a mine in the Hunter Valley. When I mentioned I needed some time off to visit Jake and explained my concerns about his whereabouts, she stepped in to help me. With all the staffing issues around Covid, she seemed desperate to keep me driving. The mine grinds to a halt when the trucks stop. She said that she knew someone and assured me she would get some action. I need to get in contact with my son. I'm very worried about him.'

'I understand, Mrs Thompson. You said that you lodged a missing person report three weeks ago. When did you last have contact with your son?'

'Nine days before that. Jake and I normally speak to each other every week. Seeing as we both work odd hours, this sometimes blows out a few days. At first, I assumed that he simply hadn't topped up his prepaid mobile phone account. This wouldn't be the first time that had happened. I'm always onto him about things like that. But he's never gone this long without contacting me. I've rung his number dozens of times, but all I ever get is his voicemail.'

Ange knew the statistics. Ninety-eight percent of missing persons turned up within a month. However, the success rate dropped off drastically after that. She needed to jump onto this before it was too late. 'I understand how worried you must be. I need to ask some questions about Jake so I can get a sense of the situation. Do you have some time now?'

'Absolutely. We need to find Jake. What do you want to know?' said the distraught mother.

'First, I know Jake was last seen in Namba Heads. Can you tell me how long he had been living there and what he was doing workwise?'

'Jake moved to Namba Heads straight after school to pursue his dream of becoming a professional surfer. I had hopes for him to go to university, still do, but he was hell-bent on becoming a pro surfer. A relative of mine owns a beach shack in Namba Heads and has kindly let him live in a self-contained shed in the back year. Jake has some part-time work on a local trawler to keep his head above water. His living expenses are minimal, and he has a sponsorship that provides him with surfing gear and helps him compete in competitions.'

This news impressed Ange. There were tens of thousands of aspiring surfers in the water every day, but only a handful ever gained a sponsorship. 'Can you give me the address of the house where he was staying, Mrs Thompson?'

'I don't have this with me right now. I'll text it to you later.'

'Great. So, where did Jake go to school?'

'Coffs Harbour. Jake grew up there. It was the only place he knew until he moved to Namba Heads.'

'Why didn't he stay in Coffs Harbour? There's plenty of good surf in the area.'

'We'd been living hand-to-mouth for years and I was worried that I wouldn't be able to support him through university. I gained my heavy vehicle driver's licence and started searching for a well-paid job in the mining industry. When Jake finished high school, I took a job driving dump trucks in the Hunter Valley.'

'OK. I understand. You said that Jake has a sponsorship. Do you know which company sponsors him, and do you think he might have some commitments with them?'

'Bell Surfboards have sponsored Jake for over two years now. I had the same thought and contacted the owner, Gus Bell, but he hasn't heard from Jake either. Gus has been very good to Jake.'

A shiver ran down Ange's spine. This could be a case of grooming. Jake was a textbook victim: young male with a single mother, isolated from family and friends, taken under the wing of a coach or mentor. She needed to consider the possibility that Gus Bell might have exploited Jake and something had gone horribly wrong.

Ange metered herself a dose of reality. Bell was the most high-profile of all the surfboard makers around Byron Bay. Everybody in town knew Gus Bell and his legendary father. Bobby Bell was a genuine surfing icon who had founded the company back in the sixties. Since then, Bell Surfboards had established a reputation as the most expensive and exclusive surfboards one could ride—especially their longboards. Ange's finances didn't stretch that far, but she was a regular visitor to the Bell factory outlet in Byron, even if only to buy some coffee and covet their gorgeous creations. Bell surfboards are a rideable piece of art. Ange planned to buy one as soon as she could spare the cash. It made little sense that someone as high-profile as Gus Bell would engage in grooming young guys. Unfortunately, Ange knew of the sobering statistics. One never knew, and she couldn't discount that possibility.

'Tell me about Jake's surfing career. How was this going for him?' asked Ange.

'I thought that this was just something that he needed to flush through his system before he woke up to himself and went to university, like I'd hoped. When he won two rounds of the Burleigh Pro Invitational at the end of last year, I knew it was for real and that he had a future in the sport. That was until Covid hit and the government shut everything down. It was lucky that Jake has his job in the trawler to keep him going.'

'Wow, the Burleigh Pro. That's quite an achievement for someone so young. You and Jake's father must have been proud,' observed Ange.

'There is no father. He scooted off years ago. A total deadbeat. I reckon he's the real reason that Jake wanted to pursue pro surfing.'

Ange swallowed before replying. Estranged parents were another group high on the list of suspects for missing children. 'How so? Can you explain what you mean by that?'

'Jake's father was a local rugby league star in Coffs Harbour. They called him a prodigy down at the footy club. Vince was being courted by two of the big rugby league teams based in Sydney when I fell pregnant with Jake. On the face of it, Vince did the right thing and hung around, abandoning his plans to become a pro rugby league player. In reality, it was the worst thing ever. Vince gradually grew bitter and resentful, blaming Jake and me for his subsequent failures. It was all downhill when he started hitting the grog and then, one day, he just up and left us. I think Jake didn't want to become his father's son and live a life regretting he didn't make the most of his opportunities and talents.'

'Have you heard from Jake's father recently and do you know how I might contact him?'

'I have no idea and I don't wish to know. It was a struggle to bring up Jake on my own. We had nothing and would never have gotten through without the support of family and friends. I seriously doubt that Vince would have anything to do with Jake going missing. He wouldn't even know what Jake looks like,' replied the woman, making no attempt to disguise the bitterness that she felt towards Jake's father. Ange mentally moved his name further down her list of suspects.

'What about friends? Is there any mate who Jake might have gone off on a trip with?'

'I've already rung his best mate, Henry Anderson. Jake and Ando are surfing buddies, but Ando hasn't heard from him since their midterm surf trip to Forster on the Central Coast. That isn't unusual for boys like them, and Ando seemed surprised that I'd called him. I was miffed to learn that Jake had taken that surfing trip with Ando. He had only been a couple of hours' drive away. I would have loved to see him,' explained Mrs Thompson, pausing briefly before providing Ange with a telling insight. 'Jake hadn't totally forgiven me for taking this job and leaving Coffs Harbour.'

Ange made a note of this. Jake and his mother might not be as tight as she had first assumed. 'What about girls? Was Jake seeing anybody?'

'Not that he had told me, but he might want to keep that to himself. Jake's always been reserved and mostly keeps to himself. As far as I know, he's never had any long-term girlfriends. It's possible, I suppose. That would be wonderful if he was just off with a girl,' replied Mrs Thompson, brightening up with the prospect of such a benign outcome.

'Do you know the name of the trawler where Jake was working?'

'No. But that shouldn't be hard to work out. Jake had said that there were only a couple of trawlers working out of Namba Heads,' said Mrs Thompson before pausing and admonishing herself. 'I guess I should have rung around, perhaps tried the marina.'

'Don't worry. I'm heading down to Namba Heads today to check all that out. Mrs Thompson, I think that's all for now. I'll ring you if I find anything or need further details about Jake. Oh, by the way, what does Jake do for transport? Does he have a car?'

'Yes, he does. An old Toyota Camry wagon. It's registered in my name, Joy Thompson. I can text you the registration details as well.'

'Don't worry. I can look that up myself. Just text me the address of where Jake was living,' said Ange before saying goodbye and hanging up the call.

For the next hour, Ange did some online searching, needing to learn about Namba Heads. She had been planning to visit for ages, having heard about the town on the surfers' grapevine. There was a local longboard surf-riders' club that seemed active, and the club's Facebook page was splattered with recent pictures. By the look of things, Namba Heads enjoyed several quality point breaks that would well suit the southerly wind which had been hanging on for the past week. As she scrolled down the list of search results, she read about the recent tragic death of a local trawlerman, a well-liked man called Dave Fletcher. Ange suspected the story behind the headline, so logged in to her work intranet to access the coroner's report. Suicides were one of the worst parts of her job, and it looked like Namba Heads was going through a rough patch.

That Jake was working on a trawler was a curious coincidence, but this was not necessarily alarming in itself. There were many logical reasons that the two events would intersect. In fact, without a job, it was reasonable that he might have left town and was drifting down the coast on a surf trip.

Ange saw she could rent a cabin at the local caravan park, so she planned to make a weekend of her visit. She was excited, but had to remind herself of the serious side of the trip.

The case was already far more interesting than Ange had expected.

Chapter 3

Bell Surfboards

After telling her boss what she was planning, Ange went back to her apartment and packed enough clothes for two nights. Most importantly, she took a moment to throw in a wetsuit and slide her longboard into the back of her Toyota Camry.

The factory outlet store for Bell Surfboards was in the industrial estate on the way out of Byron. Hoping she would catch Gus Bell before she drove to Namba Heads, Ange swung into their car park and made her way into the shop. She approached the young surfer guy attending the counter that doubled as a coffee shop. 'Hi. Is Gus Bell in today? I'd like to speak with him if I could.'

'I saw him around earlier. Can I ask your name and what you need to speak with him about?'

Ange flashed her badge, a ploy that she had never felt comfortable with. 'Detective Angela Watson. I'd rather speak with him in person, please.'

Despite her misgivings, the badge did the trick. The guy fiddled with his mobile phone. 'He could be in the factory. I've just sent him a text.'

While she was waiting, Ange admired the gallery of beautiful Bell surfboards. A short and wide fish design caught her eye. As she admired its lines, a confident voice came over her shoulder. 'It's a good-looking board, isn't it? We're best known for our longboards, but we've been moving into shortboards as well lately. The one you have in your hand is a five-foot-ten fish design. Despite its shortish length, you can see we've added in extra width and volume to make it easier to paddle. The combination of a swallowtail and the twin fin configuration make it super-fast and manoeuvrable. It's loads of fun in smaller conditions.'

Ange placed the board carefully back in its rack before turning to face the man.

He held out his hand and smiled warmly. 'Gus Bell. You wanted to speak to me about something?'

'Hi, Mr Bell. Detective Angela Watson. Is there somewhere we can talk?'

'Call me Gus, please. Mr Bell is my father, although nobody even calls him that. How about we find somewhere to sit in the courtyard? Would you like a coffee?'

'A flat white would be great, thanks.'

Gus led Ange back to the shop counter. 'Archie, can you grab us a couple of flat whites, please? We'll be in the courtyard.' He turned towards Ange with a large open smile. 'We're only allowed to sell takeaway coffee with all the restrictions over this pandemic. I guess you won't arrest me, seeing as I'm not going to let you pay.'

Ange smiled at Gus Bell's disarming manner. 'Of course not. I'm not that sort of police.'

Gus led Ange outside towards a shady table in the far corner of the courtyard. Although she knew not to be influenced by such things, she could not help but admire his form. A touch over six feet tall, fit and ruggedly handsome, his longish blond hair framed with a fashionably stubble beard. Gus Bell moved with ease and exuded a relaxed, confident air. He certainly didn't look like a molester of young boys, although Ange knew those types came in all shapes and sizes.

'So, Detective Watson. How can I help?' replied Gus Bell with a smile. His casual manner was not that of someone guilty of anything.

'It's about Jake Thompson. I understand you sponsor him?' asked Ange.

'Jake is a really talented young surfer and we have big plans for him,' replied Gus.

'Have you heard from him lately?' asked Ange.

'No, I haven't heard from Jake for a while now. All the competitions and events have been cancelled because of Covid-19, so there has been little going on with our sponsored surfers. Although, we recently sent some new boards down for Jake to try. I'm a bit surprised we haven't heard from him with some feedback. Jake's a good young kid with a bright future. I hope he's OK and not in any trouble. His mother rang me last week as well,' replied Gus.

'How long have you sponsored Jake?'

Gus Bell looked up and to the right, thinking carefully through his reply. 'I guess he's been with us for a touch over two years.'

'How many surfers do you normally sponsor?'

'It depends. I guess we usually sponsor between four and six. Jake's a bit of an anomaly.'

'How so?'

'As I said, we're best known for our longboards, and that's traditionally been where our sponsorship dollars have been channelled. However, I've been moving us into shortboards so that we can access a younger customer base. Jake is our youngest ever sponsored surfer.'

'Why Jake Thompson?' asked Ange, still needing to probe her more sinister scenario.

'Let me tell you how I stumbled across Jake.' Gus paused while Archie walked over and laid their two coffees on the table. 'I had driven down to a secret surf spot called Flat Rock. I gather that you're a surfer and would know that there are plenty of Flat Rocks up and down the east coast., which makes it a pretty good name for a secret spot. Flat Rock is a heavy left-hander and a goofy-footer's paradise when it's working, which is hardly ever. The break needs a large, deep swell coming from the north, which, as you would know, is uncommon in these parts.' Gus paused briefly to take a sip of his coffee.

'The surf was on fire that day and was being patrolled by some fierce locals. You know the type, warriors who think they have some sort of self-appointed ownership of the take-off zone. I was struggling to get a wave and was sitting down the line, picking up the odd crumb alongside these two kids, one of which was Jake Thompson. I could hear them grumbling about how hard it was to get a decent wave. Then, suddenly, Jake paddled up the line inside all the other surfers. You should have seen the looks that they gave him as he paddled past. Jake plonked himself so far inside that everyone assumed he would just sit there. One guy even yelled out at him, urging Jake to catch a wave. The locals knew it was almost impossible to make the first section from where he was sitting, and they wanted him to eat some reef and bugger off. Even worse is that Jake surfs natural—backhand at Flat Rock. Anyhow, after ten minutes, an enormous set came through and Jake paddled for the second wave. It was a monster and I could see it sucking the water back off the reef as it reared up. What happened next was incredible. I'd seen nothing like it,' said Gus.

The story had Ange totally transfixed. She sat and waited patiently while Gus drank some more of his coffee.

'Jake never really took off. The best that I can describe is that he sort of blended into the wave like quicksilver. He was up and going immediately, and there was no time to make a bottom turn. The wave was a beast, a runaway freight train. Jake pivoted halfway down the face and stayed high before he grabbed the outside rail of his board with his right hand, stretched out his left, and moulded himself back into the wave face. Immediately, Jake slotted into a thundering tube. It was his only viable escape path to avoid a painful altercation with the reef. I can tell you, he certainly had everyone's attention. The line-up all turned and waited to see the inevitable tombstoning of Jake's board. We were all certain that he would get chewed up by the wave and smashed on the reef. The lip covered him up for ages and I was holding my breath, fearing for his life, if I'm honest. It was that heavy.'

Gus paused again. Ange found that she too was holding her breath.

'Then, suddenly, the roaring wave shot Jake out of the spray as if blown by a jet engine. His mate was cheering and whooping like crazy. Even some locals couldn't control themselves and yelled out their appreciation for what he had just done. Jake had no trouble in the line-up after that. I'd never seen such tenacity and natural talent in my life, so I offered him a sponsorship as he paddled past. He thought I was joking and all but ignored me. Despite looking cool, I suspect that there was some serious adrenaline coursing through him. I waited for him on the shore after the session and convinced him to come on board.'

'Wow, that's quite a story. How much contact do you have with Jake?'

'Not much lately. However, after he won through those first two rounds of the Burleigh Pro, I had secured him lots of invitations, even overseas events. I was mapping out his schedule and working through the finances when the pandemic hit and all surfing events were cancelled.'

'Do you know where Jake lives?' probed Ange.

'I know the address. Not offhand, but we sent him surfboards and other kit to an address in Namba Heads. I can get it for you, but I've not visited him there, so I couldn't tell you exactly where it is in the town.'

'No, that's OK. His mother texted me the address. I'm on my way down to Namba Heads now. Tell me, did Jake have a girlfriend that you know of?'

'We didn't have that sort of relationship. Jake keeps to himself. I've been mentoring him and giving him advice about his training, but his personal life is his own business. I might get involved if he fell into drug problems or something dodgy, but I never had those concerns about Jake. Like I said, he's a good kid.'

Ange retrieved a business card from her wallet and handed it over. 'Thanks, Gus. You've been most helpful. I'll be in touch if I need anything further. Please ring me if you think of anything or hear from Jake.'

'Will do. I hope that Jake's OK. Can you keep me in the loop where you can?'

'Thanks,' was all that Ange was prepared to say as she took her leave. All too often, she had offered to keep someone abreast of developments, only to disappoint them when she needed to remain quiet for reasons of confidentiality.

Ange was as comfortable as she could be that Gus Bell was no child molester, but she fought hard to remain objective in the face of Gus's all-around appeal. Time would tell on that front, thought Ange as she settled into her drive down to Namba Heads.

Chapter 4

Not a Fishwife

Sharon and Dave Fletcher were stuck in the commercial fishing industry, waiting for the day that someone 'with a dream of the open sea' would come along and offer them a good price for the operation. Nonetheless, they both loved the sea and loved living in Namba Heads with their two unruly boys. Childhood sweethearts, the pair had married young, and the boys had arrived in quick succession.

Dave had never wanted to follow in his father's footsteps and become a commercial fisherman. He and Sharon had plans to buy a van and meander around Australia, like gypsies on a long, permanent holiday. Unfortunately, the couple had to abandon these wanderlust ideas when Dave's dad became suddenly sick, forcing Dave to take over the trawler. When the boys came along, it seemed as if their future was settled for good.

Sharon was your quintessential surfer girl, but underneath the blond hair and freckles there lurked a no-nonsense doer, not to be underestimated. Most everyone liked Sharon, or 'Shazz' to her close friends, even the local girls who had once batted their eyelids at Dave. Sun exposure, hard work, and having two kids had inevitably taken a bit of a toll, but Dave always beamed when other guys commented on how attractive she was.

Sharon had gumption and opened a fish and chip shop at their fisheries co-op. Fresh produce, some picnic tables, a few umbrellas, a woman's touch, and the place became quietly successful. Weekenders and holidaymakers mostly frequented her quaint waterside eatery, keen to taste the sea after a day on the beach. The extra income helped keep the boat in the water. There was always something else to fix on the damn thing. At least they had both smelt of fish all the time, a thin silver lining to all this hard work.

Being a commercial fisherman is a tough life, and only tough characters should apply. Uncertain income, constantly rising fuel and maintenance costs, weather, dwindling fish stocks, the list went on and on. Dave had run the gauntlet and operated uninsured for a period last year. They just didn't have the cash to pay the premiums at the time.

It seemed as if everyone hated commercial fishermen these days, yet everyone loved eating fish. 'Where do they think the stuff comes from?' Dave would exclaim when he took yet another death stare from a holidaying Sydneysider driving past the marina in their flash SUV. Namba Heads owed its very existence to a fishing heritage, and its residents supported their shrinking fishing fleet—and their skippers.

Then there was the time when Dave docked at the wharf to find a 'Karen' waiting for him.

'I have the right as an Australian citizen to inspect the catch and make sure no laws are being broken,' the woman blurted, loudly in fact, sounding like a deranged vigilante.

Sharon marched out of the fish and chip shop in full flight and promptly tore into her, angrily dispatching 'Karen' and her Volkswagen Beetle in no time. Sharon's best friend was also called Karen, and she was super annoyed that her name had become stereotypical for entitled 'I demand to speak to the manager' types. Dave had been desperately proud of how Sharon had stood up for him and their business that day.

Dave had always loved the ocean. It excited and calmed him at the same time, alive with possibility. He said that there was always something going on and something to learn. However, the ocean was changing as well, right before their eyes.

Fishing catches were always variable, and the couple often endured 'dwindling fish stocks' discussions at school BBQs. They usually turned the other cheek, knowing that there were no winners in that discussion, just as there were no silver bullet solutions. Dave himself only targeted sustainable fish species, knowing that his family's future depended on fish stocks remaining sound. He mostly fished in close, leaving the large pelagic fish like tuna and mackerel to the longliners, those using baited hooks strung out behind their boats. He was also concerned about the estuaries and maintaining viable breeding grounds to support future catches.

After a life at sea, Dave knew how complicated and interconnected the ocean truly was.

There was a longliner operating out of Namba Heads, and Dave sometimes ran into him over a beer at the pub. He seemed to do it even tougher than Dave and blamed 'those bloody foreigners', complaining loudly to anyone who would listen about the number of tuna hoovered up by huge overseas outfits, often just out of Australian waters. With their massive ring nets, they took out entire schools, unrelenting until their gigantic holds were full.

Despite the dwindling tuna schools, there seemed to be more sharks around. Dave had commented to Sharon how the sharks seemed to have learned the sound of his boat, coming around and following him, sometimes damaging his nets. Occasionally, Dave encountered massive great whites, moseying up to the boat to check out what was going on, as big as a Kombi van, ominous and scary-looking. He said that it was mesmerising, watching these massive creatures from the safety of the trawler, something he hoped to avoid when he was out surfing.

Then, suddenly, Dave was gone and their life together was in ruins.

Chapter 5

The Aftermath

There is simply nowhere to hide in a small town like Namba Heads. After dealing with the gruesome formalities, Sharon Fletcher had retreated to the safety of her family, her inescapable daily chores performed on autopilot. With no one capable of taking over, Sharon shut the fish and chip shop for a while. This respite from her work duties didn't really assist her mental state, and in some ways gave her more time to dwell over the tragedy, sometimes blaming herself, sometimes others.

Almost the entire town turned out for Dave's funeral, wanting to pay their respects to one of their lovable sons and his grieving family. Sharon still refused to believe it, but the coroner's report was clear in its finding that Dave had hanged himself. There had been plenty of evidence to support the coroner's view.

That the bank had knocked back their recent loan application back increased Dave's financial pressures, and Dave had spoken freely about his challenges when catching a beer or a wave with his mates. The girls at the co-op had vouched for how terrible Dave had looked the day before his death.

The town was in mourning. It was one of those terrible periods in the history of a close-knit community. The locals all rallied behind the family, dropping off meals and doing what they could. The look on the face of those poor boys at the funeral had been heartbreaking. Dave's mother was clearly a broken woman. Other than the funeral, nobody had seen her since the tragedy, conspicuous by her absence at the Bowls Club.

Sharon was made of tough stuff, and she tried to keep a brave face, but the façade would crack often enough. Townspeople just didn't know what to say when they came across her in the street or at the supermarket. Some tried to avoid the discomfort, others gave their awkward condolences. Sharon was never a hugger, so the whole situation was distressing, to say the least.

The community took a long hard look at itself, confronted and uncomfortable with its reflection. They questioned why they hadn't heeded the signs, and everyone was constantly looking over their shoulder, wondering who else might be struggling with their own demons.

Some blamed the banks, who were a convenient target. The manager of the local building society had felt like he had caused the tragedy. Unfortunately, with the new stricter lending rules, small family outfits like Dave and Sharon's were simply not bankable. If the Fletchers had put forward a plan to sell in a year or two, he probably would have gotten a small loan to tide them over. The bank manager still felt terrible and had sought counselling from the head office. None had been forthcoming.

The boys took a long time to fully comprehend that their father wouldn't be coming home each day, tired from a hard night's work and reeking of fish. Some nights they cried for hours, fatigue finally offering the refuge of sleep. Dave's mother was worse, withdrawn and uncommunicative. Dinners were sombre affairs; gone was the noisy banter of the boys and their dad, replaced by silence and despair. Sharon knew that time was supposed to heal all wounds, but she simply couldn't imagine life ever being normal again.

After a couple of weeks, Sharon knew she had to pull herself together. The boys needed her, and a sense of responsibility slowly overtook the lethargy of helplessness. Dave's mother had aged ten years, and it was as if the tragedy had sucked the life out of her, rendering her unable to even help around the house. Their old life was over, and Sharon realised she needed to move on. Alone.

She knew deep down that it would be a complete waste of time, but she had a tough conversation with someone at the superfund, who told her that their insurance policy didn't cover suicide.

The boat needed to be sold as quickly as possible. It was the family's biggest asset, one that was deteriorating with every idle moment. After doing some searching online, she contacted a boat broker from the Gold Coast, one who had a string of excellent reviews. The broker had told her that there was renewed interest in trawlers. There were plenty of investors looking for a safe haven, and plenty of former skippers who wanted to leave their dreary jobs in the city and resume a life at sea, safe from the coronavirus.

Going down to the boat again was the most difficult thing that Sharon had ever done. The image of Dave hanging there amongst the netting still haunted her nights; memories of him around the house haunted her days. The nightmares just wouldn't go away.

The whole thing still made no sense to her, as her relationship with Dave had been better than ever during those past few months. Sure, there had been some bad days when Dave had been distant and troubled, but nothing wildly out of character for someone who had basically been living hand-to-mouth for years. She knew Dave had regretted his decision to take over the trawler from his father, but they had carved out a pleasant life for themselves, despite the many challenges.

Everyone adored Dave. It made her angry that Dave hadn't seen that. 'Why would he take his own life when so many people loved him?' she thought as she lay awake at night, staring at the ceiling, struggling to comprehend the incomprehensible.

Taking a deep breath, Sharon opened the door to the wheelhouse. She stood outside for ages, unable to cross the threshold. There were so many memories, some bad, but mostly good ones. Sharon had even lost her virginity on this boat, sneaking into the wheelhouse for some privacy. Dave knew where his father kept the spare key, and they had lots of sex in the relative discomfort of the bench-seat-cum-daybed in that little cabin.

Sharon remembered her panic that time in grade twelve when she'd thought she was pregnant, their choice of natural contraception laced with risk as it was. Surreptitious schoolyard condoms had been hard to come by within an all-seeing, all-knowing village like Namba Heads. On the other hand, questionable school-yard sex advice was readily available. Sharon had never told Dave about that scare.

She reached up into the hidey-hole where Dave had safely clipped a spare key, the same place his father had used. It was still there. Dave was a creature of habit, and it briefly saddened Sharon that this little ritual would not be passed down to another generation. Being a mother was hard enough, let alone the added responsibility of guiding her two boys toward manhood without Dave's help.

Shaking off those memories, Sharon pushed herself into the wheelhouse and started work. The broker already had someone who wanted to inspect the boat as soon as possible, so she had to get it ready and check that everything was in good working order and ensure that all the paperwork was available for inspection. Sharon did the best she could, but that was one of the toughest days of her life.

Sharon kept meticulous records and soon had all the certificates, invoices, and service logs ready for the broker. Luckily, everything was up to date and shipshape. It hadn't always been this way; there'd been times when they were short of money and had to cut corners, like they had with the insurance the year before last. Sharon hoped desperately that the potential buyer would be pragmatic and turn a blind eye to these small failings. She couldn't have been more wrong.

Chapter 6

Something Stinks

The broker brought someone down to inspect the boat within the week. Apparently, the inspection went well, and the broker asked Sharon for her permission to allow the buyer to contact the shipyard and talk through the maintenance invoices. 'At least something is going right in my life,' thought Sharon.

It surprised her to get a call the next day from the broker, telling her that there were some discrepancies in the maintenance records.

'What do you mean? What discrepancy?' she asked in a testy voice.

'Well, it seems as if the repairs for the last job were more extensive than the invoice showed. The buyer is concerned that the boat is not as represented and is reticent to spend the money on the survey without some assurances,' explained the broker.

'Leave it with me,' said Sharon sharply, and she immediately rang the shipyard.

'Barry the Boatbuilder' was what Dave used to call him jokingly. He had liked Dave, and Barry had driven down for the funeral, as depressing a day as there ever was. He sounded nervous when Sharon told him why she was calling.

'Look, we don't want to get sued for misrepresentation, so I had to tell them the truth,' he stumbled defensively.

'What do you mean? What truth?' Sharon shot back sharply.

'Well...,' said Barry. 'That time when Dave hit the sandbar caused a fair amount of damage. The bill came to seven thousand, two hundred dollars after we gave him a discount.'

'But Dave said it was nothing. Your invoice was only for two thousand, two hundred,' Sharon quickly retorted.

Barry paused before answering. 'Well... Dave paid five thousand in cash. He told us to make the invoice out for two thousand, two hundred. I assumed you knew, and that the cash had come from the fish and chip shop.'

Sharon took all this in before asking Barry to send her a report on letterhead detailing the actual work done on the boat. She planned to provide this to the broker and hoped it would settle the buyer down.

'Where the heck did Dave find that much cash?' thought Sharon after she hung up. She needed the sale to go through, so she quickly rang the broker back and apologised that she had forgotten to explain that invoice.

'Things have been crazy from my end,' she said. 'I've been distracted lately and forgot that Dave had negotiated a discount for some cash. I just hadn't gotten around to putting it through the books properly.'

The broker was understanding and thought that the buyer would be fine with it all once he had the report from the shipyard.

'The work had been done properly. Dave had been meticulous about keeping the boat in perfect running order. You need everything to work properly when you're out at sea. I'm sure the survey will be fine,' Sharon said before she hung up from the call, speaking with far more confidence than she really felt.

Sharon grabbed the boat keys and marched down to the marina. When she went to unlock the boat, she realised she had picked up Dave's set of keys instead of hers. On the key ring, there was a small key she had never noticed before. 'What on earth is that key for?' she thought, confused.

Sharon started in the wheelhouse, looking for anything unusual. She slid herself up under the console, where Dave stowed the life jackets, flares and the locator beacon, the most likely place for Dave to hide something. 'Nothing out of the ordinary here,' she said to herself after moving everything aside. It was a tight squeeze, and as she rolled over to pull herself back out, she noticed the small metal box tucked under the dash and duct-taped to some wires.

Sharon immediately knew what the key was for and realised that this was where Dave had probably stashed his cash. There was nothing in the box, so it didn't help answer the question of where Dave had found the five thousand dollars used to pay off their account at the shipyard. Bewildered, Sharon even sniffed the box, vainly hoping that it might have contained nothing more than a common vice, something normal that Dave had wanted to keep from his wife—cigars or tobacco, perhaps. A chill ran up her spine. She knew it was nothing so banal.

Sharon needed to think about this development, so she put the box back where Dave had hidden it and went home.

She desperately needed to sell the boat and make a new life for herself, hopefully pushing this tragedy behind her in time. However, Sharon knew something wasn't right. She still didn't believe that Dave was the type to take his own life, although she now understood that nobody really knew what that 'type' was. She also dreaded that her boys might go through life believing their father had killed himself, escaping his troubles in such a terrible and heartbreaking manner.

Sharon rang Jake's phone, but it went straight through to voicemail. She then rang Cory, the most sensible of Dave's seasoned deckies.

'Hi, Cory. It's Sharon Fletcher here. Had Dave been doing anything unusual over the past six months?' she asked, getting straight to the point.

'Oh, hi, Mrs Fletcher. Nothing other than the work he was doing for Dr Bjorn, picking up his whale tags from time to time. We still feel terrible about Dave,' replied Cory openly.

Sharon knew that Dave's deckies were basic guys, certainly not brain surgeons. She was not so easily fooled.

'How many times did this happen?' she asked.

'Four or five, I suppose. Dave used to give us fifty dollars for the extra time it took,' Cory explained. 'Dr B had given Dave this contraption that he used to locate the tags in the ocean. It was a nice change from pulling in nets, actually.'

'What contraption?' thought Sharon after she hung up. There was nothing like that on the boat. She went back down to the marina and undertook a more thorough search, even down in the engine room, smelling of oil and diesel. She found nothing out of the ordinary.

'Why would Dave hide something like that? He would have told me about helping with whale research. It makes no sense,' she questioned herself out loud.

Sharon certainly recalled the yarn about Dr Bjorn that Dave had acted out one night over dinner. Dave had the family in stitches when he made a complete botch of a Scandinavian accent, gleaned from watching Scandi Noir crime series on TV. Dr Bjorn, sometimes Dr B, became the name given to any Scandinavian-speaking person after that. Once the laughter had subsided, Dave had filled them in on his encounter.

Dave had been getting the boat ready for a night's fishing when this guy had approached the boat, looking very official in his khakis. Dave's immediate instinct had been to look the other way, hoping he wasn't guilty of some breach of the rules. It was hard to keep up, as there was always at least one new regulation ready to catch them out. The guy had stood alongside the boat, intent on gaining Dave's attention. Mid-thirties, blond, good-looking; he certainly hadn't looked or sounded like an officious inspector. Dave reckoned those types simply demanded attention.

Dr B was looking for a boat to help locate a whale tracking beacon that had become dislodged. The tag had six months' worth of valuable data, and Dr Bjorn was eager to retrieve it before the weather turned sour. Even though he had offered to pay, Dave was getting ready to go fishing and would be out overnight.

Interested in anything to do with the ocean, Dave had asked how Dr Bjorn went about tracking whales. Apparently, when a whale came up for air, Dr Bjorn's tag usually had just enough time to fix some coordinates and store them, sometime even ping some coordinates via mobile phone. The tags eventually dislodged and then wallowed aimlessly around in the ocean, alerting the researcher to the problem.

Dr Bjorn told Dave that he used a handheld receiver and a directional aerial to home in on a beacon. Because the system used VHF radio signals, and it was all low power, it required a rough idea of a beacon's location and then a direct line of sight once nearby. Dave had suggested Dr Bjorn try one of the fishing charter boats operating out of the marina. They had the added benefit of a tuna tower used for spotting fish and seemed better suited to the task.

When Dave asked about the state of the whale population, Dr B had explained that the outlook was bright. Populations had fallen dangerously low by the 1970s, but they were now back to where they had been before records had begun in the early 1800s. Everyone around these parts knew that Byron Bay had once been a centre for whaling in the region, now a black mark in history. The closure of the industry had been great for the whales, but not for the whalers of the past, which was a sobering thought for a modern-day fisherman and something that kept Dave and Sharon awake at night.

Dave had laughed when Dr B had walked off looking for a more suitable boat.

Seeing a guy in khakis striding their way would make any boatie sweat. Dave swore he could see the fear in their eyes, worried their catch might include some undersized fish. He heard later that one of the charter fishing boats had earned four hundred dollars finding Dr Bjorn's precious whale tag. Not bad for an hour and a half's work.

Chapter 7

The Sergeant

Sergeant Darren 'Dazza' Billings had been in charge of the Namba Heads police station for almost seven years now. A tall and hawkish man, perhaps even handsome in some eyes, Darren had considered himself quite the ladies' man back in the day. He wasn't into surfing or fishing and knew the job for what it was, an outpost to keep him tucked away and out of sight.

Darren had once been quite ambitious. Some would say fuelled with far more ambition than talent, Dazza had walked with a confident swagger, acting like a man on his way up. When not in uniform, he considered himself a snappy dresser, the best-dressed guy at the party no less, the irony being immediately apparent to even the most casual observer.

He enjoyed his study at the police academy in Sydney, one of those students who was a bit of a know-it-all during the semester, but cagey after the results came out. After graduation, everything went according to plan.

Following a steady but unexceptional career as constable, Darren was promoted to senior constable at Muswellbrook, a smallish town inland from the NSW Central Coast. Darren held that position for a few years, an unremarkable stint free of blunder. When the vacancy had come up for a sergeant in Newcastle, Darren had put his best foot forward and scored the job.

Newcastle was closer to the action and Darren had his heart set on becoming a detective as soon as possible. He imagined himself as a super-cool homicide detective in Sydney, resplendent in a well-cut suit and a smart silk tie. Newcastle was way too small a place to house an ego as large as Darren's.

Darren was doing a great job cosying up to his superiors, and things were progressing perfectly until that fancy recruit showed up at work. 'Strewth, isn't she a looker?' thought Darren that first time she walked into the station. He fancied his chances and went on the charm offensive—well, at least in his eyes, anyway. You see, Darren had a problem with body language and reading the signs, which really wasn't a great trait for a detective, if one was being honest.

Shocked to be hauled in front of the boss, Darren was told that there had been a complaint lodged against him for sexual harassment. 'What do you mean?' Darren thought. 'I never even got anywhere near first base.' He tried to remonstrate his innocence, but this only made matters and the reprimand worse.

'Typical, always believing the woman over the man,' Darren said under his breath, just loud enough to be heard, frustration boiling over as he left his boss's office. Darren rationalised this 'gross miscarriage of justice' as a response to the #MeToo campaign. In his mind, he was being totally screwed by an ambitious young woman using the system.

'She probably realised that I was getting in the way of her career,' Darren told his drinking buddies that evening down at the pub. Never for a moment did Darren consider he was at fault in any way.

The posting to Namba Heads put Darren out of the way and avoided a messy arbitration or potential lawsuit. Luckily for him, he never did approach first base, so the reprimand and transfer were all he copped in the end. Oh, don't forget the counselling and being forced to attend a course on sexual misconduct.

'What a snoozefest those engagements turned out to be. The world is going crazy,' Darren told his new best mates at the Namba Heads Returned Services Club. Anyone with a modicum of sensitivity would have kept quiet about the whole affair, but not Sergeant Darren Billings.

Upon finally accepting that he was in Namba Heads for the long haul, Darren had married a few years back. Cheryl was a divorced teacher from Lismore, and Namba Heads was far enough away from her ex, but close enough to Kyogle and her parents. Cheryl was no oil painting, but the pair got on well enough, each resigned that this was probably the best that they were ever going to do, partner-wise, that was. Darren still liked to patrol the beach in his police 4WD on the weekends, a uniform teamed with Ray-Ban Aviators providing the perfect cover to ogle the pretty young girls in their skimpy bikinis.

Darren and Cheryl were married on the headland one Saturday, as one does. The Namba Heads headland was a nice little earner for the local civil celebrant, seeing as it hosted a wedding or two on most weekends, weather permitting. Not only locals, lots of countryfolk, and more than a few Asian brides in their finery, all eager to secure their hero shot over the bay.

Darren was often tempted to yell out 'You'll be sorrreeey' as he drove by. His old man had invariably embarrassed Darren and his mother this way whenever they drove past a Saturday wedding at their local church. His father never thought for a moment to consider the feelings of his wife sitting obediently beside him. It was their summer Saturday ritual, drop his father off at the pub, whilst his mother took Darren to cricket. Both older parents, he had been their only child.

She was the team scorer, which suited Darren just fine. He could always talk himself into a few more runs once his pads were off. 'I hit that boundary, Mum. You scored it against the wrong person. Didn't you see my cracking cover drive?' Darren would proclaim confidently. His mother couldn't distinguish who was batting anyway, all that way out in the middle of the oval. She was usually happy to indulge her son, even kindly helping to correct the opposition's scorebook. Stressful stuff, scoring cricket for the under-twelves.

The pair would always enjoy takeaway fish and chips in the park after the game, Darren's favourite meal of the week. His father would finally arrive home at all hours, reeking of booze and ill temper. It devastated Darren when his mum passed away. He shed no tears at his father's funeral.

Chapter 8

Brushed Off

Darren Billings was trying to catch up on some early-morning paperwork when Sharon Fletcher marched into the station, ranting and raving that there was 'definitely something wrong about Dave's death. Dave loved his family and would never have taken his life,' she implored.

'As if I don't have enough to do already,' thought Darren before replying. 'The coroner's report was conclusive, Sharon. Do you really want to relive this tragedy over and over again? What makes you so sure it wasn't suicide?'

Sharon mumbled some nonsense about money, but Darren wasn't really listening. 'It's always about money with women. This affair needs to end once and for all,' he told himself.

Sharon was adamant. Darren didn't respond well to the requests of assertive or confident females—'bossy bitches' he called them. In the end, just to get rid of her, Darren promised to take another look at the evidence, assuring Sharon that he would be in touch should he find anything of interest. To make the point, Darren went and pulled the coroner's report from the dusty beige government-issue filing cabinet and put it on his desk.

He had absolutely no intention of doing anything whatsoever.

Sharon had left the station feeling flat and abandoned. She knew Billings didn't believe her. She felt completely adrift, without support. To add to her distress, as soon as she arrived back at the co-op, the broker rang to say that the buyer was twitchy and reluctant to go to the expense of a survey.

'Any sensible buyer will want a boat survey, Sharon. You should think about commissioning this yourself, now that you're determined to sell her,' explained the broker.

'How much would a proper survey cost?' asked Sharon.

The broker paused while he did some mental arithmetic. 'For a boat like yours, my guess would be something between five and six thousand dollars.'

Sharon grimaced at the thought of such an expense, given how tight things were financially. 'Could you try to secure an offer from the buyer subject to a satisfactory survey? Perhaps the cost of the survey could be added on at the end, if the sale proceeds?'

'Probably. It's certainly something I'll put to the buyer.'

'OK. In the meantime, I'll think about getting the survey underway,' Sharon concluded.

The broker gave Sharon the names of a couple of survey outfits he used. He finished by pointing out that there were distinct benefits of going this way. She could discuss anything unusual with the surveyor before they put it on paper and head any potential deal-breaker off at the pass.

Sharon thought about this all morning. It would exhaust the last of their Covid cash boost if she went ahead. The broker had made sense, though, so Sharon rang both names he had suggested, requesting quotes. She received these later that day, and Sharon accepted the lowest at $5,500, including tax, who also had the advantage of being available to start Monday. He would drive down to Namba Heads first thing, and Sharon asked him to come and see her at the fish and chip shop.

Sharon hoped she was doing the right thing, gambling much of their savings on the survey as she was. With some luck, she could get through this and navigate her family towards sunnier times. She could not possibly have anticipated the dark storm that she was heading into.

Chapter 9

First Look

As Ange drove out of Bell Surfboards, headed for the highway, she became excited about this little 'roadie' down the coast, although it was little more than an hour's drive. She had missed all the 'peak hour' traffic, and the new highway was superb. Ange hadn't travelled this way since it had opened and remained alert for her exit, knowing that just a solitary road connected Namba Heads with the Pacific Highway. Finding her exit easily, she turned to the east, where the narrow bitumen road meandered through an extensive coastal bushland reserve. The outskirts of Namba Heads suddenly appeared out of the bush just on 8 a.m.

The first job was to reconnoitre the town and connect the imagined Google Map in her head. Namba Heads was classic Northern Rivers, a large headland protecting the picturesque and appropriately named Sandy River from the prevailing southerly winds. The town tucked into a bend on the northern bank of the river and sported a large riverfront caravan park. The far and southern side of the river contained the marina, the fisheries co-op, and more houses perched up on the headland. She saw a large school, tucked into the bushland reserve to the south, and imagined hordes of noisy children flooding the beaches and river on weekends and holidays.

As any surfer would do, Ange made a lap of the headlands to identify the surf spots that she had seen on the surf-riders page. A growing interest in surfing, and the resulting surge in crowds, had made everyone cagey about exactly where their surfing selfies had been taken. However, Ange could connect a few dots and recognised some locations. Most of the surf spots seemed to be on the southern side of the river and they all looked brilliant. Hopefully, she would have time for a late-afternoon surf.

Ange drove back down into the town, along the river and past the marina, finding her bearings on the position of the town centre and the major facilities. All the major attractions seemed only a short walk from the main street. Ange found a cafe and ordered some coffee and raisin toast. 'Nice town,' she thought, 'a very different feel to Byron.' Ange felt quite at home in Namba Heads, more country than coast if one could look past all the surfboards and fishing paraphernalia.

She paid the cafe tab. The coffee was excellent, so she would be a regular this weekend. Along with 'Another Arsehole Exposed', 'Bad Coffee, Bad Mood' was a favoured 'Ange Adage', the term her girlfriends had coined for these little gems.

Recharged after her breakfast, she next checked in to pay her courtesies at the local police station, although locating it took longer than she expected. Most country police stations were smack bang in the middle of things, but this one looked like a converted house in a backstreet amongst the burbs. Low-set, dull brown brick, badly oxidised aluminium sliding windows, faded red roof and guttering, a few scrappy bushes as landscaping, the station literally drained any life out of the street. A veritable outpost.

Namba Heads reminded Ange of hundreds of country New South Wales towns, with its wide, unadorned streets and single-level houses set back from the road. Ange could have parked a road train on any of the streets, let alone her police-issue Toyota Camry.

The screen door jangled as Ange entered the station, unsettling the midweek stupor that had already descended on the quiet backstreet. Some flies that had been hanging around buzzed in behind her. A young male constable eventually appeared from a back room somewhere.

Ange introduced herself with a smile, showing the constable her badge. 'Is the sarge in?'

'Out the back. I'll go get him.'

Ange looked around the small, drab, depressing reception area. Classic police-issue, devoid of any flair and not somewhere to linger. Other than Ange and the flies, the only sign of life was a gecko, sitting patiently in the cornice hoping for an opportune lunch. A poster explaining how to stay safe with Covid-19 had been tucked out of the way behind a door. Another more prominent directive implored people to keep their cars locked and their valuables secure. Ange couldn't see any missing person flyers.

Sergeant Darren Billings came out of his little office and checked her out from the legs up, eventually reaching her eyes as he extended a hand to deliver his opening greeting. 'Hi, Sergeant Darren Billings, what can I do you for?'

Ange had only been in town a short while, but it seemed the coronavirus was yet to truly show its face in Namba Heads. As if Billings' wandering eyes weren't awkward enough, nobody shook hands in Byron anymore.

'Better not, Covid and all that,' explained Ange as she deftly dodged his handshake whilst avoiding his gaze.

'Of course,' said Billings with a flippant smile. 'Thirty-plus years of having the importance of a firm handshake drummed into you makes it a tough habit to shake.'

Ange explained she was following up on a report about a missing person and summarised what she knew. Billings scratched his chin, as if deep in thought, before affording Ange his learned opinion.

'Don't know him. Can't recall seeing him before. There are so many unfamiliar faces in town with the Covid exodus from the cities, it's hard to keep track of everyone.'

'Unhelpful and uninterested,' thought Ange as she handed her business card over, assuring him she would check in before leaving, asking him to call her if he thought of anything. Ange left the station with a strong sense that a case-breaking call from Sergeant Darren Billings was most unlikely.

Back in her car, she then entered the address that Joy Thompson had texted into her phone, arriving at the little beach house where Jake Thompson had been living in no time. 'What a great fifties beach house; fully asbestos, I bet it will last forever,' she thought.

Parking her car on the grassy verge, Ange walked across the yard and found the shed out the back that Jake's mother had described. She peered through the windows of the shed. It was all spic and span, totally empty, and certainly no surfboards lying around. She walked around the building. The doors and windows were all secure.

She looked around at her surroundings. The property was the last on a small dead-end road, tucked up against the bushland reserve. Whatever the place lacked in terms of any water views, it made up for in terms of privacy. She saw some kangaroo spoor on the grass and figured that the unkept lawn would represent an attractive and peaceful dinner destination for them. Other than the bushland itself, there was only one neighbouring residence, and Ange walked over to that house to see if anyone was home.

There was an older woman inside who was friendly enough. Pointing back to the shed, Ange asked, 'Can I ask if this is the place where Jake Thompson lived?'

'Well, I didn't know his name, but there was a young kid who had been there for several months. I was worried when he moved in, but he seemed a nice kid and kept to himself pretty much,' replied the neighbour.

'Do you know if he moved out? The shed doesn't appear to be lived in at the moment,' Ange responded.

'Not sure,' the neighbour replied. 'Come to think of it, I haven't seen him for a while. Although I heard some noise during the night, some weeks back. He must have moved out then.'

'Did it seem odd that he never said goodbye?' Ange inquired.

'Not really. As I said, he kept to himself. He was certainly no trouble as far as we were concerned, and it was nice to have someone in the house. With all the van people around, we constantly need to deal with squatters,' explained the neighbour.

Ange knew exactly what she meant. Keeping camper vans off the streets, even in people's private driveways, was proving a huge problem back in Byron. Ange said her goodbyes to the woman and wandered back towards the street. Pulling up Joy Thompson's text again, Ange leaned against her car and rang the number for Henry Anderson. She was in luck.

'Henry Anderson, my name is Detective Angela Watson. I'd like to ask you some questions about Jake Thompson. Do you have a moment?'

'Is everything OK with Jake? His mum rang me a week or so back. I'm now becoming worried about him.'

Ange had no answer to the question about Jake's well-being. 'When did you last see or hear from Jake?'

'I haven't heard from him since our last surf trip,' replied Anderson, pausing as if to do the math. 'That was over six weeks ago now, in winter during uni holidays. Mid-July. I can't remember the dates exactly, but I can work it out if needed.'

'That's OK. We can come back to that later if necessary. That seems a long time not to have had any contact. Is that unusual?' asked Ange.

'Not really. Jake's not exactly the greatest communicator, certainly no chatter-box.'

'Where did you go on your surf trip and how did Jake seem to you?'

'Normal. We surfed around Forster and had a great time. Jake was just Jake. I hadn't seen him since I moved to Sydney for uni, early in the new year. We're best mates and just picked up where we left off. Jake had a bunch of new boards to try from his sponsor. It was fun surfing all the different breaks around Forster and trying out his new boards. We were staying at a beach house owned by my uncle.'

'Did you ever think of joining him and becoming a pro surfer?'

'No way,' replied Anderson emphatically. 'Jake is a way better surfer than I could ever be. Even though we learned to surf together, Jake could always out-surf me. He's also super committed and would force us to paddle out even when the surf was total rubbish. He said it was good practice for when the surf was good. Somehow, Jake can find speed and create a decent ride out of knee-high northerly slop, while I'm struggling to even catch a wave. His ability really pisses me off sometimes,' replied Anderson, before catching himself. 'In a good way. I love Jake. He's my best mate.'

'How did Jake take it when you left for university?'

'I think Jake was angry when Mrs Thompson up and left for the job in the mines. I know she desperately wanted Jake to attend university along with me. She was not pleased when Jake announced his plans to become a pro surfer. Leaving Coffs Harbour and his connections would have been difficult, but Jake's pretty tough. I knew that he'd been thinking about turning pro for ages, so his decision didn't surprise me.'

'Do you think Jake had a future as a pro surfer?' asked Ange.

'Absolutely. Jake's super dedicated. Even after a full morning's surfing, Jake would then go off and do his training while I had a rest or hit the books. He was gutted when Covid cancelled all the surfing comps he had ahead of him. I guess you heard about his performance at the Burleigh Pro. I was his board caddy and general dogsbody. It was so cool getting to meet all those surf stars after he won those two heats. They treated Jake like one of the crew.'

'How upset was Jake with Covid and the disruption of his plans?'

'Not enough to do anything stupid, if that's what you're suggesting. Jake reckoned it was an opportunity for him. He's been training harder than ever for when surfing events come back online. He feels certain that some of his competitors won't be as diligent and as committed as him.'

'In your opinion, would Jake have gotten involved in drugs or anything illegal?'

'Jake? No way! He used to chuck off at other surfers who fell for that crap,' replied Anderson with conviction.

'OK. Do you think Jake might have gone off on a surf trip without letting his mother know?'

'Yeah. I suppose. That sounds like Jake. We'd always spoken about taking a surf trip along the coast through South Australia and the Southern Ocean, then up the West Australian Coast to surf the Indian Ocean. There are loads of cracking surf spots along that stretch. Maybe he's taken that trip given he had no commitments to compete in any surf comps.'

'Surely not on his own?' probed Ange. There was no chance that she would contemplate such an adventurous solo surf trip. The southern and western part of the Australian coastline was rugged and remote, famous for lonely and heavy surf breaks, tuna fishermen, desert, massive great whites, and not a whole lot in between.

'I reckon he would. Jake's happy in his own skin and with his own company. As I said before, he was angry with his mother about leaving Coffs. I think it's possible that he wouldn't tell her what he was doing. I remember asking Jake if he planned to visit his mum when we were surfing in Forster. Hunter Valley was only a couple of hours' drive away.'

'What was Jake's response to your suggestion?'

'There wasn't any. Jake just mumbled something, and we moved on. I guessed she wasn't in Jake's good books at the time.'

'Ok. Thanks, Henry. I'll be in contact if I have any further questions. If you hear from Jake, can you ask him to ring his mother straight away? She's anxious about him.'

Once Ange had hung up from the call with Henry Anderson, she gazed across at the little beach shack where Jake had been living and thought through the implications of that conversation. It seemed quite plausible that Jake was off on a surfing trip somewhere and wouldn't necessarily keep his mother informed of his movements. If he was down in southern or western Australia, surfing at some remote surf break, it was also possible that his mobile phone would be out of range and any calls from his mother would go straight to voicemail. If that were the case, then tracking him down would be almost impossible, at least in any sensible time frame. The other key piece of information she'd learned from Anderson was that Joy Thompson might have been exaggerating about how often she spoke with her son. This whole affair might simply be the case of a guilty mother and a wandering surfer.

A vehicle pulled up alongside and pulled her from those thoughts. The passenger-side window slid down.

'What are you looking for over here? Anything interesting that I can help with?' asked Darren Billings, not even bothering to get out of his police-issue 4WD twin-cab.

'All good,' replied Ange. 'Just following up a few leads.'

'OK. I'll leave you to it. Let me know if you need any help,' replied Billings as he peered over his sunglasses in a patronising way.

As Billings drove off, Ange mumbled to herself, hoping that he wouldn't follow her around like a minder, or worse, a puppy dog. That would really piss her off.

Chapter 10

The Marina

Ange's next stop was the marina, which was sensibly tucked into a gentle bend in the river, between the bridge and the breakwater. Ange drove slowly by the marina, taking in the range of boats moored securely against the persistent southerly wind. She tried to imagine who owned the boats, what they did, what they looked like, what secrets they held. It was a game she commonly played. Ange was sure that this little habit made her good at her job. Whether or not that was true, she certainly maintained a terrific imagination. As a young girl wandering around the farm, Ange had been a prolific daydreamer, often dreaming about the life she was planning to have. 'I wonder what my ten-year-old self would think if she could see me now,' she mused as she drove slowly past the boats. Ange reckoned that any ten-year-old would be impressed, except of course for the lack of a husband or boyfriend, a future state that had fascinated her and her girlfriends back then.

As she scanned each vessel, she could readily imagine the day tripper, the aficionado, the escape-from-it-all couple, the money pit and the 'biggest mistake of my life' guy, the weekend sailors, or the 'I just don't have enough time to get out' types. She easily identified the charter fishing boats, the longliners and the trawlers. She spied a man working on a weather-beaten trawler and pulled over in a makeshift parking area, used by boaties when they needed easy access to their poison. The trawler was no pleasure craft; beaten, worn and badly in need of a coat of paint, function having comprehensively won the battle over form.

Ange walked alongside and the man looked up as she approached his boat, his crusty weather-worn face a clue to a long life at sea. The man hardly gave her a second's glance before he dived back into his repair job. Ange peered over the gunwale at what the man was working on and saw a large winch in pieces, its innards strewn across a large canvas sheet laid out across the deck. It looked like a long and messy job ahead. 'Hi. I was wondering if you knew a young deckhand by the name of Jake Thompson. I understand he was working on a trawler based out of here,' inquired Ange. Her voice carried easily over the jingle of rigging as it flapped around in the stiff southerly breeze, singing the unmistakable melody of a packed marina.

The man looked up from his pile of parts and held his hands up, like a surgeon might. Ange could see that they were covered with heavy grease, the type that contaminated everything within reach, given half a chance. 'He didn't work on my boat. I'd suggest you check with Sharon Fletcher over at the fish co-op.' The man turned and used one of his blackened hands to point out a low-level building at the end of the marina, the end closest to the river entrance. 'I saw her car pull up earlier. Poor woman. She's only just come back to work,' said the man.

'Is she the wife of the trawlerman who committed suicide?' asked Ange.

'Yep. A real tragedy. We all liked Dave and none of us saw that coming,' said the man, his voice trailing off with thoughts unsaid.

Ange thanked the man and walked over to the co-op. She saw a doorway protected by blue and white strips of plastic, hanging vertically, an unsightly decoration aimed to thwart the squadron of flies buzzing around, dead fish being one of their favourite delicacies. 'Surely those strips must do more harm than good,' thought Ange, thinking back to her days on the farm and never having been sure if they kept flies out or in. She pushed through the flapping doorway. An omnipresent smell of fish hung in the air. She was in the right place, that was for certain. She approached a young boy, working away at the counter where the lunchtime crowd would shortly place their fish and chip orders. 'Is Sharon Fletcher about?'

'Sure,' came the young boy's reply. 'Mum's out the back, I'll get her.'

Ange stood and surveyed the bins of fish scattered around the perimeter of the shop. She peered into the bins and saw some of the product was whole and some filleted, all displayed neatly across a thick layer of ice. She came to a bin filled to the brim with silver whiting fillets and felt a rumble in her stomach. The thought of her favourite fish amid the wafting scent of salt and vinegar was almost too much to bear. Soon enough, Ange was relieved from her gastronomic torture when a woman in her late thirties or early forties walked through a doorway and over to where Ange stood. Sharon Fletcher wasn't quite what Ange had expected. Her first impressions were that of a confident, attractive, observant woman, holding herself with some pride. Ange introduced herself, adding her commiserations for Sharon's loss. A tragic look flashed across Sharon's face before she quickly regained her composure.

'To be frank,' Sharon commented, 'I thought Darren Billings had just brushed me off again—like usual.'

Ange thought this comment curious. Staying on track, she got to the point of her visit. 'I wanted to ask you a few questions about Jake Thompson, a deckhand on your husband's boat.'

'Oh, I thought you were here about my concerns over Dave's death. Billings promised he would look over it again. I guess not. He even conned me by pulling out Dave's file and putting it on his desk, as if he was planning to get straight on the job,' Sharon lamented, a sour look on her face.

An awkward silence ensued, broken by Ange. 'How about you help me with Jake Thompson, and I'll be happy to go over your concerns about your husband?' she ventured.

This seemed to please Sharon, and she immediately opened up. 'Jake is a nice kid. He keeps to himself and doesn't mix with the other two older deckies. Dave said that he's a brilliant surfer. Apparently, he won a couple of rounds of the Burleigh Pro back in February, before Covid hit.'

'When did you last see him?' inquired Ange.

Sharon's brow furrowed as she thought for a moment. 'It was a couple of weeks before Dave's passing. Actually, it must have been at least that. Sometime in late August, I guess?'

'Any idea where he is now?' asked Ange.

'I presume that you've already checked out where he lives. Other than that, I can't be of much help. Like I said, Jake keeps to himself,' said Sharon.

'Thanks, now tell me about your concerns regarding your husband,' asked Ange.

'How about we sit outside at one of the picnic tables outside and I'll fill you in?' suggested Sharon.

She picked two bottles of water out of a large drinks fridge and led Ange outside. Evidently, there was some meat to this story.

The pair sat opposite each other at the picnic table, soaking up the warming winter sunlight. Sharon Fletcher resisted an urge to don her sunglasses, needing this smart-looking detective to see the sincerity in her eyes. She took a sip from her bottle of water and then looked directly at Ange, pausing, gathering herself, sizing up the detective opposite and measuring her against Billings, a poor yardstick in her opinion. Hesitant at first, she told Ange the same story that she had told Billings. At the end, she realised how flimsy it all sounded, especially when flying in the face of the coroner's report.

'I understand how hard it must be to accept this, Mrs Fletcher.'

'Call me Sharon, please.' She paused again, sensing that her story hadn't convinced the detective that anything was amiss. She took a deep breath before wading into much deeper water. 'There was something that I didn't tell Darren Billings. Somehow, I have never totally trusted him. Can I rely on your discretion, Detective?'

'I can't guarantee that, Sharon. I will do what I can,' replied Ange.

Sharon paused and weighed up the situation, realising that the detective opposite would need to do her job above all else. Taking a deep breath, as one might just before jumping into deep water, Sharon then told Ange all about the five thousand dollars which Dave had used to pay the shipyard, along with the cock-and-bull story he had told the deckhands about the whale researcher and the beacons. 'It was Cory Young who told me that the how many whale tags they'd recovered. Dave had two regular deckhands, Cory and Reece. Cory is the more sensible of the two.'

'Do you have Cory's number, Sharon? I'll need to interview him,' suggested Ange. Sharon read out each digit of Cory Young's phone number while Ange entered it into her own phone.

'That was all highly convenient,' said Sharon. 'There had, in fact, been a researcher down from the Gold Coast looking for a dislodged whale tag. That must have been in January or early February, but that seemed like a one-off to me. I can't believe that he would need Dave to pick up four or five of them, and at exactly the same time as Dave was going fishing. It all sounds fishy to me. Excuse the pun.'

Ange said that she would check Dave's story out in case it was true, before asking Sharon if she'd found any equipment on board that might have been used to locate anything floating in the ocean. Sharon told Ange that she had searched the boat from end to end and had found nothing out of the ordinary, then bit her lip before telling Ange about the cash box that Dave had hidden under the dash.

'Would you mind showing me?' asked Ange.

They walked across to where the trawler was berthed. Stepping onto the boat, Sharon unlocked the wheelhouse and knelt down to show Ange where the metal cash box was hidden. Ange took a few pictures with her phone and then walked back to her car to retrieve some gloves and evidence bags. Putting on the gloves and carefully removing the duct tape, she removed the box and slid it into an evidence bag. Ange asked Sharon if she had a key for the box, and Sharon slid a small key off her key ring and handed it over.

'Dave had two, one on his boat set and one with his ute keys. I'll get the other one when we go back to the office. The boat is for sale. I really need this sale to go through so we can get on with our lives,' Sharon explained.

It would have been helpful to have known that Sharon Fletcher had just commissioned a survey of the boat for Monday.

Chapter 11

A Long Story

The pair made their way back to the office to collect the second key to the small cash box. Although Ange was eager to get cracking on the real reason that she was in Namba Heads, she sensed a connection between the death of Dave Fletcher and the disappearance of his young deckhand. She had more questions than answers and certainly didn't believe that coincidences like these were mere happenstance. She paused at the picnic table they had just left and suggested they take a seat. Ange was pleased that she was still carrying her bottle of water. This might take some time, and Sharon could retrieve the key from her office later.

'Can we go back to the start? How was Dave leading up to the tragedy?'

Worry and pain creased Sharon's brow. 'That's the weird thing. Life had been better than ever for the past few months. It was the happiest that our family has been for ages. We'd hit a rough patch when the boat was damaged, coming off the back of all the Covid disruption as it did.'

'How was the boat damaged?' asked Ange, wondering if this was the source of some tension around Dave Fletcher.

'When Covid hit, the government restricted us to only serve takeaway. This proved uneconomic, seeing as there weren't any tourists in town, so I ended up shutting the shop completely. It just made little sense to open for just the odd takeaway meal. Fortunately, the demand for fresh fish from the supermarkets was strong, and Dave was busy. That was a turn-up, as the fish and chip shop had been keeping the boat afloat for years. A working trawler is so damned expensive to keep running. Anyway, Dave had scored a tremendous catch, but he'd stayed out too long and missed the tide. With all the extra weight of the fish on board, he hit the sandbank on his way across the bar. Wooden boats are almost like living creatures, and she soon started leaking. Unfortunately, we just didn't have enough cash to get her fixed. With the fish shop closed, the boat was our only source of income. I tried the bank, but they weren't interested. It was a terrible time until the government announced the Covid support measures and I learned we were eligible for a cash boost. Dave obviously lied to me about the cost of getting the boat repaired,' replied Sharon wistfully.

'What about the days leading up to his passing? Was there anything out of the ordinary that you noticed?' probed Ange.

'I've lain in bed on countless nights, tossing and turning for hours and running through those last days,' replied the woman, grief still written in bold letters across her face. 'There was a huge weather front coming through and Dave wanted to get in one last fish before it turned ugly. This surprised me, as he was normally cautious with the weather, but he said he was worried about our finances. Dave came in late that evening and woke me up as he crawled into bed. I could tell he was shaken. Apparently, the front came through early and caught them out wide. He said that it had been one of the worst trips of his life. I was worried that the boat had been damaged again, but Dave assured me it was OK and I went back to sleep. The next day was pretty normal, although Dave still looked beaten up from the night before. It had been a poor catch, especially considering all that trouble, so there was little work to be done. Dave went for a surf that afternoon, which seemed to cheer him up a little. We hardly spoke over dinner that night.'

'Was this the night he died?' asked Ange, unsure of the timeline of these events.

'Yes. I guess it was around midnight when Dave said he wanted to check on the boat. The wind was brutal. I thought nothing of it and went soundly back to sleep. When I woke up to go to the toilet around three a.m., I noticed Dave hadn't returned to bed and became worried, so I went down to the boat to check on him.' Tears formed in Sharon's eyes at the memory of what she had found on the trawler.

There was nothing that Ange could say. Finding your husband dead like that would not be easy to recover from. Clearly, further questioning would be cruel and insensitive, so Ange left Sharon Fletcher to her grief, promising to keep in touch.

As she drove away, she saw the poor woman staring blackly at her half-empty bottle of water. Ange felt terrible for having stirred up such depressing memories; that was an occupational hazard that she would never be at ease with. Retrieving the spare cash box key could wait for another day.

There were no earthly witnesses to Dave's final fateful trip, but Sharon Fletcher had imagined it during the dead of night, lying awake and staring blankly at the ceiling, worrying about her family. She had been out on the boat plenty of times, helping her husband whenever they were short-staffed. Commercial fishing is a tough job and Dave had only ever let Sharon accompany him when the conditions were perfect. She could see the appeal.

Sharon remembered how it felt as they crossed the bar, standing watch on the bow and tingling with anticipation, gazing into the deepening blue of an open sea, the soft light of a sinking sun behind, an uncertain night's fishing ahead. She loved the smell and the feel of the soft ocean breeze as it brushed her face, seeing the sea life exploding all around, falling into sync with the rhythm of the ocean, the vibration and hum of the big diesel engine adding a comforting bassline to this symphony. It was equally satisfying to return safely into the river the next morning with a boatful of fish, watching the dolphins surfing the boat's bow wave, leaping, and diving over a job well done.

Dave's last run would have been nothing like that. The sky would have been dark and ominous, and the sea breeze would have been heavy and oppressive. The outward journey would have been easy, one of those grey oily seas that precedes a change in the weather. As the barometer dropped, the birds and sea life would go crazy—as if they knew bad weather was on the way and needed to fill their bellies ahead of it. It was not a stupid idea for Dave to take advantage of this frenzied activity. He would have made a few runs in close, hoping to fill the boat and avoid going out wide. Having no luck, he most likely would have taken a south-easterly track as he headed further out. That way, he would have ensured a following sea on the return journey back to port.

If he'd been caught with the nets out when the front came through, he would have had a devil of a time. Once the sea was up, even turning the boat back to port would have been a perilous task. The boat would have rolled wildly the moment it turned sideways to the swell. Even at full throttle, it would have been largely out of control and at the mercy of the rising sea. That was the most dangerous time, when the boat would wallow ahead of the next big swell beaming down, aiming to slam into the boat abeam and smash it to smithereens.

Sharon had imagined Dave standing in the wheelhouse in the dark, weakly illuminated by the glow from the boat's instrument panel, peering through the angled windscreen over the running lights mounted on the boat's bow. Sheets of rain and salt water, picked up by the raging wind, would have been sweeping across the bow of the stricken boat, obscuring any hope of seeing what was ahead. Dave would have been relying on technology to bring him home safely, GPS and radar helping ensure he stayed clear of the headland or any other nearby vessels stupid enough to be out in such conditions.

In such a heavy sea, Dave would have been desperately clutching the wheel, straining to keep both himself and the boat upright. His track back to port would have forced him to run diagonally to the swell and wind at times. This would have delivered a hairy ride, the boat rolling wildly when abeam, then broaching and yawing whenever he turned ahead of the following sea, even surfing the odd wave that threatened his well-being. Once safely into the lee of the headland and in sight of the river, Dave would have cut the throttle and taken stock, checking that everything was in order before he braved crossing the bar.

In her wildest thoughts, Sharon could never have known the truth. Things had been far from being in any sort of order.

Chapter 12

Caravan Park

Ange was keen to blow off the cobwebs and catch a few waves. However, she first called Jim Grady to check in and give him an update. 'Something isn't quite right here, boss. I'll keep looking over the weekend, but I might need to stay another day if that's all right,' suggested Ange. Grady agreed.

'Oh, by the way, can you see if someone can track down a whale researcher from a university on the Gold Coast who may have been in Namba Heads recently?' Ange asked. 'Apparently there was someone down here in late January or early February this year, supposedly looking for a lost whale tag.'

'Another clash with the greenies?' asked Grady.

'No, just verifying a story,' she replied before hanging up.

Her last stop before hitting the surf was to check into the cabin she had booked at the caravan park. Ange could not believe how massive the Namba Heads caravan park was, probably the most important driver for tourism in town, she thought. Nestled between the main surf beach to the east, the river to the south, and the town to the west, it was perfectly located for anyone wanting a cheap vacation by the water.

As Ange drove in, she could see families setting up their tents and camper trailers for the weekend, excited kids running around and riding their bikes. Its flat and tree-covered park was almost too good to be true, even enjoying its own little beach on the river. The caravan park would be a developer's dream, and Ange wondered if this was a point of tension in the town.

After finding her bearings, Ange located the manager's office. 'Great spot,' said Ange by way of greeting as she walked into the small office.

The manager smiled. 'Yes, it's been busier than I would have expected, given all the travel restriction and border closures. On top of our regulars, there are lots of people exploring their own backyard instead of tripping up to Queensland or over to Bali. How can I help?'

Ange gave her name and the booking reference, asking about the prospects of extending another night if needed. The manager said that things were quite busy, but he could keep her cabin clear until Sunday morning, asking Ange to let him know her plans early.

'Fantastic,' said Ange as she waved her credit card over and around the EFT-POS terminal, vainly searching for the right spot. 'Why is it that every terminal scans from a different spot?' Ange thought, finally securing the comforting beep of success.

'Where are you from? I haven't seen you around before,' asked the manager.

'I work up in Byron,' Ange answered. Immediately sensing by the look in his eyes that this was not a welcome answer in Namba Heads, she quickly added, 'I work in the police service.' Ange normally liked to stay under the radar, so when the manager asked if she was visiting because of work, Ange casually replied, 'No, just down for a relaxed weekend's surfing.'

The manager appeared to take her excuse at face value. However, not wanting to continue that line of inquiry, Ange hurried the discussion on, asking where the best place might be to eat in town.

'That depends,' answered the manager. 'If you want to meet the locals and the families, the Services Club is the place to go on Friday nights. Saturday or Sunday nights, I suggest the beer garden at the pub across the road. They have live music and it's very popular.'

'Sounds good. Thanks for the tips,' replied Ange.

Finding her cabin provided somewhat tricky, as the numbering system seemed rather random. Clearly, the rambling park had been expanded multiple times. Ange eventually found her digs, still not believing her luck at unearthing this gem. Seeing as she'd only brought a small duffel bag, there was no unpacking to do, and her surf gear could stay in the car. As soon as she had changed into something more comfortable, she drove around to the closest of the point breaks that she had seen earlier.

Getting into one's wetsuit is always harder than it should be. Like many a surfer before her, full of anticipation and excitement about getting into the water, Ange was like a kid on Christmas morning, wrestling to open her presents. A total lack of restraint extinguished any grace she might have possessed. Her toes got stuck as she awkwardly pulled on the legs of her 2mm steamer, only to find she had it on back to front. Back to square one, eventually achieving success after an inelegant little dance fighting with the zipper. Ange figured that her ungainly gyrations could substitute for a proper warm-up.

After a cursory scrape of some wax on her longboard, Ange walked into the surf. Once she had paddled beyond the breakers and taken in her magnificent surroundings, she felt her cares dissolve into the sea. Whilst it was not the best session Ange had ever had, she managed a paddle and a saltwater rinse-off. She felt great, savouring the luxury of her afternoon surf and the brief respite from the growing investigation. Her antennae were already fully up, warning her of the dark undercurrent that was flowing beneath this tranquil setting.

Chapter 13

Meet the Locals

After rinsing her wetsuit and hanging it up with her towel on the front porch, Ange took a shower and fashioned a quick spruce-up. Wearing jeans and her current favourite Bell tee shirt, Ange wandered along the river foreshore to the local Services Club, following the sage advice of the caravan park manager.

The wind had already dropped out, and the river was glassing off. She noticed the thousands of flying foxes in the pink-and-lavender sky, heading out into the bush to feed. It was a spectacular sight amidst a stunning evening.

Ange had listened to a great podcast about how incredible bats and flying foxes are, and she knew the crucial role they played in plant pollination. Given a bad rap because of their love of fruit, they also carried the dangerous lyssavirus, along with a relative of Ebola called the Hendra Virus. Ange had been called to deal with difficult run-ins involving angry green activists, local farmers and flying foxes. Despite her farming background, and much to the disdain of her family, Ange remained squarely on the side of protecting these peculiar creatures.

The Services Club was in fact the Returned Services Club, one of thousands built around the country to support returning veterans. Entering the foyer of the massive club, she decided she might well become a regular visitor to Namba Heads, so impulsively joined up as a member, paying the token fee by EFTPOS. Now 'a fully paid-up member', she entered her number into the members' draw for that evening.

The place was busy. One would not exactly describe it as 'pumping', but the club was noisy with the cheerful chatter of local families and groups. Like many such towns up and down the coast, Namba Heads showed a somewhat split demographic. Lots of retirees at one end, and young families at the other, equally drawn by the lifestyle—and a good state school, of course. Each of these demographic groups, and more in between, were on display that Friday night.

The mood was pleasant and relaxed, and all the essential elements were in place. The Friday night rugby league game was running on several prominent TV screens, Keno was running through some others, and the gaudy flashing lights of the pokies seemed to attract ample custom. Ange approached the bar, showing her freshly minted membership card like a true local, and purchased a glass of New Zealand Sauvignon Blanc. She sat at one of the shared tall tables, which seemed like the best place to watch the fun.

Some kids came up to her asking if she would buy some raffle tickets to support their expedition to climb Mt Bartle Frere up near Cairns, part of their leadership training. 'It was going to be Mount Kilimanjaro, but Covid killed all that,' the two lovely high school students informed her. Ange was happy to buy some tickets and support their goal, even if she was unlikely to be around for next week's draw.

A booming man's voice came over the public address system, calling out a sequence of numbers in a broad Australian accent, announcing the winner of the first meat tray. 'Who first came up with that idea?' she reflected to herself. 'Let's get everyone at the pub to buy a chance to win some raw meat!' It is funny what we accept as normal sometimes.

Sergeant Darren Billings was there with some mates, ensconced in front of a large-screen TV that was showing the Friday night action. Ange quickly changed seats to ensure she remained out of eyesight, as she had no desire to talk shop with Billings.

She wasn't long perched on her stool before she noticed the glances of a ruggedly handsome man in a Hawaiian shirt. 'Probably an arsehole,' thought Ange instinctively before smiling to herself. 'I need to check my cynical side—not all men are arseholes.'

Ange liked men. Some of her friends had met wonderful guys and were happily married, but like any relationship, there were highs and lows. Ange wondered if she had become too picky and expected too much of the men she dated. Many of her single friends were obsessed with finding the perfect man, when they themselves were far from such.

Ange had enough self-awareness to acknowledge this relationship-killer trait in herself, but it didn't help that she also often saw the worst side of humanity in her job, where drug and alcohol-fuelled violence against women and children was all too common. It was hard not to assume the worst. Perhaps places like Namba Heads, with its clean sea air and open space, would enjoy better statistics. Seeing all the smiling faces around her, Ange hoped that was the case.

She shook off those dark thoughts as the guy eventually headed towards the bar, walking past and saying hi on his way. He looked surprised when Ange smiled back and asked, 'You look like a local—what's the best meal on offer in the bistro?'

'Well, seeing as we're a fishing village, I would go for whatever locally caught fish is on the menu tonight,' he replied.

'That makes sense. Why didn't I think of that?' she said, laughing, causing her smiling face to light up. Her lovely natural smile was one of Ange's greatest assets, drawing people towards her.

'Are you just passing through? I haven't seen you before,' he queried.

'I work up in Byron. Embarrassingly, this is my first visit to Namba Heads,' Ange revealed, as if apologising for her ignorance of such a delightful place. She motioned in the direction of the caravan park. 'I've rented a cabin for the weekend. It's really nice.'

Glancing down at her Bell Surfboards tee shirt, he commented, 'I guess that you're a surfer?'

'Obsessed novice—but improving quickly,' was Ange's reply. Taking advantage of the opportunity, she asked, 'Where would you suggest I head tomorrow?'

The guy didn't hesitate in his reply. 'Well, the wind is expected to remain southerly, and the swell's holding up, so I think Sliders will be the go. That's the southernmost point. It should be protected from the breeze. Cross the bridge, and then head through the scrub to the Bushies Beach car park. I think there's a signpost just past the marina. Sliders is an easy twenty-minute walk south along the beach. Oh, and the tide will be too full early on, so there won't be any rush.'

'Brilliant, nothing better than a surf report from a local,' Ange commented.

He held out his hand, saying, 'I'm Brett, by the way.'

Funny, unlike with Sergeant Darren Billings, Ange didn't feel weird shaking hands this time around. 'Ange. Perhaps I'll see you in the surf tomorrow?'

'Hopefully,' Brett replied.

'Smooth,' thought Ange to herself. 'Interested, but not gushy.' Ange hated gushy men.

She expected Brett to make a move, but he looked apologetically back towards his table, 'My shout, catch up later,' and walked away.

'Maybe not an arsehole?' Ange silently hoped.

After a second glass of wine with a delightful meal of flathead, salad and chips, Ange realised how weary she was, deciding it was time to hit the sack. She took her leave and strolled towards her cabin. It still wasn't even 9 p.m., yet Namba Heads revealed an overpowering sense of tranquillity, the sort of peace and quiet reserved for country towns alone. The streets had emptied, people were in their houses, or tents in the case of her holidaying neighbours. A safe haven.

The walk home proved quite a stark contrast from Byron at this hour on a Friday night, where the pubs and restaurants would be heaving. Despite sharing a similar coastline, the two towns had very distinct personalities. Ange decided she liked them both, for their similarities and their differences. She most definitely did not want her friend Kerrie to post any images of Namba Heads on her lifestyle page.

She was keen to catch a good night's sleep, and the quietness and peaceful mood of the town was working wonders. Ange slept deeply, waking up to the squawking of some noisy parrots, themselves having been awoken by several raucous kookaburras just before dawn. 'Only in Australia,' she thought.

Chapter 14

Sliders

Checking her emails first thing the next morning, Ange noted that the guys at the station had located the whale researcher from the Gold Coast. Dr Soren Pederson had been in Namba Heads in February looking for a whale beacon. He remembered speaking to some local trawlermen, but he certainly had asked no one to pick up another since then. The email briefly described the VHF receiver that the researcher used to locate his whales and their beacons. She would need to speak with Dave Fletcher's deckhand to gain a description of the VHF receiving and tracking device that Fletcher appeared to have been using.

Taking the advice of her handsome local from the previous evening, Ange decided that a lazy start to the day was in order. She pulled a tee shirt dress over her bathers, donned her Havaianas, and headed to her new favourite cafe. As she read the latest news on her phone over coffee and toast, the horror of the global pandemic racing around the world struck Ange. It was a stark contrast to her relaxed, sunny morning in Namba Heads, where life seemed to go on as per normal—if one could say that a missing person and an increasingly suspicious death were normal.

Breakfast complete, Ange threw her wetsuit and towel into the car and drove across the river and over the headland, until she spotted the turn-off for Bushies Beach. A small bitumen road wound its way through the coastal scrub, ending at a small car park with a view of the ocean. It was still early, just on 7.30 a.m., but the tide was dropping, and a few more cars pulled up as she packed her gear into a small backpack. It looked a decent walk around to Sliders. 'Even better,' Ange reasoned to herself. 'More effort means fewer people and more waves for me.'

Ange tucked her longboard under her arm and wandered down onto Bushies

Beach. The walk over to Sliders was magnificent; however, by the time she arrived, she wished she had a set of those surfboard wheels she had noticed supporting the longboards of some locals. Such a great idea. Ange would ask around to find where she could buy one for next time. Perhaps Bell Surfboards might stock them?

The surf was small but clean and looked like lots of fun. There were a handful of surfers out already in the crescent-shaped bay, accompanied by a pod of dolphins lolling around further out from this semi-remote headland. She knew it was more folklore than fact, but Ange felt better when there were dolphins around, with their reputation for keeping sharks away. There had been plenty of tragic shark attacks this year, and the prospect of meeting a monster great white was the sinister and scary side of surfing. That the sun was shining and the water clear gave some comfort, at least.

Ange watched the surfers catching some nice long rides whilst she did her stretching, put on some sunscreen, and then donned her wetsuit—this time with patience and a great deal more grace than the previous afternoon. After swiping some wax onto her board, Ange followed the moves of the locals and walked along the headland to a jump-off point amongst the rocks.

The water was still in winter's clutch, taking her breath away as she ducked under the first wave. It was a short paddle to the take-off zone. Some other surfers smiled and said hello. 'Wow,' thought Ange, 'what a pleasant change from the death stares I sometimes get thrown as I paddle out at The Pass back in Byron.'

Ange smiled back as she propped up, sat on her board, and looked around. Sliders occupied the furthest and southernmost point in Namba Heads, and the view back north caught several headlands and their secret beaches. It was amazing, and definitely the most picturesque place Ange had ever surfed at so far.

Ange knew she cut a svelte form in her wetsuit, and she had learnt that being an attractive female was a definite advantage in the surf. Despite more and more women getting involved, surfing was still very much a macho sport, and men outnumbered women at least fivefold on any given day. Ange was never in the least bit fazed by this gender imbalance, often using it to her advantage to gain a few more waves in crowded conditions.

The waves were bigger than they looked way back from the beach. Before long, one of the older locals ushered her to take a nicely formed wave. Ange was no Steph Gilmore and fumbled a sketchy take-off. Once up and away, she tentatively made it through two sections, pulling out of her wave halfway down the break.

As she paddled back out, the guy from last night said hello. She hadn't recognised him at first, but gathered herself to respond with a casual smile. 'Morning, Brett, almost butchered that one.' Ange stopped and sat on her board just past him and looked back just as he caught a nice wave. He surfed smoothly and confidently, stylishly matching his moves to the rhythm of the wave, impressing Ange greatly.

She caught more waves that morning than ever before in a single session. Everyone was cruisy, taking their turn and sharing the waves. 'Just like the old days used to be,' according to some of her old-timer Byron surfing buddies. The dolphins even got into it, speeding along the waves beside her. Her heart still skipped a beat when a dark shadow shot underneath her legs, even though she knew it was a dolphin.

After a couple of hours in the water, Ange was contemplating 'one last wave' but realised she was weary and her surfing was deteriorating anyway, so she walked back to her gear for a rest, rather than make the trek out to the jump-off point again. Stripping off her wetsuit and wiping down, she stood with her towel, basking in the sun and the exhilaration of what she had just experienced.

Ange saw Brett come out of the surf. She admired his form, tall and fit, as he walked over. 'What do you think of Sliders?' he asked.

'What do you reckon, Brett?' Ange laughingly replied, the two agreeing that the morning had been superb. Standing there in her bikini, Ange was pleased that she kept herself fit and her body taut. It was a turn-on standing there talking to this good-looking stranger.

'So, you're a detective from Byron Bay?' asked Brett. 'There aren't any secrets in Namba Heads,' he added with a knowing smile.

'Note to self,' thought Ange. 'The bush telegraph is alive and well in Namba Heads.' This was quite a contrast to her days in Sydney, where apparently fifty percent of residents didn't know their neighbours.

'Yes, I came down looking for a missing person. Jake Thompson, a young guy who moved into town at the start of the year. A hot surfer, by all accounts. You didn't know him by any chance?' inquired Ange.

'Not really,' Brett replied. 'I have seen him surf. He was by far the best surfer in the water.'

'When did you last see him?'

Brett thought about this for a moment. 'Not for weeks, perhaps even months ago. I hope you find him. Too many young surfers drift into the wrong crowd and off the rails.'

'I'm sure he'll turn up soon; most missing persons do. His family is understandably worried,' responded Ange, failing to mention that the success rate drops off markedly after each successive week.

After a short pregnant pause, Brett said, 'I must get going, a few jobs to do. What are you doing this evening? Fancy catching a bite at the pub? They have live music.'

Ange agreed to meet him around 6 p.m. for a drink before dinner. 'Great, catch you then,' Brett said with a broad smile.

After an hour's recuperation on the beach, Ange paddled out for another session, surfing until her arms felt leaden. When she started missing her take-offs, she knew it was time to pull up stumps and head into the beach.

Ange basked in the sun's warmth and the glow of a sensational surf session. As she slowly walked back along the beach and up the track to the car park, she stopped and chatted with a middle-aged couple on their daily walk. Further on, she had to stand aside when a large family came down the narrow track towards her, struggling with mountains of paraphernalia as they herded their boisterous children to the sand. A typical Saturday at Namba Heads, Ange reasoned.

The drive back to her cabin took Ange past the marina, so she swung into the car park and entered the fisheries co-op, hoping to buy some fresh prawns for lunch. Sharon Fletcher was serving another customer. 'I guess keeping busy is the best thing,' thought Ange. Once Sharon was free, she turned towards Ange.

'Hello, Mrs Fletcher,' said Ange before she was cut short.

'Please call me Sharon. I think we've reached first-name terms now. How can I help?'

'Which prawns do you suggest?' asked Ange.

Based on Sharon's recommendation, Ange purchased half a kilo of the cooked tiger prawns. Sharon was all business, with a drawn and tired look on her face. Ange felt bad asking her to retrieve the spare key from the mystery cash box. Sharon trudged off to her small office and soon came back, carrying an envelope containing the keys. Sharon handed over the envelope in silence.

Another customer came into the shop, closing off any chance of small talk. The pair exchanged an insipid goodbye before Ange turned to leave. It was quite awkward, really. Excusing her distracted manner as that of a grieving widow with lots on her mind, or perhaps she was regretting opening up, Ange walked back to her car, the smell of the cooked prawns making her stomach growl.

After a shower and tidy-up, Ange strolled down to the river and found a shady spot under a large Norfolk pine, where she could eat her prawns. Immediately out in front, she would see kids frolicking in the shallows and some anglers pumping yabbies on the sandbank. Ange loved the Norfolk pines that festooned most coastal towns on the east coast, conjuring up lovely and vivid memories of lazy summer holidays at the beach with her family.

The theory was that the trees, originally planted long ago by sailors on the tall ships, would make perfect masts, a sensible insurance policy for getting back home should they suffer a break during heavy weather. The Norfolk pines they planted had grown tall and straight, finding the Australian coastline to their liking. Unfortunately, what had seemed like a smart idea at the time had proven an abject failure. Unfortunately, the shipwrights discovered that a mast made of Norfolk pine snapped easily and abruptly under the load of a large wind-filled sail, leaving the trees to grow old gracefully.

'Their loss was our gain,' thought Ange as she enjoyed her shady lunch spot, savouring the prawns whilst taking in the scenery. Walking over to the water's edge, she instigated a feeding frenzy for a school of small bream and whiting, her prawn scraps a tempting berley for these hungry little fish, forever wary that something bigger might come along to make a lunch of them.

Chapter 15

Bella Vista

After lunch, the combination of sun, surf, strenuous exercise, and a full belly of prawns took its toll. A deep lethargy suddenly came over Ange. She struggled back to the cabin and did something that she never did, took a luxurious afternoon nap. Not a twenty-minute power nap, or an 'I'll just rest my eyes for a minute' nap—this turned into an hour-long stupor. She awoke feeling more tired than before and she struggled to gather the energy needed to escape her bed. Still in a daze, she shuffled outside to find that the wind had freshened from the east. Ange knew the surf would be blown out, even if she could have summoned the strength for another session.

There was something Ange wanted to see before she started getting ready for her dinner date. 'Tea Trees' was a failed residential property development that had achieved legendary status amongst green activists. Some years ago, the local Council had approved a midsized residential development on the outskirts of the town. Wallowing on some low-lying land between the road and the beach, Tea Trees was a marginal site. Ange found it ironic that developers seemed compelled, even obligated, to name housing estates after the thing that they had displaced or destroyed. 'The Meadows,' 'Daisy Hill' or 'Forestville' sprang to mind.

Once approved, the developer had immediately sent in the bulldozers while the Council kept activists at bay. The first stage of the development was completely finished and ready for families to build their dream homes. However, before any of the eager housebuilders could start, the activists took both the developer and the council to court.

She shuffled outside to find that the wind had freshened. Some kitesurfers were making the best of the fierce conditions and their colourful winged kites flashed across the white-capped sea. Ange pondered that kitesurfing might be something to be explored once she had mastered normal surfing.

Turning her back on the ocean, she drove west towards the highway in the direction she deduced Tea Trees to be. After a few false starts, she eventually found the overgrown entrance to the abandoned estate, blocked by a locked gate of sturdy construction. Parking her car, Ange slipped around the gate like plenty had before and walked into the eerie estate. It was incredible. There were roads, roundabouts, gutters to direct rainwater into a string of large stormwater pits—even the streetlights were still there. Not to be outdone, the tea trees themselves were having the last revenge, reclaiming the housing blocks and eventually even pushing themselves through the asphalt to take back the roads. It looked like something from an apocalypse. Ange found this a sobering image given the world was in the grip of a global pandemic.

Mesmerised as she walked along a couple of streets, she felt a shiver run down her spine and glanced at her watch, well and truly ready to leave this sad, dark place and get ready for dinner. Back at her car, she crossed paths with a middle-aged man who was getting ready for a night's fishing off the beach. He had seen Ange come out of the estate. He saw the man take in her bland, nondescript Camry, screaming 'public servant' as it did.

'Spooky, isn't it? That's what you get for trying to destroy the environment,' said the angler. As he made this proclamation, the man waved an arm around expansively, the one not holding a fishing rod, his weapon that would soon be used to kill some fish. As she drove back into town, Ange contemplated that there are at least two sides to every story and often many divergent perspectives.

Fears over Covid-19 had seen the real estate market boom in places like Namba Heads, people keen to escape high-density living for some open space. Ange figured that Tea Trees had likely become a highly valuable development site once again.

Ange took a shower and threw on some makeup before deciding what to wear. Her selection was limited, as she had not certainly been expecting to go out on a date—if you could call it that. Forced to put her jeans back on, she tried on every top in her bag before finding something that was marginally acceptable. As 6 p.m. approached, she strolled back through town to the Bella Vista Hotel.

Smack bang in the middle of town, the Bella Vista was a lovely art deco brick building that would have been the height of style when it pulled its first beers. Ange reasoned the hotel would once have enjoyed a marvellous view down to the river mouth, before the trees grew up and the town expanded, rendering its name incongruous. It would also be a spectacular development site.

She did the right thing and checked in on her phone using the Covid Safe App. After six months, scanning the little QR code and confirming her details was almost second nature. Entering the large open beer garden, Ange scanned the crowd along the way. Any anxieties about her attire were overblown. The Bella Vista was very casual. The laid-back music was competing vainly with the chatter of people, happy to be out and enjoying the company of others. Ange saw her date wave from the corner of the busy venue, guarding a spare stool beside a large open window fronting the street. It impressed Ange when he stood as she came over.

'Welcome to the Vista,' Brett said confidently. 'What can I get you to drink?'

Ange suggested a glass of Australian Riesling if they had it by the glass; otherwise, a Sauvignon Blanc from New Zealand would work. As she waited, Ange fell into her usual habit of scanning the crowd and imagining their stories. She noted a woman with a somewhat extravagant haircut and figured she worked at the 'Cut Above' in the main street. Ange had often imagined the disappointment of the person who first came up with this clever play on words but never had the foresight to franchise or license the name, thereafter appropriated by hundreds of salons around the country.

She sat there, perched on her bar stool, and marvelled at all the stories that could be told by this crew. Happy, sad, tragic, inspiring, and everything in between. Her date came back with the drinks, shaking Ange from her daydream by asking about the rest of her day.

'Thanks, cheers,' she said, holding up her glass and clinking his beer. 'It's been a good day. I had another long session until my arms were shot and I couldn't make my take-offs anymore. I also picked up some prawns from the fish co-op and even had an afternoon nap. I hope I'm not too stiff tomorrow. Another surf would be good. Sliders is amazing. You're so lucky to have it as your home break.'

'I'm glad you enjoyed Sliders. There are one or two others that I like just as much, but it all depends on how much sand is around the various headlands. It changes all the time, which keeps things interesting,' Brett commented.

'Oh, and I went and had a look around Tea Trees, that abandoned estate on the edge of town,' Ange said.

A shadow passed briefly across Brett's smile, and he mumbled something about it being a disgrace. Clearly a sore point, Ange quickly moved on and asked Brett how long he had been in Namba Heads and what he did here.

'I moved to Namba Heads just on two years ago. I was looking for a change of scenery after a messy divorce. We have two children, aged nine and eleven. They live in Sydney with my ex-wife, still living in our former family home,' answered Brett, the fleeting glimpse of regret that flittered across his eyes forewarning Ange to suppress her detective's instinct and refrain from probing this topic.

'I like it here. The locals are super friendly and I get to surf a lot. I dabble in a bit of investing and property development, which keeps me off the streets. The kids come to visit over the school holidays. Namba Heads is a kids' paradise, and we always have fun together,' Brett elaborated. Ange struggled briefly to connect the image of the relaxed surfer with that of a doting father.

'What about you?' he asked Ange, clearly not wanting to talk anymore about himself.

'Well, I grew up in Tamworth, before attending boarding school in Armidale for my high school years. Boarding was hard at first, but I fell into it and ultimately really enjoyed my school years. I then went on to Sydney University to study arts, that degree to take when you don't know what you want to do with your life,' Ange explained with a smile. She took a sip of wine before continuing. 'During my undergrad, I took a couple of criminology electives and found I really enjoyed them. So, after graduating with my bachelor's degree, I enrolled in the police service. I really like my job. It can be demanding and stressful at times, but I suppose that's true of most professions. I've been in Byron Bay around four years now. I'd never surfed before moving here, so this has been an unexpected highlight.'

They talked easily and covered the usual suspects—music, favourite surf spots, movies. At around 7.30, they ordered their meals. More fish and chips for Ange, and a rump steak for Brett.

Just as the meals arrived, Ange heard a police car racing across town, siren blaring. As a police officer, she was especially attuned to this ear-piercing sound.

'Not my problem—over to you, Billings,' she thought happily. She was only part way through her tasty fish meal when she heard the chopper in the distance, heading this way.

'Now it's serious,' she thought to herself. Her phone pinged before she could take another bite. It was a text from her boss.

Are you still in Namba Heads by any chance?

'Sorry, Brett, my boss—I think something just came up.' Ange stopped eating and texted back.

Yes, what's up?

The phone rang immediately. Ange excused herself and walked outside before taking the call.

'It looks like we have another missing person case. An immediate alert has gone out for any officers in the area to help with the search,' explained Jim Grady.

'I'm on it,' Ange responded. She made a hasty apology to her date and raced back to her car, pleased that she had only had time for a single glass of wine. At least she didn't need to change out of any finery.

The commotion seemed to come from First Point, on the south side of the river where she had enjoyed that late-afternoon surf yesterday. It was dark by the time she arrived. Parking her car, she showed her badge to a uniformed officer and ducked under a string of blue-and-white checked bunting that had been used to cordon off the area.

She soon found Darren Billings. 'What's up, Sergeant?' asked Ange. 'I just received a call from my boss asking if I could lend a hand.'

'We have a report of a young woman not coming out of the water following a late-afternoon swim in the surf,' Billings explained.

'Does anyone know her?' inquired Ange.

'Not yet. We think it may be one of the van-life people. A witness described a tall, slender hippie-looking girl with long, braided dark brown hair,' said Billings.

'OK. Do you want me to question the witness or look around for any signs?'

asked Ange.

'We already questioned her, but it would be good if you had a chat, woman-to-woman like. We also found a towel and some sandals on the rocks that nobody has claimed yet.'

'Those could be anyone's—people leave stuff around all the time. There could be some kid who lost their stuff being hauled over the coals by their mother right now,' observed Ange.

Ange approached the woman. By now, quite a few police had arrived, their searchlights dramatically combing the shoreline as the chopper searched the ocean. The sea was up, and a body would be difficult to see at night. If she had drowned, her body would have quickly sunk and would likely remain submerged for the next twenty-four hours.

The woman told Ange that she had been sitting on a park bench, looking west towards the sunset. The missing woman had walked right by, said hello, and then commented on the stunning sunset as she passed.

'I mentioned it was getting late for a swim, but the woman said that she wanted to clear her head with a quick dip in the sea. She said she didn't plan to be in the water long. Anyhow, I was sitting here the whole time, watching the sunset and the flying foxes, but I never saw her come out,' the woman explained, clearly still upset.

Ange thanked her. The locals had her details already, so she went back to speak with Billings.

'It's going to be difficult finding her before morning if she drowned,' Ange commented.

'We have to consider a shark attack as well,' said Billings.

Ange agreed with him, commenting that the description given by the witness didn't sound like someone who planned to commit suicide. Ange concluded that her planned surf tomorrow was already toast.

Chapter 16

Councillor

When Terry Scott heard the blaring police car race while enjoying an early dinner, he immediately thought of a robbery. There were so many blow-ins passing through the town since Covid hit. People living the van life were proving an issue, breezing through without a care in the world, posting their 'glamorous' lifestyle on their social media profile. Terry couldn't think of anything worse. Living out of a tin can parked in a car park, using public toilets—or worse. Crime rates had jumped, kick-started during the bushfire evacuations last summer, and Terry couldn't believe it when thieves looted his house during the evacuation. Serving as a local councillor for some eight years, Terry was highly protective of the township he loved.

'Thanks goodness the police caught the bastard, and he's back in jail where he belongs,' Terry had told his fellow councillors at the time. Residents had become more cautious since, but opportunistic passers-by were a constant annoyance. It sure had been a tough year.

It was his wife, Jenny, who first heard the helicopter over the top of the rugby league game the couple was watching on television. Terry loved his footy, and this distraction was deeply annoying. He walked outside onto his balcony overlooking the river and saw the chopper, following it until he saw it hover somewhere near First Point. He went inside only to find that St. George had just scored a try. 'Bloody hell!' he exclaimed to Jenny testily. 'I'll need to check out what's going on over there.'

Terry lived up on the headland and walked down to First Point, figuring that an angler had been swept off the rocks. A few years back, the government had mandated that rock-hopping anglers needed to wear life jackets in certain locations. 'You just can't legislate against stupidity,' thought Terry at the time. In his mind, it had made matters worse, with some types taking on more risk, thinking that their life jacket would keep them safe. It didn't.

The checked police bunting offered no barrier to Terry, and he quickly sought Darren Billings. If he didn't know better, he would have sworn that Billings was avoiding him—a futile ploy.

'What's going on, Darren? Another fisherman?'

'A girl appears to have gone missing. Someone saw her go in for a swim and didn't see her come out. We've found nothing other than a towel and some sandals so far,' replied Billings.

'I hope it's not a shark attack,' said Terry immediately. 'That's just what we don't need coming into summer off the back of Covid. Keep me informed the moment you find something.'

Billings did not look pleased with that prospect.

When Ange had finished speaking to the witness of the disappearing swimmer, she saw an older man speaking with Billings. She could tell by the body language between the pair that the man was someone of authority. Ange made a point of catching up with him when he'd finished with Billings and was making his leave.

'Hello, sir. My name is Detective Watson. I wondered if we could have a chat?' asked Ange, extending her hand to greet the man.

'Terry Scott. I'm the local councillor. Where do you come from?' asked Terry brusquely. Despite his obvious reticence to get involved in another conversation, Ange noticed his handshake was firm and direct.

'Byron Bay,' Ange responded before quickly adding, 'but originally from Tamworth.' Ange could tell Terry was a bushie. She had grown up around country people and thought them easy to spot. His tanned and weathered face showed the patina of a busy life outdoors, his bearing that of someone used to being the boss.

The plan worked. Terry looked at her sideways and asked, 'Watson, heh? What did your family do? I might have known them.'

'Cattle and sheep mostly,' replied Ange.

'Thought so. I come from Narrabri and I used to dabble in selling used farm equipment. I sold your father a tractor once. How are they coping with this terrible drought?' Terry asked, looking especially pleased with himself that he 'knew' this smart-looking Byron Bay detective.

'Small world,' quipped Ange, happy that they had made this rural connection. 'The drought has been really hard on everyone. Fingers crossed they get a wet season this year. I'm not sure how long they can keep going without some decent rain soon.'

'I feel for them. Drought is one part of living in the bush that I do not miss. How did you get here so quick?' Terry asked her with a direct stare.

'I was already in town, looking into a missing young man who was last seen in Namba Heads. I like to surf, so I stayed on for the weekend. I'm booked into the caravan park. Nice town you have here.'

When Darren Billings saw that Ange and Terry were talking, he rushed over, evidently seeking to stamp some of his own authority. Terry turned and addressed Billings in short order. 'Why don't I know about this other missing person, Sergeant?' snapped Scott.

'Darren' when things were going well and 'Sergeant' when he displeased Terry—Billings knew the drill.

'She only arrived in town yesterday,' pleaded Billings. 'A young surfer off on a surf trip, most likely,' he added, as if brushing it away would prove any explanation.

'There wouldn't be a detective snooping around my town if the guy was just on a surf trip,' countered Terry. Pointing to the scene before them, he added, 'And this better not be a shark attack.'

'As if I can do anything about that,' muttered Billings beneath his breath. Terry Scott's withering stare closed down any further comment.

Ange left Billings to wallow in discomfort before breaking the ice. 'I'll need to come by and see you sometime, Councillor, just to get some background.'

'Appreciate that—any time,' responded Terry.

Ange wanted to speak to Terry away from 'all ears' Darren Billings, who was giving Ange the distinct impression that he was strong on virtue signalling but weak on action.

Turning to look Billings directly in the eyes, Terry added pointedly, 'Like I said, Sergeant, keep me informed. Certainly better than you did about this last little surprise. Now, I've got a game of football to watch.' He glanced at Ange before abruptly walking away, the resigned look in his eyes showing a hint of amusement. Ange instantly decided she liked Terry Scott.

As he wandered back home, Terry prayed that this latest incident really wasn't another shark attack. The past few years had been dreadful for shark attacks in this section of the coast. Terry had been a powerful voice in getting drum lines and electronic tracking of sharks to protect his constituents. The good news was that these initiatives seemed to work. Terry checked the monitoring app on his phone and was relieved to see that Namba Heads wasn't showing up on the alerts.

It was no guarantee, of course, but the system tracked tagged sharks previously caught on drum lines and released. Terry wasn't squeamish about killing animals, when necessary, but he knew there needed to be a balance. He hoped the region was striking this right balance. The monitoring was expensive, but nowhere near as costly as the economic and social carnage a grisly shark attack brought to a coastal holiday destination like Namba Heads.

Terry had his own theories about the apparent increased number of shark attacks. Some said that it was simply that more people were in the water nowadays, with Australia's population swelling around its narrow strip of green coastline. Terry couldn't see how this applied to his region, as the rise in shark attacks seemed disproportionate to population growth.

Others blamed the fact that sharks were now protected, arguing that we couldn't keep decimating fish stocks whilst leaving the top predator protected at the same time. Eventually, sharks would experiment with new, more viable food sources. The usual climate change proponents found a tenuous connection amongst all of this.

The first of Terry's two favoured theories was that large sharks moved with the exploding population of humpback whales as they migrated up and down the coast. Namba Heads was one of the most easterly points of Australia, and whales passed close to the coast on their biannual migration. This was to the delight of tourists and whale watchers as they sat patiently on the headland, scanning the ocean for a fleeting glimpse of these massive creatures.

A whale had been a rare sight only a few years back. Now you could stand on the headland and see dozens during autumn and spring. At times, you would hear them slapping the water with their tails or pectoral fins, sometimes leaping into the air before crashing down amidst 'oohs' and 'aahs' from their watching admirers. Whale calves were also a favourite food for great whites and other large sharks. It stood to reason that some of those sharks would check out the coastline as they swung by.

As sharks were opportunistic feeders, attacks often dismissed as 'wrong place, wrong time' events. However, Terry also knew that sharks were habitual. He understood from his spearfishing mates on their annual trip to the Swains reef in North Queensland that sharks were quick learners. His mates had commented on their last expedition that waving anything that resembled a spear in the water would bring multiple sharks in an instant. Terry was no spearfisher, but he also knew how difficult it had become to land a decent coral trout fully intact. More often than not, if the fish was of any size and putting up a decent fight, Terry would ultimately pull up just a head, the body and all the meat neatly excised. Terry never swam on those fishing trips.

As a farmer, he'd spent half his life observing biological systems, and he knew from experience how complicated they were and how little we really knew. It was always tempting to conjure up a silver bullet, but he knew that there were always many interrelated factors at play.

Against Terry's better judgement, he hoped fervently for a silver bullet, one that would rid his peaceful town of the dark forces that seemed to be circling.

Chapter 17

Mysterious

Ange headed back to her cabin as soon as they called off the search just before midnight, hoping to secure a few hours' rest. She was now even more pleased to have caught that afternoon nap. Nonetheless, Ange crashed into a deep sleep the moment her head hit the pillow, undisturbed until her raucous avian friends erupted into their morning chorus.

On her way to grab some coffee, she walked by the manager's office, hoping he was also an early riser. The door was open, and Ange hadn't even made it inside before the manager said, 'I guess you'll need that extra night, then.'

'At least that,' replied Ange.

'Already crossed out the next few days for you,' he said, smiling wryly before adding, 'By the way, did Brett Tompkins track you down? He came in yesterday morning around eight a.m. looking for you.'

Ange thought this curious. Brett Tompkins knew exactly where she would be. He was the one who told her where to go surfing.

'Yes, he did,' responded Ange casually, then adding, 'Do you know much about him?'

'A bit of a mystery man. I guess he arrived in town a couple of years ago. Dabbles in investments and property development is all I've heard, whatever that means. He must have a few bob. Drives a nice new Land Cruiser and they aren't cheap anymore,' replied the manager.

With that food for thought, Ange swung by the cafe to pick up an extra-large triple-shot flat white to kick-start her brain, teamed with a bacon and egg toastie to help fuel her body—both to-go. She drove over the bridge towards First Point, arriving to see the search already in full swing. The sun was out and the seawater clear, so they should be able to find the woman's body—if it was there. As she ate her takeaway breakfast, Ange counted four police jet skis, the coastguard, and a police inflatable boat searching the coast between the surfers, who seemed unperturbed by all the activity.

A medium-sized twin-cab truck pulled up, manned by four police investigators, and filled with forensic equipment. One of them knew Ange from another job and waved to her. Suddenly, Ange remembered the cash box from the trawler, so she retrieved the evidence bag containing the small metal box and keys from her car and handed it over.

'Would you mind running this by the lab at some stage?' Ange asked. 'I don't think it's connected with this, but you never know. Could you ask them to look at what was being stored in the box, and perhaps any fingerprints or skin fragments that could help? Also, see if they can pick up any fingerprints from the keys,' she asked nicely.

Ange was naturally kind and respectful to the forensic staff. It always amazed her when other front-line colleagues acted superior and officious. Not only contrary to Ange's style, but it was also not strategic for when a favour was needed. Her forensic colleague made a note of her requests and promised to get right onto it.

Ange decided she couldn't add much to the search and a chat with Councillor Scott seemed in order. Before driving off, she read his brief biography on the council website to get a sense of where his interests lay. Ange found the address easily. 'Nice house,' she thought as she knocked on the door. Jenny Scott answered, and Ange showed her badge and introduced herself before asking to speak with her husband.

'Sure, come in. Terry was expecting you to pop around. Would you like a cup of tea or coffee? We have an espresso machine,' Jenny Scott inquired. As the Scotts were a farming couple, Ange had assumed theirs would be an instant coffee household. Pleasantly surprised, she knew it was going to be a long day, so she asked for a flat white.

Terry was on the balcony, speaking on his phone. Ange admired the expansive view that covered a large part of the river. She could even glimpse the beach to the north of the breakwater. 'Impressive view,' she commented as Jenny brought her coffee. Appreciating the effort, Ange thanked her and took a sip. The coffee was excellent, but the view was better.

Terry finished his conversation and turned to Ange. 'The phone has been going crazy this morning about this missing woman. The town's petrified of receiving more bad news,' Terry explained. 'How can I help?'

Ange asked if he had seen a tall, slender young woman with long hair as described by the witness.

'Yes, I've seen her walking around with her boyfriend and their dog over the past six months. Handsome couple, although I don't like tattoos myself. Nice-looking blue cattle dog. I guess she would be five foot ten with long brown hair. He would be six feet or thereabouts with short, dark hair. He looks fit, like he pumps weights,' Terry replied confidently.

'Do you think you could identify them if needed?' asked Ange.

'Definitely,' Terry Scott confidently replied. 'What about the young surfer who's gone missing? Where are you at with that investigation?'

'I've only just started my investigation, Terry.'

This sidestep was no obstacle for Terry Scott. 'Do you think his disappearance has any connection with Dave's suicide? That tragedy gutted our town. None of us saw it coming.'

'It's more likely an innocent connection than not, but I'm still looking into it,' Ange replied, ducking and weaving as best as she could.

'It never rains but pours,' concluded Terry with a disappointed look on his face. 'The town can't take many more hits right now.'

Ange said her goodbyes and realised that Councillor Terry Scott was worth keeping in touch with. He clearly wanted the best for the town and its residents—just the right type of nosey in her experience. She couldn't overstate how valuable observant citizens often proved to an investigation. Passive surveillance was a powerful tool for fighting crime, and she wished more people kept their eyes and ears open to help protect their own community.

The drive back around to First Point took Ange past the marina, where she saw that some fishing boats were arriving back at the boat ramp. She parked her car amongst the boats and trailers and wandered over to the fish-cleaning benches, where two anglers were cleaning their catch and reminiscing about their day and the 'big one that got away'. Ange stuck her head into the action, asking about the various fish the men had caught, establishing a connection with the cheerful men.

'What is the prevailing ocean current at this time of year?' Ange asked one of the more elderly anglers.

'Well, in my experience, the predominant current runs north along the coast. The warmer northern current coming down from Queensland and the Gold Coast meet the cooler southern current at Byron Bay. As I guess you realised, Byron Bay is the most easterly point on the east coast, so this sort of makes sense,' replied the man.

'If you dropped something overboard, where do you think it would end up?'

The man debated this with his fishing colleagues before replying. 'We all reckon that it would drift north, parallel to the coast, until it eventually washed up onto the beach. Where that might be exactly would be a complete guess.'

Ange thanked them for this useful information and went to her car, noting how the smell of dead fish lingered.

Chapter 18

Outplayed

Ange arrived back at First Point to find that nothing had transpired. By midday, the searchers had covered every inch of the coastline around First Point. Conditions were good, but when the northerly sea breeze freshened, they decided to call off the search and play the waiting game. Either a dead body, or part thereof, would turn up in the ocean or a live one on land.

There was a news reporter with Darren Billings, resplendent in full uniform and clearly relishing the attention. Ange wandered over to hear what was going to be on the evening news. She caught an odd but brief glance of acknowledgement from Billings before he focussed on the reporter.

A confident-looking Sergeant Billings gave a fair enough description of the incident. Getting any credible feedback from the public would be hard without a photograph. However, the police sketch artists were working with the solitary witness to prepare something to accompany the news report.

'Police are asking anyone who has noticed anyone missing since yesterday evening to come forward immediately,' said Billings, peering gravely into the camera. Ange had the distinct impression that Darren Billings was enjoying his spot in the limelight.

Once Billings had finished his well-rehearsed spiel, the reporter went in for the kill. 'Do you think that woman might have been the victim of a shark attack?' she asked. To his credit, Billings handled that question well.

'We have no indications that this is a shark attack, and there were no tagged sharks near Namba Heads at the time of the incident,' he said, confidently looking the attractive reporter in the eye, appearing happy that he had batted away the reporters' provocative question.

'But given she was last seen at dusk, surely a shark attack is a real possibility?' she retorted.

Taking the bait, Billings floundered. 'We just don't know, but I would urge people not to swim in the ocean at dusk.'

This was no doubt meant as a general and sensible warning, but Billings' face suggested he'd instantly realised that the report would likely read, 'Police urge people not to swim at dusk after a woman goes missing at Namba Heads'. Game, set, and match to the reporter. Terry Scott would be apoplectic.

It was hard for Ange not to break into a smile. Even though she knew that fronting a reporter on location was always difficult, Billings had delivered a real stinker. 'And he was going so well...' Ange smiled to herself. There was no actual harm done to the investigation, but she imagined Terry Scott would not be happy. Not trusting herself to keep a straight face, Ange made a hasty retreat and headed back to the caravan park to do some more background checking.

She pulled out her iPad and set herself up on the small kitchen table in her cabin. It would have been easier with a second screen, but she would have to make do. She opted to focus on Jake, at least until something broke on the missing woman situation. Ange reasoned she was the only one looking into Jake's circumstances, so she could leave the other incident to Billings and his crew.

Ange first went through Jake's calls and text messages, starting back in February. She made a note of the regular numbers and checked them off against known contacts. Jake made regular calls to his mother, as she had mentioned. There were a lot of different numbers around the date of the Billabong Pro event, which Ange decided would relate to the event, so she put those aside for the time being.

She checked off the numbers for Dave Fletcher and Gus Bell that she had in her notebook. There were several interactions with both. There was only one number she couldn't explain, so she rang it. A woman answered, whereupon Ange introduced herself and explained why she was calling. The woman turned out to be the relative of Jake who owned the house. She hadn't heard from him since that last call and confirmed that he had not mentioned that he might be leaving.

'I hope you find him. His mother rang me about her concerns. The whole family is worried sick about him. He's a really nice kid.'

'I'm sure he'll turn up. Is there a way for me to access Jake's room at your house, just in case I need to have a look around?'

'I have a spare set hidden for when I forget my main set of keys. Go around to the far-left corner of the main house and put your hand around and under the house. My spare set is resting on the ant capping that protects the corner post.'

'Thanks. I'll make sure to put them back in the same place, if ever I use them.'

'Please do. I forget my main set all too often. I'll keep in contact with Joy about Jake.'

After hanging up from that call, Ange turned her attention to the transcript of Jake's text messages, starting with the most recent exchange involving Dave Fletcher.

Fletcher: RU available to work tonight?
Jake: Planning to head south on a surf trip. Weather forecast looks ugly?
Fletcher: Some good fish about, planning a few runs in close before front hits. Weather bad for a few days. Surf trip seems a good idea
Jake: OK
Fletcher: CU at boat by 3pm. Back on high tide before midnight
Jake: OK
Fletcher: Don't worry, plan to be back on high tide, well before front hits

That was it. No more calls or texts after that date. Ange was becoming increasingly concerned.

She checked his social media accounts, but there was nothing of note, other than some great surf shots. Ange recognised some of the scenery around Namba Heads, but many of the locations were foreign to her—probably some secret spots hidden in there somewhere. Jake seemed to go on regular surf trips, so it was plausible that he had up and left straight away, still surfing at some hidden location. However, even despite Jake's frugal communication style, it seemed out of character that he would stay out of touch for this long.

She pondered what to do next. The brief exchange of texts was a flimsy basis to order a forensic investigation of the boat, not to mention a bit late. It would disrupt Sharon Fletcher's plans to sell the boat. Ange reasoned she would wait to see if the analysis of the cash box turned up anything suspicious before taking that next step.

Ange needed a break and to stretch her legs. Donning her exercise kit, she tucked her hair under a cap and headed off toward the headland. She noted how friendly everyone was, saying hello as they walked by. Even teenagers would look her in the eye and ask her if she was having a nice day. It embarrassed Ange that she felt surprised and almost uncomfortable by this. 'What is happening to me, that I would find friendly people strange?' she lamented. Namba Heads very much reminded Ange of the country towns from her childhood in the bush.

The headland enjoyed a spectacular view, and she found some narrow sandy paths that meandered through low, windblown coastal scrub. As soon as she entered the scrub, the wind died out, and all she could hear were the twittering small birds and the odd cicada, reminding her that summer was just around the corner. She could see the diggings of echidnas, made whilst they foraged in the sand for ants. Ange hoped she would get to see one of these curious creatures.

She saw an expansive grassy headland ahead and, as she emerged from the scrub, she startled several large grey kangaroos. They looked quizzically at her before easing away. Ange could feel the thump of their hops reverberating through the ground. The headland boasted a thick covering of coastal couch grass, which was so perfect that Ange almost expected to find a greenkeeper's shed. 'Ah,' she thought, 'those guys are the greenkeepers.' Ange watched the kangaroos effortlessly hop through the thick, scratchy scrub and appreciated how well suited this strange and endearing animal was to the countryside.

The headland offered a spectacular 270-degree panorama. The sea seemed to go forever. Ange found a pleasant spot, sat down on a cushion of thick, springy grass, and gazed out into the blue expanse. The breeze carried the spray from the waves hitting the headland and refreshed her face. The tension from the past twenty-four hours drained out of her. She lay back and gazed at the clouds as they surfed the breeze, almost falling asleep before reminding herself that she had work to do.

On the walk home, a white Toyota Land Cruiser slowed down beside her, and Brett Tompkins stopped to say hello.

'Any luck with the missing woman?' he asked.

'Not yet. We're hoping for someone to call in after this evening's news,' Ange replied. 'Did you know her?' she added.

'No, but I had seen her around with some guy. I assumed they were surf nomads. I saw the guy in the water a few times—pretty good surfer. She was hard to miss, tall and attractive, if you like the bohemian look,' he commented.

They said their goodbyes, and Ange swung by First Point once more before heading back to her digs, something that proved more interesting than she had imagined.

Chapter 19

Bad News Travels

Terry and Jenny Scott sat down to watch the 5 p.m. local news before they settled down to dinner. The missing swimmer was big news locally, but not that important in the grand scheme of things. The Covid-19 crisis and the duelling state politicians defending their border restrictions dominated the headline stories, so they had to sit through ten minutes of doom and gloom until Namba Heads featured.

'That Billings is a complete imbecile!' exploded Terry as the interviewer signed off with 'here at Namba Heads,' as if to ensure everyone knew exactly where the sharks were circling, driving yet another nail in the coffin of the town's finances. Now that the border restrictions were softening, Namba Heads was banking heavily on seeing a spike in bookings for the approaching summer holidays.

'I need to head to the police station before this idiot does any more damage,' Terry said, as he snatched up his car keys and headed out the door.

Terry despaired at the seemingly insatiable appetite for sensationalism nowadays. After being elected onto the council, he had been privy to the truth behind some of the juicy stories about council corruption and dodgy developer deals. His motto was, 'It's never as bad as they say, and never as good as they say.' Social media had made things more difficult, and Terry was sometimes dragged into the fake news quagmire, so he understood how careful one needed to be. Billings was clearly out of his depth.

Meanwhile, arriving at First Point, Ange walked out onto the breakwater to watch the waves and observe how the water moved in the bay. Breaking first on the point, the waves peeled a hundred metres down the headland before closing out in a small bay. Needing to escape, the water that the swell had carried then rushed out and around a small rocky outcrop, ending with a short, steep, and otherwise uninviting beach set against the southern wall of the breakwater. Finally, having nowhere to go, the water rushed out to the east along the breakwater and back to sea. Deep, choppy, and with lots of water moving around, it was not a good swimming spot. There were several signs telling swimmers that this was not the place to take a dip.

Ange could see how the undertow could quickly suck out unwary swimmers. Dangerous to swimmers, these same often-concealed currents and rips were godsends to surfers, whisking them out to sea with a minimum of effort, safely afloat on their surfboard. She had become quite the expert on rips once she started surfing.

She wandered along the breakwater, admiring the view and chatting to the odd angler on the way. Nobody was catching much as it was bang on high tide; they were waiting for the tide to turn and some run to come into the current. Ange spoke to one nice man who gave her a lesson in how the currents shifted as the tide changed. Ange concluded it would be more difficult for a swimmer to be swept out during a slack tide, and much easier once a making or ebbing tide was in full swing. She made a mental note to check the state of the tides when the swimmer had gone missing.

As she walked back down the road towards her cabin, a white Isuzu twin-cab ute slowed down beside her. Terry Scott asked Ange if she needed a lift; he was heading down to the station to speak with Darren Billings after that 'disaster of an interview' just shown on the local news. The prospect of Terry 'speaking' to Billings delighted Ange. Enthused by this entertaining event, she quickly agreed and jumped into Terry's twin-cab.

During the drive over to the station, Ange asked if there were many drownings at Namba Heads. 'Very rare,' said Terry. 'We have an excellent Surf Lifesavers club here. You should see all the kids on Sunday morning. People come from all over. It warms my heart to see all those kids getting some fresh air and learning about the surf.'

Terry explained that the tourists and holidaymakers who came to Namba Heads were mostly from the country and the surrounding regions. International tourists were a more common casualty in the surf, not appreciating the power and danger of the Australian coast. However, being off the beaten track, Namba Heads didn't see many international visitors.

'What about shark attacks?' asked Ange.

Terry gave her a full account of the measures that the council had put in place. They had banded together with a couple of councils to the north to embark on a wider program in their efforts to limit interactions between sharks and swimmers.

'Bloody expensive, but it seems to work,' said Terry. 'We even joined forces with a university in Queensland to trial drones and artificial intelligence to identify sharks in the water. Amazing stuff. It's like something out of a science fiction movie.' His face soured. 'We had a hell of a battle with the conservationists and greenies to get it all approved. I realise we need balance, but their intractability and dogmatism infuriate me. Very few sharks have died in our program. One thing I learned that surprised me is that there are only around seven hundred and fifty adult great whites in the east coast population, and they sometimes travel all the way over to New Zealand and back. They mostly prefer to eat stingrays, seals, dolphins, whales and the like, not humans as we imagine. Anyway, great whites only account for one-third of worldwide shark attacks.'

'When was the drone trial?' inquired Ange, interested that perhaps this type of innovation might make her own surfing safer. She was not at all convinced of Terry's apparent comfort with great whites.

'Still going,' said Terry. 'I can give you the number of my contact at the uni. Very impressive young woman—I like what she's doing. Tell you what, I'll ring Jenny, and why don't you come back home for dinner tonight? It's a bit later than normal, and I think Jenny was planning pasta, so I'm sure we can feed another mouth.'

Ange liked Terry and felt he would be an excellent source of background information for her investigation, so she readily agreed. As they walked into the station, Terry was on the phone, warning his wife about their unexpected dinner guest. Hanging up, Terry briskly pushed through the door and said to the constable, 'Is your boss in? I need to speak with him.'

'In his office, Councillor Scott,' came the deferential reply. 'You know where it is.' Clearly, Terry was a regular visitor.

Ange followed along behind, amused by the prospect of what may happen. Rounding the doorway, Terry launched straight into the hapless sergeant.

'What the bloody hell do you think you're playing at, Billings? One pretty reporter flutters her eyebrows, and you give up the farm. That little headline has probably cost the town tens of thousands of dollars these holidays, money that the town desperately needs.'

Darren Billings was like a rabbit in the headlights, sputtering and stuttering lame explanations. Not wanting to get into any debate about it, Terry cut him off. 'Don't speak to the press again unless you let me know first. This town can't afford you as its representative,' he concluded. Terry turned abruptly and quickly made for the door, affording Billings no chance to respond. Ange had trouble suppressing her mirth.

Ange surmised that Terry Scott would have felt quite at home in the US, where county police answered to their elected officials. That New South Wales state police were not beholden to a local council was clearly no obstacle for Councillor Scott, and Sergeant Billings was clearly no match for his local councillor.

As they walked to the car, Terry exclaimed in exasperation, 'God help us, what did we do to deserve that imbecile being posted in our town?' He dropped Ange off at the caravan park and suggested she come to their home as soon as she was ready. 'Say twenty minutes?'

'Time is money' would be a favourite saying of Terry Scott's, thought Ange. Luckily, choosing a dinner ensemble from her meagre collection wouldn't waste any of it.

Chapter 20

The Lay of the Land

It was a bit of a rush, but Ange arrived for her impromptu dinner at the prescribed time, knowing that a punctuality fail would be a black mark in Terry's book. Jenny Scott answered the door and seemed genuinely pleased that Ange could join them. They had set dinner up on the balcony overlooking the magnificent river and coastline. By this time, the flying fox squadron had dispersed amongst the bush; however, there was still plenty of birdlife to substitute for dinner music, the Scotts clearly not being audiophiles.

Jenny asked Ange what she would like to drink. 'Whatever white wine you have open,' Ange offered. Terry was having a beer and Jenny joined Ange in a glass of South Australian Chardonnay.

'What do you think of our little town?' inquired Jenny, kicking off the conversation, knowing that her husband was still fuming over Darren Billings.

'I'm loving it. So quiet and peaceful. It reminds me of growing up in a country town, only by the sea. Of course, it doesn't hurt that I love surfing, and Namba Heads has some impressive breaks,' Ange replied. She went on, 'One thing that I really appreciate is the lack of development along the coast. Sitting out the back at Sliders the other day and looking up and down the coastline, I could hardly see a man-made object. It creates a very special experience.'

Terry entered the conversation by discussing some of the history of the town, how it grew from a small enclave of beach shacks for local farmers to support the fleet of fishing boats. There was a big jump in growth after World War II, when land up and down the coast was released as part of the Soldier Settlement Scheme.

'That helps explain some of the architecture,' commented Ange.

Terry explained that the coastal land that Ange spoke of had been returned to its traditional owners, the Bundjalung people. While some locals had concerns that this spectacular land might one day end up as a series of housing developments, Terry felt that this was implausible.

'I have quite a bit to do with the Bundjalung Land Council, and I enjoy working with them.' Terry explained he was firmly in the camp that wanted people to visit and experience the coastal bushland, reserves, and parks. 'Why would people vote to protect these places in the future if they don't get to love them?'

'Who maintains the land?' asked Ange, giving the couple a description of the walk that she had undertaken that afternoon.

'The land is held in trust and there are locals who volunteer for bushland regeneration and preservation. They make a real difference, keeping noxious weeds and pests at bay where they can. Regular bushfires help eradicate non-native species and are also important for native seed germination. Unfortunately, concerns over global warming, air quality and dogmatic green groups have made it difficult to strike a sensible balance on burning, so noxious weeds create an immense problem,' he explained. 'The trouble is that if we don't allow regular smaller fires, we end up with a massive fire because of the high fuel load—like we had last summer. There's an active group of retirees who patrol the tracks, and we get the occasional complaint about overzealousness on their part. You know the type, life's self-appointed police officers. However, our volunteers do a great job overall and keep a watchful eye against damage to the scrub or erosion to the headlands.'

Ange nodded and agreed that better community surveillance was something that needed fostering in Australia. They covered a lot of ground over dinner, including their former rural lives. The Scotts were interested to know how Ange had gone from a country girl to a surfing policewoman. Ange laughed and gave them the same story she had given Brett Tompkins. Terry and Jenny explained how they used to visit Namba Heads for family holidays and retired there once they'd sold the farm.

'How did you become a councillor, Terry?'

Jenny Scott answered for her husband with a wry smile. 'Terry is easily bored and retirement wasn't quite working out for us. Serving on the local council for the last eight years has been a godsend to me. He would have driven me crazy.' Her affection and admiration for her husband were obvious.

'I can see that Terry isn't in it for the fame and glamour,' Ange quipped.

'We just need some more economic activity and stability,' Terry explained, bouncing the conversation away from himself. 'The town needs to grow a bit and we need more young families. Retirees like us are all well and good, but it's the young families that bring life and prosperity to a small town like ours.'

Ange mentioned that she had visited Tea Trees. This was clearly a sore point and Terry became animated over what a terrible outcome that had been for the town. 'Namba Heads can't ever be a glamour location like Noosa Heads or Byron Bay,' Terry explained, 'but to have that development turn to ruin was a travesty,' Jenny added that this development had divided the town for years, half for bringing it back online, and the other half dead against.

'Actually,' said Terry, 'it was a bloke from up your way that started all the trouble. A green activist by the name of Joe Kramer who heads a not-for-profit mob called the Byron Bay Coastal Preservation Society. Every time there's even a hint that the Tea Trees development is being reconsidered, he comes knocking on my door threatening legal action. A real piece of work. Apparently, his organisation is funded by well-heeled Brisbane and Sydney environmentalists. I sometimes feel that he has our council chamber bugged.'

Terry advised her to keep an eye out for Kramer and his tricks. Having lost the fight with developers at Noosa Heads, Byron Bay and its surrounding region had become the battlefront for the anti-development movement. 'That's not to say they don't have a point, occasionally,' said Terry. 'There had been some pretty ordinary coastal development over the years.'

'I'm pretty sure I met Joe Kramer at one of his information nights with my friend Kerrie. I can assure you that conflicts between developers and green activists regularly come across my desk,' Ange offered, seeking some common ground with Terry over this issue.

Ange told them how impressed she was with the surf breaks around Namba Heads, as well as the relaxed nature of her fellow surfers.

'It's those other things in the water that I'd worry about,' said Terry, showing that surfing was not an interest they shared. Terry went on to explain his theories on the rise of shark attacks, whilst Jenny rolled her eyes before disappearing to make some tea. Evidently, Jenny had heard this dissertation many times before; however, Ange found Terry's ideas sensible and plausible. They both agreed that nature struck a delicate balance, and the fabled butterfly effect was more fact than fiction.

It had been a pleasant and informative evening. As Ange said her goodbyes, she remembered to ask Terry for the number of that drone researcher from Queensland. Terry disappeared into his office and emerged with a business card.

'I wrote her name and number on the back—give her my regards if you speak with her. For future reference, I also added the number for Joe Kramer, but I hope you never need his help. That guy would stop his own mother from building a deck on her house if he saw some publicity in it,' Terry added dryly. Kramer was clearly not on the Scotts' Christmas card list.

Chapter 21

Big Brother

Ange woke up early again, courtesy of her fine-feathered alarm clocks, and walked over to the surf, hoping she could grab an hour in the water first thing. Unfortunately, the northerly was already blowing, and the swell was gone, leaving a sloppy, unrideable mess. In this part of Australia, wind out of the north-easterly quadrant was bad news for surfers and anglers alike, and today was no exception. She walked back to her cabin and packed her meagre possessions, needing to head back to Byron and meet with her boss.

The manager was up early as usual, and she paid her account. 'I'll probably be back tomorrow sometime, or the next day at the latest. How do the bookings look for the rest of the week?' Ange asked.

'Already blocked off your unit,' he said, grinning at her. Even though Ange hardly screamed 'police officer', the word was out around town about this attractive no-nonsense detective staying at his caravan park.

'Oh, by the way,' Ange asked the manager as an afterthought. 'I don't suppose you ever came across the missing woman who was on the news last night?' Ange reasoned that, even if the woman was part of the van-life set, she couldn't have stayed around town for too long before getting in trouble with Billings or a council inspector.

'Come to think of it, I do,' he replied. 'She was with some bloke. Driving an old van. I remember they had a nice-looking cattle dog. We don't allow pets, so I told them to try the real estate agents in town.'

Even though she had decided to stay clear of this investigation, her night with the Scotts had piqued her interest. Ange rang her boss and gave him an update. 'Hi, boss. I'm about to head back to Byron Bay. I don't know why, but I somehow feel that something connects all these deaths and missing persons. The local sergeant, Darren Billings, is completely useless. Did you see his botched interview last night on the news? Talk about inept. Anyhow, I thought I might make a few inquiries about the woman before heading back. Is that OK with you?'

'I laughed out loud at his performance. Sure. Just don't tread on too many toes if you can help it,' came the voice of bitter experience.

It was too early for the real estate agents to open, so Ange sat down at the nearby cafe for coffee and some delicious avocado toast. She checked the news on her phone, finishing with the latest surf report. This awful northerly would be around for a couple of days before a south-easterly change kicked in, bringing some fresh swell towards the end of the week. It's a thing with surfers—even if they have zero chance of getting in the water, they'll still religiously check the weather forecast in case the surf magically improves.

Just after 9 a.m., Ange wandered over to question the two letting agencies in town. As soon as she showed her badge, they both asked if she was there about that woman who went missing the previous evening. 'Wow, word sure travels fast in this town,' Ange marvelled to herself.

'Stupid woman,' the first agent had commented. 'Who would go swimming at dusk? She never came in here,' she added, dismissing Ange brusquely.

The second agency knew the woman and dug out the address of the 'cheap and cheerful' shack the agent had rented her and her partner. The agent sheepishly admitted that the couple had agreed to pay cash. They paid one month in advance and moved in the same day, provided the agent dispensed with the paperwork and any need to furnish identification. This was a tricky move by the agent, as it was against the law to rent out housing to anyone with no identification.

'Why didn't you insist on identification, as you're supposed to?'

'They were adamant on that point. The owner was keen to earn some income on the place and wanted to take the deal. We've had all types through here since Covid hit, and they seemed nice enough, so we just ran it through the books as casual letting. I hope we didn't do something wrong. They've been trouble-free tenants and always paid the rent on time,' said the agent, as if this was a reasonable excuse for fudging the rules.

'Not my jurisdiction,' said Ange, opting to keep the agent onside rather than enforce this relatively minor infraction of the rules.

Relieved, the agent commented the house was due for an inspection, leaving a convenient opening for Ange in the future.

Ange found the rental house on the edge of the town, tucked away just off the river. There was no answer when she knocked on the door, and there didn't seem to be anybody there. She would need to come back with the real estate agent.

Before starting the drive back to Byron, Ange rang Cory Young, the more sensible of Dave Fletcher's deck hands according to Sharon Fletcher, on the off-chance that he would be available to answer a few questions about what she had learned from Sharon Fletcher and the mystery whale tags. She was in luck. He would be home all morning. Ange jotted down his address and told Cory that she would be there soon.

Her navigation app told Ange that she was only fifteen minutes' drive away, and she figured that this was time to make another call she had been sitting on. Before setting off, she typed the number of the drone researcher in Queensland into her phone. Waiting until she was clear of the town and on the open road, Ange rang the number. A woman answered.

'Am I speaking to Dr Jacqui Hansen?' Ange asked. Having confirmation, Ange introduced herself and inquired if she could come and speak to the researcher tomorrow or the next day in Namba Heads. The researcher explained she was in Queensland, having braved the Covid-19 border restrictions the previous evening.

'I wanted to ask you some questions about your drone surveillance program,' Ange asked nicely, only to be surprised somewhat by the exasperated reply.

'Not another complaint!' Dr Hansen lamented. 'We have all of our permits, and what we're doing is totally legal,' she explained defensively.

Ange quickly reassured her that this wasn't the purpose of her call. Dr Hansen described how her team had suffered countless complaints from 'Big Brother Surveillance' conspiracy theorists. Some of her researchers had suffered direct verbal abuse.

Ange asked about the program, how long it had been running and how often they deployed the drones.

Dr Hansen seemed pleased. 'We've been running the program for almost six weeks now, and we're due to finish up the trial at the end of the month. We try to deploy our drones every day, weather permitting, usually during the morning to take advantage of lighter winds and calmer seas. We mostly operate off First Point and the southern break wall, as the water seems consistently clearer on that side of the river mouth.'

Ange asked how they kept track of the drones and if they needed to pilot them by hand.

'Once we plot a surveillance area, the drones mostly look after themselves,' Dr Hanson expanded. 'We have someone there watching them and monitoring the video feed on their phone, but this gets uploaded into the cloud and analysed back in the lab.'

'So, you keep the video feed, then?' Ange asked hopefully.

Dr Hansen explained how she used the stored video to train their artificial intelligence engine, running the feed through their algorithms many times over. 'It's painstaking work initially, but the AI engine learns quickly and gets better each time at correctly identifying objects in the water. Ultimately, identification, authentication and tracking will be in real time.'

Ange asked if it would be possible to gain access to the footage for the past week, explaining the current investigation around the missing swimmer. Dr Hansen was aware of the incident, having seen the news and recognised the scene of the television interview. 'That police sergeant probably helped us secure another round of grant funding,' she laughed.

Dr Hansen promised to discuss it with her team, but she felt confident that this would be OK. 'Would you mind shooting me an email with your request? You'll need to deal with confidentiality. We see real commercial value to our research, so we need to protect our intellectual property.'

Ange pulled her car over and wrote down Dr Hansen's email address, committing to send something as soon as she got to her desk that morning.

Before ending the call, Ange asked, 'Do you think the drones will help? I'm a surfer myself. I find what you're doing is really interesting.'

'Absolutely,' Dr Hansen replied confidently. 'This technology is amazing. Watching the drone identify and follow a shark is mesmerising. One day we hope to have squadrons of drones patrolling popular swimming and surfing areas. The public will even be able to log on and view the live video feed. We've already helped local surf lifesavers twice, where the drone has successfully identified a shark and pinged an alert.'

'Keep up the good work, and thanks for your help,' Ange said, finishing the call by telling Dr Hansen to expect her email shortly.

Chapter 22

Backwaters

Ange arrived in the small riverside town of Deepwater soon after her call with Dr Hansen. Following her navigation app, she quickly located the small walk-up block of flats where Cory Young lived. Maintenance was obviously no priority for the owner, as the flaking and faded building was badly in need of a coat of paint. It was built amongst the flatlands, in an area Ange figured was likely to flood often, and the street exuded a swampy, dank feeling. Mosquitoes would definitely be a problem during the summer.

After parking her car on the grassy verge, Ange walked up the rickety wooden staircase and knocked on the door of flat number three. A shortish man of non-descript features answered the door. Ange guessed he must be in his mid-twenties, and he reminded her of the roustabouts who travelled with the shearers to her parents' farm each year, itinerants who were hired for their muscle rather than their brains. Ange inwardly named his haircut as a prepubescent mullet, which seemed an appropriate style for someone who worked on a fishing trawler.

She flashed her badge. 'Hi. Cory, is it? My name is Detective Watson. I called earlier.'

'Sure. Come in,' replied Cory. He motioned towards a young girl, perhaps in her late teens or early twenties. 'This is my fiancée, Talia. We're getting married soon. Tarls is pregnant.'

Ange took in her surroundings and concluded that the combined kitchen-cum-lounge-room seemed a perfect match for the exterior of the building. A chipped kitchen table sat to her left and a tattered beige couch sat in the co-joined living room to her right. A large flat-screen television presented a substantial incongruity to this thrift-shop decor.

Talia remained slouched across the couch and fixated by whatever she was watching on television. Going by the noise, MTV or some other music program was showing. She rolled her eyes in annoyance when Cory asked her to turn the volume down.

'How can I help you?'

'I have some questions about some whale tags you helped Dave Fletcher pick up out at sea,' said Ange.

Cory cleared the remnants of breakfast off the kitchen table and quickly swiped it clean. Given the state of the greasy rag that Cory had fished out of the sink, Ange doubted he had achieved much. Once finished, Ange tentatively sat down in a rickety kitchen chair, keeping her hands off the table. Evidently no domestic goddess, Tarls remained glued to the screen and made absolutely no moves to assist her husband-to-be.

'Oh, those things. They were a fun diversion from pulling up nets. Dave always seemed pleased when we found them and slipped us a pineapple at the end of the trip.'

Ange knew that pineapple was slang for a fifty-dollar note, which might have seemed generous to Cory but would have been a small fraction of Dave Fletcher's recompense for those deep-sea collections. 'How many times did this happen?'

'Four or five,' said Cory. He paused and undertook some mental arithmetic. 'No, we definitely picked up five tags. I remember that Reece and I saved up and used our two-fifty to buy some concert tickets. Reece is the other regular deckie who worked on the Fletchers' boat.'

'OK. So how did it work, picking up the tags?'

'It was pretty straightforward. Dave would navigate to a set of coordinates that Dr Bjorn had given him. Dr Bjorn is a whale researcher from the Goldie who Dave knows. Apparently, he uses tags to track the whales, and needs someone to pick them up once they come loose. I don't know why he bothers; those things are in plague proportions out here. We were always worried about hitting a whale or one getting caught in our nets.'

'It must have been hard to find something so small in the ocean. How did you manage that?'

'Dave had this contraption that Dr Bjorn had given him. When we arrived at the coordinates, either Reece or I would take the helm, and Dave would direct us to the tag. Once he could see it bobbing around, we would ease over and Dave would pick it out of the water with a boat hook.'

'How could he see it at night?'

'Trawlers have massive lights. It's like daylight out there when we're sorting the catch,' explained Cory.

'I see. What did Dr Bjorn's contraption look like?'

'I never saw it close up, but it looked like a handheld UHF unit, the type like the police use. That's you guys, I guess. It had this weird aerial coming off the front which reminded me of a hammerhead shark. Dave used to wave this around and I guess it helped him home in on the tags.'

'How long would it take to find a tag and hook it on board?' asked Ange.

'That depended on the sea. If it was calm, it would only take ten minutes once we'd reached the coordinates. If the swell was up, we could spend up to an hour looking for the thing. Dave said that the signal given off by the tags was really weak and easily messed up by the swell.'

'Great. I get the picture. Now, tell me about the tags you picked up. How big were they?'

'Not much bigger than a mooring buoy. Not round, more the shape of a teardrop. I guess that shape would be more aerodynamic for the whales to pull around in the water.'

Ange imagined the forces on the alleged tag caused by a whale diving deep down in the ocean. A floating object like the one Cory had described wouldn't last long at all, tens of metres underwater, at best. She reasoned Cory hadn't aced physics at school. 'What happened then?'

'Dave would stash the tag and the contraption in the wheelhouse and we'd either head back to port or keep fishing. I presume Dr Bjorn had the tags picked up from the boat,' answered Cory.

Ange carefully studied Cory's body language. His reply showed no guile or concern that he might have been wittingly involved in any illegal activity. Cory might have been deploying a clever poker face, but Ange didn't feel this was his natural style.

'OK. Thanks. Can you tell me about Jake Thompson? How well do you know him?'

'Nice enough guy. Keeps to himself. A cracking surfer. Did you know he won two rounds at the Burleigh Pro last year?'

'Yes, Mrs Fletcher told me that. Have you seen him lately?'

'Not for ages. I reckon six weeks at least. He only worked the odd shift for Dave, so we never saw him all that often.'

'What about the night before Dave's death? Were you on the boat that night?'

'No, thank Christ. I didn't realise he went fishing that night. What was he thinking? The weather was putrid,' replied Cory, spitting out the word putrid like a rotten piece of fish.

'Where were you then?'

'We were up in Tweed Heads at the Services Club for that concert we had tickets for. Reece and his girlfriend were with us. Tarls drove, seeing as she can't drink and all that.'

'Would Dave ever go fishing on his own?'

'I doubt it. I think some of the small prawners operate solo sometimes. Dave's boat would be a handful without a deckie or two on board, especially if the weather wasn't perfect.'

'So, what are you doing now? Have you found another job as a deckhand?'

'No. I've got some work labouring on the new highway. It's not as much fun as the trawler, but the pay is much better and I guess we need the money, what with Young Cory on the way. It's really sad what happened to Dave. I would never have picked him as somebody who'd top himself. He was brilliant to work for, and the Fletchers are nice people.'

Ange concluded she had all the confirmation she needed. 'Thanks, Cory. You've been most helpful. Sorry for the intrusion, Talia.'

With some apparent effort, Talia raised her eyes in a silent reply. No other appendage moved.

As Ange eased herself down the wooden staircase, a wave of despair came over her as she contemplated the hand-to-mouth, struggle-street existence that awaited their new child. She hoped that the young family could stay afloat now that Cory's trawler career had been sunk. An even worse prospect was that Cory Junior would become a future police statistic in one form or another.

Chapter 23

Moving Day

On the drive back to Byron, Ange pulled into a service station and grabbed some lunch to go, arriving at the police station just before lunchtime. She went straight to her desk to eat her sandwich and scan her inbox for any emails she'd missed on her phone. She saw one from forensics containing their report on the cash box. Opening the attachment, Ange first grabbed a cup of coffee before settling in her chair to read it.

She skipped quickly through the usual preamble and chain of custody blurb, going straight to the conclusions. The analysis was consistent with contamination from bank notes, as Ange had expected. There were biological traces consistent with fish residue—they even found a fish scale stuck inside the lid, none of which was surprising. What caught her full attention was the traces of narcotics, notably cannabis and cocaine. 'What on earth did Dave Fletcher get himself involved in?' thought Ange. The report had images of several fingerprints, presumably all from Dave. They shouldn't have any trouble assembling a decent set of his fingerprints from the boat and other personal effects.

Armed with the forensic report, Ange went straight to Grady's office to brief him on what she had discovered, reiterating her concerns that something was not quite right in the town.

'I think it's important that I head straight back to Namba Heads and push on with this investigation, boss,' stressed Ange.

'Fine, Ange. I hope this isn't a case of you dreaming up connections that aren't real,' replied Grady.

Ange was on a roll and pushed the envelope. 'With all that's going on here, boss, I sure could use some assistance. Is anyone available to help me out? Well, anyone other than Walton or Lynch, of course.'

'OK, I'll allocate Billy to help you,' Grady offered reluctantly, staffing a persistent challenge.

Ange was pleased about this, as she liked Billy. Although he was fresh out of training, she found that these new graduates were highly skilled in IT and tech. Whilst Ange considered herself quite competent, she was no match for these digital natives and their innate understanding of technology.

After getting his orders, Billy came over to ask Ange what he could do. 'First up,' said Ange, 'I want you to read the forensics report carefully and let me know if you see anything. Second, I want you to familiarise yourself with the report on the woman who went missing two nights ago at Namba Heads, as well as the report on Jake Thompson, a young guy reported missing a couple of weeks ago.' Ange turned to her computer and emailed the three reports to Billy, sending him straight to work.

She remembered that she still needed to email Dr Hansen. Ange contacted the legal department and explained the type of email she needed, telling them it was part of a live investigation. She then went over to Billy's desk. 'Later today, I should have access to some drone footage for the past seven days that I want you to go over. See if you can identify the missing woman or anything else unusual.' Ange went on and gave Billy a summary of the drone program and her conversation with Dr Hansen. Billy thought that this was 'super cool' as Ange had known he would, so she figured that this tedious task was in safe hands.

'Oh, and one last thing. I want you to do some digging into a group called the Byron Bay Coastal Protection Society and its head, a guy called Joe Kramer. See what you can find and give me a summary of where and when they've been in the media,' Ange said.

Billy looked chuffed and headed back to his desk to start work. Ange saw legal had sent her a draft email. It read well, so she simply copied the relevant text and sent the requested email to Dr Hansen. Ange took advantage of this momentum and went to see her boss again.

'I think I should get forensics to look over the fishing boat. I have a feeling that Jake Thompson disappeared during their last fishing trip. While they're in town, they could also look over the shed where Jake Thompson was living,' Ange said as she poked her head in his office. She knew that a proper forensic analysis was expensive and time-consuming, and not something to be squandered on a weak hunch.

Grady looked her directly in the eye. 'Will we need a warrant, or can you get the consent of the owners?'

Speaking with more confidence than she truly possessed, Ange assured him she could secure both consents. She was certain that the owner of the shed where Jake lived would be no trouble, however, Sharon Fletcher might be difficult.

'OK, so long as you can get consent and keep this as low-key as possible,' replied Grady warily, perhaps suspecting that he was being snowed.

'Let's see how that goes,' thought Ange, knowing that forensics showing up in Namba Heads to look over a closed case was likely to ruffle the feathers of one Sergeant Darren Billings.

Ange spent the balance of the day tidying up some admin before going home to drop off her dirty clothes and pick up some fresh ones. This time, not really knowing when she might be back, Ange packed a larger bag and a wider selection of clothes.

She saw an email from Dr Hansen on her phone. The researcher had organised a folder in a file share service and uploaded the last seven days' worth of drone video. Dr Hansen reiterated her stipulation that they could only use the video material for assisting in the investigation and implored Ange to respect the confidentiality of her research material. The email contained a hyperlink to access the folder, along with a username and a password. Not wanting to go back to the station, Ange sent a reply directly from her phone to reassure Dr Hansen and thank her. She then forwarded the email through to Billy, stressing that the video was strictly confidential and asking him to ring her if he saw anything interesting.

It was now dinner time, and Ange was tired and looking forward to a night in her own bed. She headed into Byron and the little hole-in-the-wall restaurant she liked in Bay Lane. In stark contrast to her past few days, the scarcity of parking spaces forced her to drive around the block three times. Busier and perhaps not as relaxing as Namba Heads, Byron Bay was always exciting and interesting.

She was sitting having dinner when her phone rang.

Chapter 24

The Survey

Sharon had endured a restless night's sleep the night before, knowing that her small cash buffer would soon be gone, but also uncertain what tomorrow's survey might unearth. Having Detective Watson in town investigating the disappearance of Jake Thompson was not helping, dredging up to the surface all of Sharon's doubts and distress over Dave's death. She desperately missed Dave; his companionship, his smile, the feel of him, knowing that he was beside her. She felt utterly alone, abruptly cast adrift in a sea of uncertainty.

Dawn finally arrived, leaving Sharon feeling bone-crushingly weary. Problems explored during the dead of night rarely get solved.

Arriving early to her little office at the co-op, she assembled all the records, licences, permits, service logs and invoices. It was quite a pile, and she reflected on how expensive and complex it was to keep a large boat in the water. The surveyor arrived down from the Gold Coast earlier than she expected and picked up the records and the boat keys just before 9 a.m. She left him to it and went back to her bookwork after a busy weekend.

Her day at the fish and chip shop did not go well. Monday was normally a quiet day, time to catch up on admin after the busy weekends. Sharon's fuse was shorter than usual when those two young women set up in her car park just before lunch, waving placards and chanting their #bantrawlers and #environmentmatters slogans. 'Clearly nothing better to do on a Monday—like work,' fumed Sharon.

Nothing could be further from the truth—the lives and livelihoods of fishermen like Dave depended on a healthy and sustainable environment. 'It's those massive illegal fishing boats they should be worried about, not community outfits like ours—we just offer more convenient parking, no doubt!' thought Sharon ironically.

She remembered how proud she was of Dave when he had the gumption to get involved and lobby the council over mooted plans to revive that Tea Trees development. Dave and his precious coastline. It was one of his passions. Sharon and her husband had not been afraid to dig in and help protect their local environment, unlike these blaring social media extremists.

It was all too easy to join the 'cancel culture' without a care in the world for the lives of hardworking people like the Fletchers, who took a practical approach to caring for their environment. She never saw those two women on the regular coastal clean-up days, scouring the beaches and picking up rubbish like she and Dave had often done. 'Too busy hashtagging,' Sharon despaired.

The surveyor pored over the boat for most of the day, dropping everything back to Sharon's office around 3 p.m. She was still fuming over her earlier encounter and was relieved when he said it all checked out so far. The surveyor needed to make a few calls and verify some of the work, but he told Sharon not to worry about this. 'Routine stuff,' he assured her. At last, something was going in the right direction. Not wanting any further surprises, Sharon explained about the five thousand dollars in cash and the invoice for the hull repairs from a few months back.

'Noted,' he said, turning to leave. 'Oh, I forgot. I found an old phone of your husband's stuck down between the deck and the gunwale.'

He handed over the phone. Sharon did not recognise it. However, she sensed this phone might be pivotal in whatever Dave had gotten himself into. On one hand, it might help prove that Dave did not commit suicide. On the other, it could expose Dave as some sort of criminal.

Putting the phone aside for the moment, Sharon needed to pick her boys up from school. She drove across town in a daze, racked by doubt about how to deal with this development. She stood waiting by the car, watching the chaos of school pickup, disoriented by how life could appear so normal on the surface, where reality was anything but.

She glanced around at all the perfect-looking mums and dads, wondering why her life was such a mess. There was Jenny from the vet clinic—everyone knew she was having an affair with one of the other fathers. She could see Phillipa—who seemed to be coping well with her breast cancer treatment. It brought some cold comfort to Sharon's own challenges, realising that complicated stories sat behind each smiling face.

She was no stranger to tragedy. Both her parents had been killed in a horrific traffic accident on a notorious stretch of the old Pacific Highway near Port Macquarie. Sharon was just twenty-six at the time, but at least she had Dave to help her through back then.

She saw her two beautiful boys walking towards her, their backpacks full of the flotsam and jetsam of school life. Monday was PE—no doubt there were sweaty clothes. She would need to get them in the wash as soon as they arrived home. Another normal thought puncturing her grief.

The two boys were chatting to some mates, and Sharon was relieved to see that they were getting some of their spark back. She marvelled at how well the boys were holding up. They seemed to cope better than she did. School life and reengaging with their mates were helping. Sharon briefly wondered if that might be the solution, letting life's trivialities displace her mind's torment.

The death of their father had been a devastating blow. The two boys had worshipped Dave. A real man's man—they had loved spending time with him, learning how to become men themselves. Now they would need to face those lessons on their own. Sharon thought that there was nothing sadder than a boy being smothered by his mother. She would need to be careful to control that instinct. It was hard enough being a mother, let alone endeavouring to fill the void left by their father.

As the boys came towards her, Sharon was unable to control her anguish. She could see elements of Dave in each of them. The solitary tear that ran down her face did not go unnoticed. They each gave her a hug, the oldest telling her, 'We all miss Dad. We'll be OK, Mum.'

'That is exactly what Dave would have done,' she thought. The boys could never have realised the comfort those few innocent words had offered.

Sharon made a special effort to treat the boys that night, making shepherd's pie for dinner, their favourite. A mother's love is a powerful force, and a fragile peace descended on their dinner table. Even Dave's mother smiled for the first time in ages. As they sat there, discussing their everyday trials and tribulations, Sharon realised they would survive this tragedy.

She needed to do the right thing. Whatever or whoever Dave was involved with needed to be dealt with. After the family had cleaned up from dinner, the boys retreated to their bedroom on the pretence of doing some homework. They had moved back in together after Dave died, each other's company helping deal with the demons that came in the night.

Sharon went back through her call register, looking for the entry for that woman detective. There was no way she would ring Darren Billings and get brushed off again—she did not trust him at all. Her finger paused briefly above the call symbol before she took the plunge, sensing that this might be a sliding door moment.

'It's Sharon Fletcher here, Detective.' Hearing the clatter and chatter of dinner in the background, Sharon added, 'Have I caught you at a good time?'

'Oh, good evening, Mrs Fletcher. What a coincidence. I was planning to call you tomorrow. How can I help?' Ange replied pleasantly.

Sharon explained about the survey that she had commissioned and the mystery phone that the surveyor had found.

Ange was in the middle of dinner in Bay Lane when she took the call from Sharon Fletcher. The restaurant was noisy, so she walked outside. Sharon then explained what had happened with the boat survey and the discovery of a mystery phone. Whilst Ange was unhappy about potential contamination and a little annoyed that Sharon hadn't told her about the survey, the call gave her the opening she needed.

'Could you put the phone aside and try not to touch it anymore? I'll come around tomorrow and pick it up.' Sharon agreed before Ange continued, 'Also, I'd like to get forensics to go over the boat, just to check that something else wasn't missed. Will you consent to this, Mrs Fletcher?'

Sharon paused a minute before answering. 'Can you keep it as low-key as possible? I do want to sell the boat.'

'That's fair enough. Let's get this done immediately. Hopefully, you can fob this activity off as part of the survey process. Can I set these wheels in motion, Mrs Fletcher?'

There was a long pause as Sharon Fletcher seemed to weigh up her options. 'OK. Let me know when to expect them. I don't need any fresh surprises right now.'

Armed with her fortuitous consent, Ange rang Billy straight away.

'Billy, we need to get forensics down to Namba Heads as quickly as possible. Get the boss to ring me if you have any problems. I think something important may have landed in our laps. Can you tell forensics to keep as low-key as possible? I'm trying to fob their visit off as routine boat stuff. They can also look through the shed where Jake Thompson was living, but the boat needs to be the priority, for the moment at least.'

'Will do,' replied Billy.

While this was an exciting development, Ange didn't wish to get her hopes up too high. In her experience, one could plug away at a troublesome case for ages, making little or no progress. Then, out of the blue, something would break, and the stars would align to point the way forward. Perhaps this was one of those events? Despite her familiar and comfortable bed, Ange did not sleep as well as she'd hoped.

Chapter 25

Drones and Phones

Ange had awoken early, keen to get on with her case. 'Or is that now cases, plural?' she wondered. After some coffee and some muesli, Ange picked up her bag and locked the door behind her, wondering how long she would be away. She threw her bag in the back of her car alongside her surfboard and surf gear. This time she added her latest purchase, a nice six-foot-eight-inch midsize board that she was itching to try out in some bigger surf. Surely, she would get some time in the water over the next few days...

As she arrived in Namba Heads, as much as it annoyed her, she resigned herself to checking in with Darren Billings. Noting the presence of his car outside and her consistently good fortune of finding him at the station, Ange concluded that Billings ventured out into the field as little as possible. The screen door clanging to signal her arrival, Darren Billings came quickly out to greet her. His forced smile couldn't hide his true misgivings about having Ange poking around.

Ange got straight to the point of her visit. 'I've organised for forensics to go over Dave Fletcher's boat.' Seeing Billings ready to explode, she quickly added, 'In relation to the disappearance of Jake Thompson.'

Billings relaxed marginally, but was clearly upset by this intrusion on his patch. Ange saw this attitude all the time, a necessary by-product of her job, poking around in other people's patches all the time as she did.

She explained that the last known location of Jake was on Dave Fletcher's boat, the night before Fletcher's death. She made it clear to Billings that the aim was to keep this quiet and as low-key as possible so as not to affect Sharon Fletcher's plans to sell the boat.

'Anything show up on the missing woman?' asked Ange nicely. She had absolutely no intention of sharing the details of the drone footage just yet.

'Nothing. If there's a body to be found, it should show up today,' Billings replied.

'OK. Keep me posted if anything happens,' she said as she headed out the door.

Ange's next stop was to check into the caravan park. The manager seemed pleased to see her. He laughed as he handed over the key and told Ange that her usual cabin was ready and waiting. 'You should know the way by now,' he added. Ange laughed with him before driving her car to the cabin and unpacking her bags. She was just about to grab some coffee when Billy rang from the station.

'I think I found something in the video footage,' he said excitedly. 'A woman who matches the description of the missing swimmer was down at First Point the morning before her disappearance. She was looking around the rocks intently, almost as if she was searching for something. I'll email you a snip of the video.'

'It's amazing stuff,' Billy went on, clearly excited by his day's work. 'Watching the drone identifying things and occasionally following something interesting is mesmerising. It reminds me of *Minority Report.*'

Ange grabbed that coffee before downloading the video. The guy behind the counter greeted her as she walked into the cafe. 'Welcome back, your usual coffee?' Ange nodded, musing that Namba Heads would be a tough place to execute a clandestine affair.

By the time she got back to her cabin, the large video file had finished downloading. She pressed the Play symbol on her iPad and watched the footage. The drone was clearly looking at something in the water, turning and moving often, but you could see glimpses of the missing woman wandering around the rocks, watching the waves, glancing back to the shore at various times. It was early morning, and she appeared to be intently checking out this location, as Billy had suggested. Ange noted it was also high tide and reminded herself to verify the state of the tide when she'd disappeared.

Pulling up the tide charts for Namba Heads on her phone, she looked back over the police report and saw that the swimmer had gone missing near to high tide. She knew from her discussion with an angler a few evenings ago that dead high and dead low tides revealed the most benign currents. Ange was becoming suspicious that this woman might have staged her disappearance.

Billy called back to say that he had now been over the reports Ange had sent him, and he could see nothing new. Also, the forensic team was heading to Namba

Heads the next day. Billy had instructed them to ring Ange when they arrived in town, and he had also insisted that they remain as discreet and low-key as possible.

Ange asked Billy what he thought about the drone footage. Pleased to be consulted, he agreed with Ange—there was something suspicious about the woman's actions that morning. Ange then asked Billy to go back through the footage from earlier days and see if he could spot the woman again and anyone she might have been with.

She drove across the river to the co-op to see Sharon Fletcher and pick up a set of boat keys and the mystery phone. Sharon looked terrible, and Ange felt for her, having to deal with this so soon after the death of her husband and the devastation to her family. They went into Sharon's small but tidy office, and Sharon pointed to a cheap, nondescript smartphone. Ange donned some gloves before carefully picking up the phone and depositing it into an evidence bag.

Ange was just getting back into her car when her own phone buzzed. It was Jim Grady.

'The hotline received a call from a woman in relation to the missing person at Namba Heads,' he explained. 'She said that she'll only speak to the woman detective from Byron Bay who was in town, which I assume means you. Apparently, she was insistent on that point.'

He went on, 'The hotline rang the station to track you down. I gave them your number and they'll put the call straight through to you when she next makes contact.'

Ange filled Grady in about the drone footage and her feeling that the woman hadn't drowned after all.

'I think we need to tread carefully here. I have a hunch that this caller might be the missing swimmer, and she's gone to great lengths to stage her disappearance. Ring me back after you've spoken to her, and we can work out where to go from there,' Grady mused before hanging up.

Ange went back to her cabin to regroup and await the call. She hoped it would come soon. She needed a break from all this tension and desperately wanted to go for a paddle, even if the surf was rubbish.

Chapter 26

The Escape

Ange waited anxiously, unable to concentrate on anything but the prospect of her impending call, wondering why the woman would have gone to such lengths. A watched pot never boils, so impatience finally got the better of her. Grabbing her phone, she walked over to the surf, which was reduced to a messy wind chop. The beach was almost deserted, and there were just a few schoolkids mucking around in the waves close in.

She walked along the beach and out onto the breakwater. Holding on to her cap against the stiff north-easterly breeze, Ange looked north from her vantage point on the rock wall. She dearly hoped that the woman was not bobbing around in the current out there in the ocean, or worse, that she hadn't already become an opportune meal for a passing predator.

She had almost arrived back at her cabin when she felt her phone buzzing. It was an unknown number. She answered, 'Detective Angela Watson.' The operator said that she was ready to connect Ange with an unidentified caller and asked if she was OK to take the call. Ange knew that the call would be recorded, but she dashed the last few metres to the cabin before giving the operator the go-ahead. Force of habit made Ange feel naked without a pen and her notebook.

When she heard the connection was complete, Ange repeated her name and asked how she could help. The caller had the voice of a young woman, clearly on edge, her words bursting out.

'I'm that missing swimmer who was on the news two nights ago. I didn't want to cause any trouble, but I needed to get away.'

'Calm down. Let's take this one step at a time. Now, why did you need to get away?' asked Ange in reply.

'I had to escape from my relationship. It had suddenly become toxic, and I was scared. Hearing that you were in town helped make my mind up.'

'I understand. You did the right thing by calling. We've been very worried about you. Can you tell me a bit more about the evening when you went missing?' Ange said in her most reassuring voice.

'Well, I walked down to First Point just before dusk. There was a woman sitting on a park bench as I walked down to the water, and I said hello to her as I passed. I may have spoken to her briefly about the sunset or something like that. Anyhow, I then left my towel and sandals on the beach, like any normal swimmer would, and entered the water. I had chosen that particular time and day because the tide was full, meaning the currents weren't too bad.'

The caller paused for a moment, perhaps reliving her escape before continuing. 'Once I was in the surf, I swam with the current around the rocks and into the little beach beside the breakwater. I was worried that I could get sucked out to sea, so I didn't swim out very far. It turned out to be easier than I thought it might. Once I reached the beach, I kept low to the ground, snuck around the rocks, and stayed out of sight as best I could. I wasn't sure my plan had worked until I heard that a search party was out looking for me.'

This was exactly as Ange had theorised. 'What did you do then, and how did you get out of Namba Heads?'

'My best friend was waiting in a car parked on the edge of the car park. Once I got level with her car, I could climb through rocks using the boulders as cover. I then snuck through the trees and into the waiting car, clearly without being noticed as it turned out. My friend had the rear passenger door open, so I quickly slipped onto the back seat and lay down, closing the car door behind me.'

'What happened then?' asked Ange, needing to keep the momentum of the conversation so that she could create a clear picture of the incident in her mind.

'Well, we drove out of Namba Heads and kept going for over an hour. I was shivering all the way, even with a towel wrapped around me that my girlfriend had brought along. Once I felt safe, we pulled over in a rest area and I got changed. I tied my hair back and kept a facemask on the entire way, a skin-coloured cloth one that I picked up at the pharmacy.'

'Where did you stop to get changed?' asked Ange, furiously jotting down notes, messy and scrambled as they were.

'I think it was somewhere south of Grafton. I had kept my head down to that point, so I'm not absolutely sure,' the woman answered.

Ange was confident that the woman was telling the truth and was indeed who she purported to be. However, just to be certain, Ange asked when she'd last visited First Point before the night of her escape.

The woman was confident in her reply that she had indeed gone down to the point early the same morning to check the high tide and reassure herself that the current wouldn't suck her out to sea 'It was the same high tide as when I had my escape planned,' she added.

'Tell me about your relationship and why you felt you needed to disappear,' Ange asked the caller.

There was a long pause before the woman answered Ange's question. 'He had become angry all the time, but more so lately. He took his frustrations out on me sometimes. I know some people won't understand, but I still like him. I think he was involved in something not quite right.'

Ange made a note to circle back to that comment, as she could tell that the woman was becoming distressed. She relieved the pressure by saying, 'I understand. I don't always make the best choices in men either. Tell me how long you had been in Namba Heads, and how you came to be there.'

'About six months. We were living in Mullumbimby and came to Namba Heads to monitor what was happening with that Tea Trees development. My partner's dad runs an environmental protection group, and they were worried that the council was planning to start work on it again,' the woman answered.

Feeling her heart skip a beat, Ange asked the name of the environmental group.

'The Byron Bay Coastal Protection Society,' the woman replied. 'I'm really concerned about what is happening in our world and the way we're destroying our environment. I wanted to do something positive to help.'

'OK,' said Ange, 'tell me why you thought your partner was involved in something not right.'

The woman replied, 'Well, he would often take off unannounced at all times of the day and night. When I questioned him, he got angry and told me to mind my own business. I also found an unusual phone in his pants one day when I was tidying up the bedroom. When I asked him whose phone it was, he became furious and hit me, accusing me of nosing around. He was always pumping weights and was into martial arts. He really hurt me that time. I became concerned about what he might do next.'

'Do you know where the phone is now?' Ange asked hopefully.

'With him, I suppose. I never saw it again. Am I in trouble? I don't want anyone to know where I am. I'm worried about getting hurt again.'

'The police are very understanding in cases like this, and you won't be in any trouble unless you've done something illegal,' Ange replied reassuringly.

'No, I've done nothing illegal. I attended a few environmental protests back in Byron Bay last year, but I don't think that's against the law. Is it?' the woman responded.

'I'm not worried about any protests, just your safety,' Ange assured her.

Ange tried to push for her name, but the woman was reluctant. Ange decided on another option. 'How can I get in contact with you? I will need to speak with you again.'

'OK. My girlfriend purchased a prepaid phone at a phone shop, in her name. I'll give you the number provided you keep it to yourself. You're the only person who can contact me. I'll hang up if anyone else calls,' she warned.

Ange promised to honour this condition. Remembering that the call was being recorded, she quickly suggested that the woman text the number to her phone, reading out her personal mobile phone number.

Ange had many more questions but sensed that this was a good time to end the call. 'Thanks again for calling the hotline. You did the right thing. You have my number now, so call me directly if you think of anything else or need to talk.'

'OK,' said the caller before hanging up. Ange's phone beeped and a phone number appeared in a text, further confirming the credentials of the caller in her mind. Saving the number in her phone's address book, she took the added protection of jotting it down on her notepad.

Ange breathed an enormous sigh. A messy doodler when she was concentrating, Ange's notes were a complete mess. She took a few minutes to sit down at her iPad and type them up. She then rang Jim Grady and told him about the call. 'Can you listen to the recording as well, boss? If you agree with my conclusions, then we need to make a call on the search. We need to respect her wishes and keep this totally quiet, but it's also no point wasting any further resources searching for her. Perhaps you could wait a day or so and call off the search, citing insufficient evidence, or something vague like that. We can then hope the story of her disappearance just dies down and people can make their own assumptions about what might have happened.'

'Agreed. Let me listen to the recording. I'll ring you back if I don't agree with your conclusions,' replied Grady before hanging up.

Gathering her thoughts, Ange rang Billy back at the station to see if he had uncovered anything further. She filled him in on the developments regarding the missing woman, extracting his commitment to keep the woman's reappearance in the strictest confidence.

'Only me, you and the boss know anything about this, and we need to keep it that way. However, we still need to identify who she is,' Ange insisted.

'I totally understand, boss. I've been through all the earlier drone footage, which picks up the woman at two separate times. She's in the company of a man on one of those occasions,' Billy said.

'That's terrific, Billy. Are you able to snip some decent images of the couple from the video and email them to me?'

'Absolutely—the footage needs to be hi-res to recognise sharks in the water, so I should be able to get you some quality images,' Billy explained, clearly now an expert in drone reconnaissance. Ange marvelled at the ability of Billy's generation to instantly adopt the latest technology as their new normal.

'Did you get anywhere with that environmental group?' Ange inquired.

'I was too busy going through the hours of video footage, but I'll get onto it right away,' Billy responded, clearly energised by all of this, before they ended the call.

Ange was pleased with the day's work and headed across to the beach for a quick swim before dinner. There was a Chinese takeaway that looked popular, and she realised she hadn't eaten since breakfast, which explained her rumbling stomach.

Refreshed from her dip in the ocean, Ange wandered over to the Chinese takeaway. The restrictions had closed many restaurants, but Chinese restaurants are nothing if not industrious. This one was doing a roaring trade—if the line down the street was anything to go by. Ange ordered a meal of ginger whiting and rice and waited outside on the footpath like everyone else, watching the comings and goings of the townsfolk and falling into her usual habit of guessing who they were and what they did.

Before she became too engrossed in her little game, Brett Tompkins drove by in his Land Cruiser. Seeing Ange in the line, he pulled over to say hello. 'I see you found the best Chinese takeaway in New South Wales,' he exclaimed, loud enough for the owner to hear.

Brett expanded that he was a regular, and Jimmy, the owner, was a good guy.

'Do you think you might have time to finish our aborted date at the Bella Vista?'

'I'm in the thick of things right now, Brett. How about I try to call you this weekend?'

'Sounds good. Look forward to it,' said Brett before he drove off.

Jimmy called out Ange's takeaway number. Clearly Chinese takeaway fraud was the scourge of Namba Heads, as Jimmy insisted Ange present her numbered takeaway slip. Verification in hand, Jimmy asked, 'You that detective in town?' Ange found it most amusing that Jimmy clearly knew the answer to that question already, yet still needed to retrieve her meal slip.

'Yes, I am, in fact,' she replied before hurrying the conversation sideways. 'I really like Namba Heads.'

'Town is changing,' said Jimmy. 'Too many blow-ins.'

Jimmy then told Ange how he had been targeted by a scammer, alleging that Jimmy's food had made the scammer sick. 'Unless I pay him five hundred dollars, he post bad reviews on social media,' he explained with a scowl on his face.

'What did you do, Jimmy?' asked Ange, now feeling on first-name terms, having successfully cleared her name of potential meal-slip skulduggery.

'I pay the five hundred dollars and ring the police. He did not know I have security camera,' Jimmy replied with a broad smile, clearly still most impressed with his own ingenuity.

'Apparently, scammer had hit twelve restaurants up and down coast. The police picked him up at motel down the road,' Jimmy elaborated before putting an extra serving of spring rolls in the plastic bag containing Ange's dinner.

Jimmy smiled as he handed the bag through his little Covid-thwarting service window. 'Everyone happy, except scammer. I like police.'

Ange walked home to her cabin, accompanied by a mouth-watering aroma wafting from the meal swinging happily by her side, pleased to be appreciated by Jimmy, but especially pleased that Brett Tompkins seemed interested. The ginger whiting and bonus spring rolls were also delicious.

Chapter 27

Downtown

The noisy dawn was impossible to ignore, so Ange figured that there was time for a quick surf. The southerly change wasn't due until evening and the wind was a light north-westerly—not ideal, but she should be able to find a wave.

She drove to one of the more open beaches in Namba Heads, parked her car and carried her board and surf gear down to the sand. The swell was small and weak, with the waves stacked up and close together. She watched the ocean for a few minutes before deciding where she would surf and dumped her stuff on the cool sand to mark the spot. Sometimes a sweep would wash you up or down the beach before you knew it, so it was good to construct a colourful marker to spot yourself with, particularly in unfamiliar territory.

There was nobody in the water yet, so Ange took her time stretching, putting on her wetsuit and waxing her board. When she saw a couple of other surfers make their way down onto the beach, she collected her board and entered the water. The northerlies were keeping the air warm, but the water felt quite cool in contrast. Once Ange's wetsuit had swelled against her skin, she soon found the temperature very comfortable.

Ange caught a couple of passable waves before a middle-aged couple paddled out. They acknowledged each other before dividing up the break and giving each other plenty of room. Her new dolphin friends swung by, which was exhilarating. After catching a nice right-hander, Ange passed close by the other surfers as she paddled back out to her spot.

'Have you found that missing woman yet?' the woman surfer asked.

'Bloody hell, it would be impossible to go undercover in this town,' Ange thought before replying. 'It's still an ongoing investigation,' police-speak for no.

'I hope it wasn't a shark attack,' came the reply, as the woman swung around a picked up a wave.

Although Ange knew the actual story, she still frequently glanced under her board, now that she'd been rudely reminded of what might share the water with her.

Ange had planned to surf until 7:15 a.m., but the appeal of 'just one more wave' meant that she didn't get back to the beach until around 7:30 a.m. Not wanting to risk keeping the forensic crew waiting, she quickly picked up her stuff and scurried back to the car park, where she hurriedly and gracelessly peeled off her wetsuit and dried herself. Wearing only a towel wrapped over her swimsuit, Ange drove back to the cabin for a quick shower.

There are few things more pleasurable than a warm shower after a bracing surf session, and Ange luxuriated a touch longer than she should have. She saw a missed call on her phone, which she rang back as soon as she was dry. It was the forensic guys, who estimated that they would arrive at the marina at around 8:30 a.m. 'Perfect,' thought Ange. She got dressed and then hurried around to the cafe for a coffee and toastie to go.

Pleased to discover she had beaten forensics to the marina, Ange parked her car near the Fletchers' boat. As she enjoyed her coffee and toastie, she studied some anglers throwing their fish skeletons to a pod of hungry pelicans. She marvelled at just how curious these large, gentle birds were, with their gigantic eyes and even bigger mouths. All eyes fixed on their prize, the pelicans behaved like pets as they waited patiently for the smiling angler. Once a skeleton was airborne, the pelicans would scramble over, squabbling noisily over who would secure breakfast. A vivid flashback of past summer holidays flashed in front of Ange—helping her father clean their catch after a successful day's fishing, delighted to be allowed to feed the pelicans and watch the birds gobble down their leftovers.

Just before 8:30 a.m., Ange noticed a nondescript Ford station wagon containing two men slowly pull into the marina. Ange recognised one of them and waved. They had even gone to the effort of dressing like tradies. In their khaki shorts and rolled-up work shirts, they certainly looked the part of someone who might work on a boat. Ange didn't need to explain their job to her forensic colleagues, so she unlocked the wheelhouse along with the padlocks that secured the hold. She explained that whatever had happened was over three weeks old now, and there had been quite a few people on the boat.

Before leaving, she gave them the burner phone she had stored in her evidence bag, asking if they could analyse it. She hoped Fletcher hadn't protected the phone with a difficult PIN. They could always get the call records from the telecom company, but it took longer and was a hassle. After extracting a promise to ring her before they left town, Ange left the guys to do their job.

She needed to figure out the identity of the missing woman and her boyfriend. Now that she had a contact number, she could always ring the woman again, but she didn't want to scare her off, potentially making life difficult down the track. Although Ange had a gut feeling about it, she couldn't be certain of any connection with Jake Thompson or Dave Fletcher. She swung by her new favourite cafe and sat down to think about it over coffee.

Sipping her latte, she watched the comings and goings of shoppers up and down the street. Ange knew the couple were living in Namba Heads for six months odd, so they must have left some trace. Ange thought over the shops that she regularly visited in Byron—groceries, bread, alcohol, pharmacy. 'Bingo,' Ange thought. There was an almost one hundred percent probability that a young woman would need to visit a pharmacy within a six-month period.

Finishing her coffee, Ange wandered across the road and into the sole pharmacy in town, asking to speak to the senior pharmacist on duty. A pleasant forty-some-thing woman came out from behind the dispensary. Ange introduced herself as she flashed her badge before pulling up the picture of the missing swimmer that Billy had sent to her phone.

'Can you remember if you served this woman in the past few months?' Ange inquired.

'Yes, I remember her. She came in three or four weeks ago to get a script filled,' the pharmacist replied confidently.

Feeling pleased with this answer, Ange asked, 'I don't suppose you can recall her name by any chance?'

'In a small town like Namba Heads, you get to know your regular customers, and it's easy to spot someone new. I remember her name quite well, actually,' the pharmacist replied, much to Ange's surprise.

'Her name is Amy Lightfoot. I remember this because my own daughter's name is Amy, and the woman sort of glided rather than walked as she left the shop, so Lightfoot seemed the perfect surname for her. It's a little game I play to help me remember my customers' names. Is this the woman that went missing the other night?'

Ange confirmed it was and thanked her before leaving. She rang Billy as soon as she was out of earshot.

'Billy, can you dig up everything you can on a woman named Amy Lightfoot? I'm guessing she'll be in her mid-twenties, supposedly tall and attractive with long brown hair,' Ange asked her increasingly busy assistant.

'Cool name,' Billy commented. 'I'm still researching the environmental group. Which do you want me to prioritise?'

'Definitely Amy Lightfoot. However, get back onto your research on the environmental group as soon as you can. Remember to include their founder, Joe Kramer, and find out if he has any children,' Ange said before hanging up.

Ange often sensed an underlying symmetry in her investigations. Perhaps this was because of her vivid imagination, but she usually found a way to discern the mosaic of interlocking connections and their intersections. Ange was forming an intriguing picture of how all these people and events might fit together.

Chapter 28

The House

Ange decided she needed to take a better look around the house that Amy Lightfoot and her boyfriend had rented. The real estate agent had showed her willingness to assist and keep on the good side of the law, so Ange had no trouble convincing her that now might be a good time for a property inspection.

Tucked away in a forgotten corner of Namba Heads, the low-set weatherboard house wasn't a complete dump, but it was badly in need of some TLC. The garden, if you could call it that, was overgrown and festooned with creepers and long grass. The place exuded an air of slow decay and Ange could see why the owner was keen to earn some income on the property. It would not be the best-performing rental in the agency's books. The estate agent unlocked the door and Ange headed inside alone. Whoever was there last had made a hasty retreat, and Ange saw that the place was messy. She recognised some of Jimmy's takeaway containers, and the kitchen needed a good clean. Finding nothing obvious, Ange walked back out, telling the agent, 'I don't want you to let anybody in the house until we're further progressed with our investigation.'

'That's fine. The property doesn't rent very well, as you can imagine. Just let me know when you need to get back in,' said the agent, keen to remain in Ange's good book, handing over her business card as they parted company.

Checking her emails back at the cabin, Ange found a recent one from Billy.

Amy Louise Lightfoot, 24 years old, no siblings. Parents are both partners at big law firms in Sydney. Grew up in Cremorne on Sydney's affluent North Shore, attended the elite Queenwood School for Girls in Mosman. Dropped out of Sydney University a few years ago, part way through a degree in environmental science. Her tax records showed some trust fund money supplemented by part-time work in hospitality.

Ange formed a picture of Amy in her mind and knew that she would have to tread carefully, seeing as both her parents were high-powered lawyers. Privileged upbringing and attending an elite school, Amy was likely to be principled, emboldened by her education, and somewhat naïve, courtesy of her cloistered upbringing. She would have left school feeling empowered and confident that she could change the world. Ange had attended an equally prestigious girls' school in Armidale, so experience formed her presumptions about Amy.

One doesn't become a partner of a big law firm without working hard and putting in long hours. Parenting potentially left to her school, her life education probably left to her equally privileged school friends. Ange had worked with some environmental scientists and knew the level of scientific rigour that this career demanded. It was a tough job, probably not unlike policing, where the popular notion portrayed on TV differed greatly from the grind of the real thing. She thought it interesting that her parents had not yet reported their daughter to missing persons.

She rang Jim Grady to give him an update.

'Boss, I know I might be clutching at straws here, but there are too many events intersecting in Namba Heads at the moment. On the face of it, the situation involving Amy Lightfoot isn't connected to what's going on with Jake Thompson and Dave Fletcher. However, seeing as we have forensics in town, I think we should get them to run their eye over the place as well, just in case. We'd kill ourselves later if we found it was an important site and may have contained some crucial evidence. I have feeling about this, boss. I admit, it's not much to go on.'

'I see no concrete link connecting the two locations, Detective. However, I will indulge you a little further on the proviso that forensics uncover something useful on the boat. These guys are hurting my budget, so I hope you aren't leading us on a wild goose chase,' Grady remonstrated.

With the forensic analysis of the boat taking on more importance, Ange went back to the marina to see how the guys were going. She knew they would need to properly analyse their samples back at the lab, and she was unlikely to find the smoking gun needed to keep them in town overnight. She would have to rely on her not inconsiderable charm.

Midway through the afternoon, the guys reported they were going well. Fishing boats are messy things, and the work had been painstaking. Ange asked them if they had come across anything interesting. After a minor professional whinge over the complexity of their job, they concurred that there were only two items of obvious interest.

First, they had found what looked like dried blood in the gaps between the decking, but they couldn't say if this was human or fish blood without a proper analysis back at the lab. Second, they had also identified possible hair follicles and skin fragments on the corner of a bench seat in the wheelhouse. They stressed the point that nothing was certain until they'd completed the lab work. Ange figured she had enough to run the gauntlet with her boss.

'How do you guys feel about spending a night in Namba Heads?' Ange asked breezily, conjuring up the most appealing smile she could find. They expressed some reluctance, citing lack of notice, but they had packed a change of underwear and their toiletries just in case the job turned difficult.

'Great. I'll circle back to you on that after you've looked through the shed where Jake Thompson lived,' said Ange. Seeing their blank looks, she explained who Jake Thompson was and why she wanted them to look through the shed.

Ange rang Grady. After a difficult discussion, she secured his reluctant consent and drove back to the caravan park to organise another cabin. The manager was out doing some maintenance in the garden but saw Ange walking towards the office and called her over. Ange explained she needed a second cabin for tonight, to which the manager replied, 'I'm sure that we can arrange something. Is it for those guys working on Dave Fletcher's trawler?' Nothing surprised Ange anymore regarding the Namba Heads bush telegraph.

Once the guys had finished on the boat, Ange had them follow her car over to the beach house where Jake had been living. While they were getting their stuff ready, Ange walked around to the far-left corner of the house and knelt on the grass. She reached up and under the house with her right hand and scratched around, pleased to hear the jangling set of keys. After a process of trial and error, Ange found the right key and unlocked the small shed, taking care not to touch anything. In total contrast with the house where Amy Lightfoot had been living, this place was spotlessly clean, almost as if it had been prepared for reletting.

While the guys did their thing, Ange drove back to the marina and dropped the boat keys back to Sharon Fletcher. 'We're unlikely to need access again, but could you limit visitors where possible?' Ange asked.

Sharon replied somewhat tentatively, 'OK. You need to know that I've secured an offer to purchase that I'm planning to accept. It will probably take a month or more before the contract settles. I can't guarantee anything after that.' She paused pensively, before asking the question that must have been playing on her mind. 'Did you find anything?'

'Too early to say. The samples will need to go back to the lab for analysis before we can make any conclusions. By the way, can you remember what the conditions were like on your husband's last fishing trip?' Ange inquired, trying to make sense of the potential evidence that forensics had observed.

'Yes, I do, actually. I remember Dave came in later than expected that night. He said that the conditions had been terrible. I remember being pleased that he was safe before I drifted back to sleep. Why do you ask?' Sharon replied.

'Nothing, really, just trying to piece a few things together to help form a picture in my mind. Oh, congratulations on selling the boat,' finished Ange with a heartfelt smile.

Ange drove back around to the beach house to collect the forensics guys. She had only just had time to call the real estate agent and organise to meet her at the house at 8:30 a.m. the next morning before the guys wandered back to their car.

'Finished already?' asked Ange.

'The place is spotless. We picked up a few odd fragments that we'll have a look over, but there were certainly no fingerprints of any value. I wish I could get the name of whoever cleaned the place so I can sack the pathetic crew doing my home at present.'

Ange thought this incongruous for digs occupied by any teenage boy. The impression of Jake that she had gleaned from his mother was that of forgetful messiness, where cleanliness and tidying up would be secondary considerations, menial annoyances which would soak up valuable surfing time.

She filled the guys in on the arrangements for the next day and they followed her back through town to the caravan park and the cabin which Ange had rented for them. As soon as everyone was suitably refreshed, Ange treated her colleagues to dinner at the Returned Services Club and the pleasures of some true local ambience.

Despite their grumbles and initial reluctance, the forensic guys opened up over a beer, suggesting that this was a much nicer idea than wasting hours driving to and from Namba Heads. They all went to the counter to order dinner, with Ange recommending the flathead, chips, and salad.

The bistro manager greeted the trio. 'What can I get you, Detective?'

Catching the surprised looks on the faces of her dinner guests, Ange laughed at her own notoriety. 'You don't know the half of it,' she commented wryly.

Seeing as it was a Wednesday night, the club wasn't very busy. Their meals arrived promptly, and they had soon finished dinner. Ange noticed that the predicted southerly change had come through and wondered if the points might be working in the morning. She pointed out the cafe to the guys as they walked back to their cabins, and they agreed to meet there the next day at 7:45 a.m. for breakfast. Ange got to sleep early, encouraged by the prospect of an early surf, psychologically prepared for the noisy dawn chorus that awaited her.

After Jim Grady had hung up from his call with Ange, he sat back in his chair and thought about his young detective. He had rarely seen anyone with such an aptitude for police investigations. Charged with a strong work ethic, she had a way of disarming people and gaining their confidence. She got along with most people, even those she didn't really like.

However, Ange had a special secret sauce that set her apart. Whether it was a sixth sense, or a heightened observation skill, or a general awareness of what was going on around her, Ange sensed connections and the flow of surrounding events better than anyone Grady had ever encountered. The flip side of this prescience was that Ange would sometimes imagine connections that weren't there, convinced as she was of her own theories and light-bulb inspirations.

Until now, her cases had all been minor, but Grady had noticed how easily Ange seemed to find the missing link that would bring a case to its end. When questioned about how she had achieved this resolution, she would express amazement, having assumed everyone would have been on the same page of something so obvious. This ease of making these leaps often put her at odds with her colleagues, and being proven correct often made matters worse. Having someone highlight one's own intellectual failings often had that effect. Like any large organisation, the police service was a cross section of society and included a fair smattering of small minds, ready and alert to take offence.

While the pros of Ange's skills definitely outweighed the cons, Grady knew Ange was going to land him in trouble one day.

Chapter 29

High Society

Ange was in the water early, but not the first surfer to paddle out at First Point. The swell was on the small side, but clean and fun. The locals all said hello to her and encouraged Ange onto plenty of waves. It was such a pleasure surfing in relaxed company and away from the hassling and aggression that tainted a surf at Byron. The early-morning crew were a mixture of tradies trying to catch a few waves before starting work, along with some older surfers who had simply lost the art of sleeping in. Ange knew she would become a regular at Namba Heads, with the longish drive being well compensated by the added enjoyment of surfing in such chilled company.

After enjoying more than her fair share of waves, she said goodbye to her new surfing buddies. Following a quick shower, she was sitting in the cafe by the time the forensic guys arrived, her still-damp hair betraying her early-morning fun.

Refuelled after some food, and alert after a couple of strong cappuccinos, they met the agent on-site at 8:30 a.m. as agreed. Ange had given them a heads-up, so her forensic colleagues came armed with a pile of evidence bags, launching into their task as soon as the house was open. Before leaving the guys, Ange arranged for the agent to lock up the house once they had finished.

'Take anything you need. It will be one less thing for the cleaners to take to the dump,' the agent suggested.

Ange checked her phone and saw that Billy had sent through some information on the Byron Bay Coastal Protection Society. She waved goodbye to the guys before heading back to the cabin. As soon as she'd sat down at her kitchen table, Ange opened Billy's email on her iPad.

Byron Bay Coastal Protection Society is a charitable organisation founded in 1992 by Joe Kramer. Their registered place of business is 57 Stuart Street, Mullumbimby NSW 2482. The organisation has a website, www.protectbyronbay.com.au, which lists that their primary purpose is to 'protect the delicate landscape and environment of Byron Bay and hinterland from overdevelopment and environmental vandalism.'

The Society survives mostly on donations and by holding events, the most profitable being the Mullumbimby Blues Festival, which has the Society listed as the charitable beneficiary. Following the Productivity Commission report into the not-for-profit sector, the Society has been under investigation for potentially inappropriate fundraising activity and accounting irregularities. A disgruntled property developer had apparently complained to the federal member about the Society's activities.

Their annual tax report shows one permanent employee, being Joe Kramer, which suggests the Society is well supported by volunteers given how active they had been in the courts over the years.

Joe Kramer is currently single but has two children from previous relationships. Edward John Kramer aka Ted/Teddy Kramer, born 18 Feb 1996, and Skye Finney, born 17 May 1999, who took her mother's surname. The photo on Ted Kramer's driver's licence matches the photo taken by the drone, making his age as approaching 25 years old.

Billy had then put together a spreadsheet summarising media activity and court appearances, supported by hyperlinks to primary sources in case Ange needed some specific information. She quickly skipped through the spreadsheet and saw that Billy had done a great job. It was clear that the Society's greatest success was Tea Trees, and that notable victory still provided profile and credibility. It seemed plausible that Joe Kramer might send his son to maintain a lookout at the scene of his greatest triumph. She quickly emailed Billy to thank him and acknowledge his great work.

Ange hoped that the forensic search would provide some hard evidence that she could use to expand her investigation into the Kramers. With no other pressing matters on her plate, she spent the rest of the day clearing her ever-expanding list of unanswered emails and catching up on some admin.

Soon enough, she got a call from the forensic team. Apparently, they had finished their work and were ready to pack up and head back to base. Ange met them with the real estate agent back at the house and walked around with her as she checked the windows and doors, before slamming the front door shut behind them. The guys had collected a substantial number of personal items, along with plenty of fingerprints. Seeing as they also had the first batch of samples from the boat, they asked Ange what she wanted them to focus on.

'Could you get someone onto the burner phone as quickly as possible, then perhaps focus on the samples off the boat? I'm hoping that something turns up to link the two locations, but that's more of a hunch than anything at this stage. By the way, now that the sun is setting, drive carefully through the bushland on account of the wallabies. They love to eat the fresh green grass shoots on the roadside and are a serious road hazard.'

Duly warned, her colleagues drove off, literally into the sunset.

Ange visited Jimmy and got some more delicious Chinese food. She could have driven back to Byron that evening, but the potential of increasing swell and an early-morning surf at Sliders was too big a temptation. For once, giving in to temptation proved the right move.

Chapter 30

Changing Winds

A nge was now embroiled in two missing person investigations, running parallel as they were. She spent the evening alone in her cabin, learning as much as she could about the Kramers. While she found scant information about Ted, not so his father. It was certainly no exaggeration to describe Joe Kramer as a media tart.

What she didn't glean from Billy's report and her own searching, she cobbled together from the Society's website and a lengthy interview in a prominent environmental magazine, perhaps best described as an expose on the life and times of Joe Kramer. Naturally, the great Tea Trees victory dominated any search of his name on the web, but the man was nothing if not industrious. Anyone carrying a shovel risked the ire of Kramer. Farmers, developers, homebuilders, utility companies, councils and governments were all fair game. She would not have been at all surprised to discover how Kramer had prevented some hapless dad from building a sandpit for his children, in flagrant breach of the little-known Backyard Grassland Protection Act, or something similarly absurd.

Joe proudly extolled his simple upbringing, attending a state-run school in one of Brisbane's burgeoning nappy suburbs, full of kids with an expectation of a bright future. According to the magazine article, Joe earned a bachelor of arts degree from the University of Queensland before enduring a series of menial administrative jobs. Then World Expo 88 came to town and opened Joe's eyes to the big, wide world. He soon left town to travel the globe. Two experiences seemed pivotal in forging Joe Kramer into the famed environmental activist that he had become.

According to the magazine article, Joe had been astounded by his visit to

Prague, home to one of the most breathtaking town centres in all of Europe, and once a global centre for science and free thinking. The Soviet Union was crumbling, and Prague offered a foothold for the West. Joe was one of the first group of backpackers to visit; tourism had only just begun. He observed the stark contrast between the magnificence and majesty of the old Prague city centre, filled with the smiling awestruck faces of international backpackers and wealthy 'I was there first' tourists, and the crumbling, nondescript, concrete-cancer-ridden communist apartment blocks of the suburbs, filled with glum, drab and desperate faces. The juxtaposition was sobering.

Prague was attracting significant inflows of international capital wanting to be associated with the old part of town. Real estate prices and rents rose rapidly, pushing the locals further and further into the crumbling suburbs. Real estate developers and property speculators were having a field day. This was often at the expense of the locals, who were stumbling out of forty years of Soviet rule, with reliance on the state encouraged and personal wealth accumulation a crime.

He met a young woman who spoke six languages fluently, a qualified teacher with a good job at a school near the city centre. Paid a pittance, she could not afford to live anywhere near her work, forced to hitchhike two hours each way. Joe learned that the two-tiered pricing system designed to protect locals had failed miserably, an unintended consequence of landlords and vendors seeking to make hyper-profits off this flood of foreign capital. Capitalism was racing through Prague like a nuclear blast, the threat of both having framed Cold War politics for decades.

Generations of autocrats and dominating rulers had built the old centre of Prague, falling to communist control as a counter to those opulent ruling classes. One set of rulers replaced by another. That same old town was now providing much-needed economic stimulus for a country grappling with market forces and globalisation. One set of problems replaced by another. The contrasts he experienced in Prague affected Joe. The insights into rampant capitalism against a backdrop of failed communism were sobering.

However, it was his second key experience that set Joe's future path into stone. Having all but run out of money, he spent several lazy months in Goa on his way home. The relaxed, communal hippie life, free from the frenetic pursuit of monetary wealth and gaining ever more stuff, struck a chord. The music and the free-loving psychedelic beach parties of Goa were legendary. There were lots of things about India that upset him—the caste system, the incredible poverty, and its contrasts to the incredible wealth. However, Goa was a paradise which changed Joe forever.

Soon after arriving back in Australia, a friend invited Joe on a trip to Nimbin in Northern New South Wales for the Aquarius Music Festival. Byron Bay, Nimbin, Bangalow and Mullumbimby were still undiscovered paradises back then, and these quaint coastal country towns proved a revelation—Goa without the poverty and challenges of a developing nation. Joe decided on the spot to move to the area permanently, choosing Mullumbimby as his new home.

Joe reckoned he became a 'greenie' naturally, an activist equally so, protective as he was of his new-found utopia. Smart, educated, travelled and articulate, Joe seemed to have had little trouble attracting members to the newly minted Byron Bay Coastal Protection Society. There was a lot to be done. Developers were moving in, trying to cash in on his utopia.

Tea Trees had been a godsend, coming just at the right time for the Society. No longer the latest fad, the interest of willing donors had been falling away. The great Tea Trees victory made them a household name and something for the despoilers to fear. The Society flourished and Joe's reputation became legend.

While Ange had formed a sharp impression of Joe Kramer, she had discovered nothing new about his son. She knew that Ted Kramer was in Namba Heads on account of his father and was certain that Ted was in too deep. However, any theory that involved Joe Kramer in murder or narcotics was mere supposition. She could waste hours upon hours of valuable time chasing his name around town. As she brushed her teeth before retiring to bed, Ange realised she was floundering in a sea of speculation about who or what sat at the centre of her multipronged investigation. All she could do was keep prodding and probing until something broke.

Chapter 31

A Bush Walker

Ange was up early again and had completed the twenty-minute trek to Sliders by 6:15 a.m. She was the first one to arrive at the headland and watched the surf for at least ten minutes before putting on her wetsuit. With the sun still low in the east, and the headland casting shadows over the water, the surf looked a touch menacing given the semi-remote location. She was pleased to see some other surfers coming along the beach, wheeling their boards behind them.

'I really must pop into Bell Surfboards and see if I can buy one of those wheel contraptions. I'll get one for Kerrie as well,' Ange reminded herself again. She whittled away some time by doing some extra stretching on the beach until the company arrived. Ange was still a nervous first surfer in the water, but relaxed a touch once she saw the other surfers suiting up.

The surf had a real punch this morning, and her first two waves caught Ange by surprise, rearing up sharply and causing her to miss her take-offs. She crashed and burned badly, her confidence shaken. Executing a good take-off and making the drop is a fluid move that relies on speed, great timing, guts, and confidence. Ange seemed to have left all those skills in the car park.

Brett Tompkins paddled out from the rocks and suggested that she move out wider and further up the line, perhaps wait for something bigger and with more water in front of it. Ange did as he suggested and nervously sat on her board, looking eastward, her heart thumping. She took a deep breath and muscled up the courage to tackle the first wave of the next set, a larger but well-formed wave she could see wrapping around the headland and lining up nicely.

Paddling into the daunting wave, she felt its power as it picked her up, accelerating rapidly. As soon as her board started skating down the face of the wave, she jumped up and powered through a long, slow, tentative bottom turn. The wave was fast, and she had to work hard to keep control over her board and maintain a positive line, lest her tail skate out and deliver an inglorious wipeout. The ride went for 150 metres, one of the longest she had ever experienced, finally delivering her into a deep gutter just before the shore break. Exhilarated, Ange paddled back to the beach and started her walk back out to the jump-off spot on the headland, grinning from ear to ear.

Still watching the surfers, she saw Brett paddling out to meet a large set wave before pivoting abruptly and executing a flawless late take-off, a move that was far beyond Ange's skill level. Confident and surfing with authority, he made three times the number of turns and manoeuvres that Ange had managed on her ride. Brett's grace, power, and skill impressed her.

She was still carefully negotiating the rocks at the jump-off point when Brett joined her, having jogged back around after his last wave. 'Nice wave,' said Brett as they both paddled back into the take-off zone.

'Wow,' said Ange, 'it was amazing. More powerful than I thought it would be. Your wave was fantastic as well.'

They surfed together for more than an hour, before Ange called out to Brett that this would be her last wave, to which he replied he would join her on the beach. A vastly superior surfer, Brett caught his wave first, with Ange following a few minutes later. They both peeled off their wetsuits and chatted about how great the surf had been. The sun was warming up, and Ange delighted in catching a few rays, standing there in her bikini, in the company of this attractive man.

On the walk back to the car park, they chatted about surfing and potential surf trips that they would like to take. Brett told her about some of his trips to Indonesia and the Pacific Islands, the thick powerful waves breaking on shallow coral reefs. He encouraged Ange to investigate taking one of these trips and recommended staying on a boat on which to travel around and sample the many distinct breaks. Ange felt she was not yet ready to confront that sort of power and danger, but it was on her bucket list.

They parted company at their vehicles, and Ange drove back to her cabin to pack up and check out. She was almost ready to leave when her phone rang.

'Detective Watson,' Ange answered, not recognising the number.

'Hello, Detective, it's Constable Thomas from the Namba Heads police station. I'm sorry to bother you, but I was wondering if you're still in town?' asked the youthful voice.

'Yes, I am. I was about to head back to Byron. How can I help you, Constable?' answered Ange, intrigued by why the young constable would ring her rather than Billings.

'Well, we had a call from one of the local Landcare volunteers. A Mrs Bernadette Williams. She rang just a few minutes ago to report something suspicious that she stumbled across in the scrub. I'm the only one on deck today, as the sergeant has flexed off on account of all the extra activity of late.'

In the background, she could hear the station's noisy screen door jangling, wondering if someone had come in, or perhaps Billings was sneaking out. She parked that ungracious thought.

'Anyhow, Mrs Williams is often reporting something or someone suspicious. She is not easily ignored, so I wondered if you would mind swinging by and checking it out for me?' continued Constable Thomas.

'Happy to. That was good thinking, ringing me,' replied Ange, putting the young constable at ease, and immediately making an ally.

'Great. Thanks. She's waiting for you in the scrub. It should be easy to find. Do you know the way to Bushies Beach—you know, the one with the car park everyone uses to walk to Sliders?' he explained.

'Sure do. In fact, I just came from a surf at Sliders this morning.'

'OK, about halfway along the bitumen road, you'll see a fire trail that runs off to the right, in a westerly direction. Mrs Williams said that she was about a hundred and fifty metres along the fire trail.'

'Got it. Thanks, Constable. I'll swing by the station before I leave town if there's anything to report. Catch you later,' Ange said easily before hanging up.

Leaving her packed bags in the cabin, she jumped straight in her car and retraced her steps from this morning, turning off the bitumen once she had identified the fire trail. She drove carefully along the rutted sandy track before arriving at a small clearing.

A fit fifty-something woman with shortish grey hair, cut practically and rather severely, waited impatiently. Bernadette Williams exuded an air of someone who was perpetually impatient. Tanned but not weathered, as if her obsession with nature was more recent, perhaps after a life spent indoors. Her stern demeanour and haircut seemed well matched. Williams nodded her way, and Ange put on her most charming voice to introduce herself. She failed miserably.

Making no attempt to be cordial, Williams gave an abrupt reply. 'You took your time. I was about to leave. Where's Billings?'

'The sergeant is off duty for the day, and the station rang me to assist, given that I was in town,' replied Ange, feeling oddly defensive under the glare of Williams' stern gaze.

Williams huffed off with Ange in tow, taking her to a section of disturbed ground obscured behind some bushes and hidden from plain sight. Before Ange could open her mouth to ask the obvious question, Williams explained she was out looking for signs of overnight feral animal activity. Her Landcare group was assisting the government with a baiting program designed to stem a wave of feral dogs, foxes, and cats that were decimating the native bird and marsupial populations.

Finding the spot in question, Ange agreed it looked highly suspicious. A sizeable area of sand had been dug up relatively recently, creating a small mound that was roughly the size of a body. There were signs of substantial recent animal activity on and around the mound.

'Thanks, Mrs Williams. I agree it looks suspicious. Leave it with me,' said Ange, whereupon Williams abruptly turned and walked off without so much as a goodbye.

Despite knowing full well that she was disturbing Billings from whatever one does in Namba Heads on a flex day, Ange rang his mobile phone. 'Hello, Sergeant, it's Angela Watson here.'

'What now?' replied Billings wearily, clearly not a happy camper about the intrusion.

'A Mrs Bernadette Williams uncovered something suspicious in the scrub and reported it to your office. I offered to come and have a look, and I agree with Williams. It looks highly suspicious. I think you need to get over here as fast as you can.'

Billings begrudgingly agreed, promising to get there as soon as possible. Hanging up from her call with Billings, Ange immediately called Jim Grady. 'Hi, boss, something has just broken here at Namba Heads. It looks like a walker has discovered a body buried in the scrub. Could I get the forensics team back down here as soon as possible? I would really like the same team, boss, now that they know the area.'

He agreed to make the call and get them back to Namba Heads immediately.

True to his word, one of the forensic guys rang Ange twenty minutes later.

'We're on our way and should be on-site in about an hour. Oh, and by the way, the tech team has already extracted the data off the burner phone, and we have a copy of this report with us. However, we haven't had time to complete any other analysis given that we only left Namba Heads yesterday. We must stop meeting like this, Detective Watson. People will start talking,' explained the investigator, alluding to their dinner at the Returned Services Club.

'I think that horse has already bolted,' Ange laughed before turning serious and attending to some practicalities. 'When you arrive in Namba Heads, you'll need to cross the bridge and then turn right, just after the marina. How about you call me when you're approaching the bridge and I'll direct you from there?'

Left to herself amongst the spectacular coastal bushland, she reflected the incongruity of what likely lay beneath. She had a terrible feeling about it.

Chapter 32

A Delicate Balance

Billings turned up eventually, and Ange immediately gave him a tour of the fresh discovery, explaining that the forensics guys were on their way. Billings was grim-faced throughout.

'Oh. By the way,' remembered Billings as they waited near their cars for forensics to arrive. 'I received a call from your boss at Byron Bay to say that the case of the missing girl has been transferred to your station. Apparently, nothing has happened, and they plan to sit tight until something breaks. Suits me. One less thing to worry about.' Billings said all this as flippantly as he could manage, the look on his face betraying his annoyance at being sidelined. 'Sounds like the work of Terry Scott if you ask me, getting the case moved up to Byron Bay and keeping it on the quiet.' Billings clearly overestimated the powers of Councillor Scott. Ange was not about to contradict him.

Eager to escape, and not wishing to get involved in any further discussion about the missing swimmer, Ange volunteered to wait at the intersection of the track with the road, so that her colleagues would find them. Billings retrieved a roll of blue-and-white checked bunting from his police car and cordoned off the site, signalling that any future walkers should stay clear. Ange donned her trusty Akubra and walked back down the sandy track towards the bitumen road.

She gazed out across the low coastal scrub as she wandered along, listening to the birds and the rustling of lizards and other small animals as they scurried off, alarmed by the vibration of her footsteps. A thick, woolly, olive-green carpet of banksias, wattles, and low shrubs stretched far into the distance. Beaten by the heavy coastal wind, this dense protective floral blanket kept the sandy topsoil from being blown away, and Ange could make out the gently undulating dunes that lay ben eath.

A fire trail crossed the landscape in the distance, revealed by flashes of white sand. In nature, straight lines are rare, and this conspicuous white welt slashing across the landscape was a glaring reminder of humankind's relentless effort to tame the natural world. Far away, near the ocean, Ange could see the gaping wound of a sand blow, where a battle was underway between the shifting sands and its delicate floral skin, exposing the truth about their fragile partnership. Ange made a note to visit this sand blow sometime.

Summer was still a way off, and the undergrowth showed an astonishing array of brightly coloured wildflowers. Free from the oppressive canopy of their bush cousins, these delightful and delicate plants seemed to enjoy the freedom and light afforded by the sandy fire trail. The soft and gentle flannel flowers were in bloom, incongruously reminding Ange of the edelweiss that she had seen in the high Alps of Switzerland during her backpacking gap year post-university. Ange could see how the scrub was relentlessly encroaching onto the fire trail, as the coastal bushland fought to reclaim its territory.

Ange reasoned that the body, buried out of sight amongst the dense scrub, would have soon been swallowed up and hidden forever, save for the observant Bernadette Williams. The sand would have presented light work, and Ange shivered at the image of these criminals on their terrible and macabre assignment, desecrating the bushland under the cover of night.

Looking off into the distance, Ange could see hundreds of grass tree spears. Reaching a height of three metres or more, they were currently in flower and a magnet for bees and small birds, paying a visit to feast on their riches. After flowering, the spears would turn black and remain through the summer and autumn. Ange imagined them as the menacing spears of defiant warriors as they protected their precious coastal scrub from invasion. In her eyes, grass trees were one of the most striking of the coastal plants. Whilst they themselves handled bushfires with ease, and their undergrowth provided exceptional and essential cover for coastal wildlife, this same undergrowth was an ideal fuel when ignited by a lightning strike.

Well adapted to this natural cycle of things, native plants survive well, and some even rely on fires for seed germination. Ange recalled her conversation with Terry Scott about the dangers of trying to eliminate bushfires. This not only increased fuel load and the risk of ever more dangerous fires, but it also paradoxically made the fires too hot for some native plants to regenerate. Enjoying the peace and solitude of this magnificent landscape, Ange pondered the law of unintended consequences, where even the most well-meaning of humans could have disastrous impacts when they meddled with Mother Nature.

A call from her forensic colleagues abruptly interrupted Ange's reverie. She stayed on the phone and directed them towards where she stood waiting, waving them onto the sandy track once they came into sight. Despite the grim task they were about to undertake, the two investigators smiled towards Ange as they slowed down and veered off the bitumen road.

'Fancy seeing you here,' Ange quipped as she hopped into the back seat of their station wagon.

The trio bumped and jumped their way to the investigation site and the waiting Billings. After Ange had made the introductions, the guys retreated to their car to suit up. Before springing into action, one of them handed Ange the report on the burner phone, which she threw on the seat of her own vehicle.

It was slow and tedious work, as they carefully cleared away the twenty centimetres of sandy topsoil, eventually uncovering what lay beneath. The object was wrapped up in thick black plastic—the type used on building sites. Taking countless pictures along the way to document their work, the investigators carefully cut open the plastic to reveal its contents.

The smell was horrific, causing Ange and Billings to gag. The two abruptly turned away and covered their noses, lest they embarrass themselves indecorously. Within no time, the first of a squadron of flies had appeared, finding this discovery very much to their liking.

Whilst one of the forensic team took photos, the other gave a commentary. 'Human body, probably male, looks like it's been here for some weeks. Liquefaction is underway, and the body is severely decomposed. I can tell you already that we won't get any worthwhile fingerprints off it.'

Ange knew the corpse would need to be carefully removed and taken to a medical examiner for an autopsy. The forensic guys paused their gruesome undertaking and retrieved a large portable gazebo from their vehicle, which they carefully erected over the gravesite. It would be a long day that would extend into the night. Ange checked the weather app on her phone, which predicted rain to arrive later that evening. She hoped that the body would be safely exhumed by then.

Ange asked Billings to organise some portable floodlighting, and she would set the wheels in motion for the body to be transported back to the morgue this evening. She also offered to organise some accommodation for the forensic team.

Whilst Ange couldn't be certain, she was sure that the body was Jake Thompson. She knew that positive ID would ultimately be made by the medical examiner but hoped that forensics would find some artefact that could assist more immediately. Ange had learnt the importance of keeping momentum in any investigation.

The forensic team felt that the body was too severely decomposed to make any visual identification. Whilst asking family or another member of the public to identify a body was a traumatic experience for everyone concerned, it was often a necessary step to help speed up an investigation. As things stood, it could take days for a positive ID to be made, so Ange hoped the guys would find something useful.

Ange went back to her car, first calling her boss to tell him of their discovery. She then called Billy and asked him to arrange for the body to be retrieved and also organise an autopsy. He should put an ambulance on standby, but she would ring later with a more accurate estimation of when the body would be ready for transportation. Pausing for a moment, she suddenly remembered the report on the burner phone, curious about what this might tell her.

The report was shorter than she had hoped, listing a series of some eighteen text messages over a four-to-five-month period. They were still sorting through the locational data, which would take more time. Ange read the texts, which contained instructions and coordinates for a series of pickups, presumably offshore. It seemed safe to assume that Dave Fletcher had made these pickups, bar one, when his boat was out of action. The phone had a tracking app installed on it, so whoever was at the head of this arrangement knew Dave's location throughout those operations.

The last exchange of texts was the most interesting, telling her several important pieces of information. Ange pulled out her notebook, finding that writing things down helped cement her thoughts.□

1. *Dave Fletcher was being well paid for his efforts, and whatever he was doing was most likely illegal. Estimate he had taken over $25,000 in total.*

2. *Fletcher sent fresh coordinates before each trip. Confirmed by Cory Young.*

3. *While offshore on the final trip, Fletcher texted someone to say that his deckie was dead (Jake Thomson?) in some sort of accident. Hard to say if this is true, or a cover for murder or manslaughter at Fletcher's hand.*

4. *Fletcher texts suggest 'he wants out' and plans to give back most of money he had been paid (stored in cash box?).*

5. *Reply text tells Fletcher to dock at marina and go home.*

6. *The next day, Fletcher receives a text asking him to meet at the marina at midnight.*

7. *Fletcher agrees to meet, which would coincide with the night that he allegedly committed suicide.*

8. *There was no further contact from that point.*

Ange rang the number of the other phone number listed on the report. It was either disconnected or no longer in service. Most likely also a burner phone, it had probably been purchased with fake ID. Ange figured it would have been destroyed and disposed of by now.

It was certainly plausible that Dave Fletcher had been filled with remorse and consequently committed suicide. However, Ange was now convinced that Dave Fletcher had been murdered and Jake Thompson killed in an accident on the boat during their final fateful fishing trip.

Ange knew she would need to work hard in order to verify her theories, so she hoped that the forensic guys would find something soon that could help her. Unfortunately, there were no known witnesses to what had happened during that wild night at sea.

The humpback sensed the boat before he saw it. Now on his umpteenth migration south, the lone whale knew to stay well clear, memories of being caught in the tentacles of another still vivid. As he paused at the top of a large swell to take on fresh air, he saw the boat off to the right, languishing in a trough and now below the colossal being. Running lights cast an eerie halo around the ungainly vessel, streaked by driving rain, an insipid beacon set amongst the deepest darkness imaginable.

Had the whale been looking more intently, he would have seen two men in the warm yellow light of the wheelhouse, wrestling over something still wet and slippery, like a super-sized coconut that had been caught in their nets. Had the whale been eavesdropping, he would have heard nothing, their shouts of disagreement whisked away by the howling south-easterly wind, drowned by the hum of the big diesel engine, idling away, sending its monotonous call to the whale through the water, reminding him of the danger these things presented. Curious creatures, these humans, always squabbling over one thing or another.

Fresh air on board, the whale dived back down into the relative calm. The surface was no place to linger on such a night.

Chapter 33

A Totem

It was already well after midday. Offering to grab some lunch and taking some coffee orders, Ange left the guys to do their job at the gravesite. Billings seemed determined enough to stay to ensure that the site remained secure from prying eyes. Although Bernadette Williams was testy, she didn't strike Ange as a woman who engaged in idle gossip.

On the way to the cafe, Ange dropped by the caravan park and organised another cabin. Coffees and sandwiches in hand, Ange swung by First Point. The swell had increased even further since this morning. A handful of experienced surfers were enjoying the powerful and demanding waves, racing towards the break wall before pulling out at the last moment. There was a lot of water moving around and the surf was far too heavy for Ange, so she headed back to the investigation site, comfortable that she wasn't missing out.

She came across a 4WD towing some portable lights parked on the side of the road near the entrance to the track. Ange pulled over and introduced herself, and they followed her down the track to the investigation site. Billings spoke to the forensic investigators, who instructed him where to erect the floodlights. After some quick instruction on how to operate the genset that powered the lights, the delivery guys scooted off. Ange saw they had surfboards in the back of their ute, so she guessed at the story they would give their boss when queried about why their delivery had taken so long. She was perhaps being ungracious with those thoughts—it was Friday afternoon, after all. Ange retrieved the food and coffee from her car and, using the bonnet of the station wagon as an impromptu table, called her colleagues over for a welcome coffee break.

One investigator walked around to the back of the wagon before reappearing with a small evidence bag. 'Definitely male, and by the state of liquefaction, the body has been here for about a month. We haven't located any wallet or ID, but he was wearing this around his neck,' he told Ange, holding the small bag in front of her eyes.

Looking closely, Ange could see that the small object coiled in the bag was a shark tooth strung on a leather thong. Ange took a picture with her phone, thanking the investigator and pondering this development over coffee. The caffeine did its trick. She had an idea. Ange suddenly jumped in her car and drove back down the bumpy track.

Ange figured that Sharon Fletcher might know if Jake had worn something like this. Sharon was the mother of two young boys, and mothers tended to notice things like this. Ange had once flipped through some cool old surfing magazines at the Bell Surfboards shop, and shark tooth necklaces had been very popular back in the day. She mused whether they wore this curious and macabre jewellery as a symbol of bravado against the surfer's nemesis, or perhaps it was a totem to keep them safe.

The fish and chip shop was quiet, gearing up for the Friday night and weekend trade. Sharon was in her office and came out to greet the detective.

'Hello, Mrs Fletcher, I wondered if you could help me with something?' asked Ange as she retrieved the picture just taken, holding her phone up for Sharon to see. 'Did you ever see Jake Thompson wearing something like this?' she asked. The look on Sharon Fletcher's face was telling.

'Yes,' said Sharon soberly. 'Dave wore a similar necklace when we started dating. I never liked it and eventually convinced him to give it away. I recognised Jake's immediately and I remember asking him about it. He said the necklace showed respect and that it might help keep him safe in the ocean. Did you find Jake?'

'We can't be certain, but it looks that way,' Ange answered soberly.

The implication of this news was not lost on Sharon Fletcher. Tears flowed, and she broke down, sobbing at the horror of what might have happened. Ange knew what she was thinking.

'We don't know how he died, or how he ended up where he did. It's just too early to speculate, Mrs Fletcher, so try to bear that in mind.' Ange knew her assurances would be cold comfort to Sharon Fletcher that evening, as she tossed and turned over this dreadful development.

Taking her own advice, Ange concluded she would not inform Jake's mother until she was completely certain. Knowing that word would soon get around town, Ange made a phone call to Terry Scott to fill him in on what they knew. Terry appreciated being kept in the loop but was most unhappy that his peaceful seaside town was now the scene of a murder investigation. He asked if there was any news on the missing swimmer.

'No news on that front. I understand that the case has been transferred to Byron Bay, which is a much bigger station than yours here. I'll certainly let you know if anything breaks, but I guess we need to wait and see. Hopefully, your concerns about a potential shark attack might blow over. Terry, I best get back to the site.' Ange abruptly hung up, thwarting any opportunity for him to probe further.

She arrived at the site just before dark, more to give moral support than anything else. The team worked into the evening before finishing just before 9 p.m. The body was now gone, and there was nothing to do but pack up, turn the lights off, and leave the site to the scrub. Ange offered to pick up some dinner on her way back to the caravan park, whilst her two forensic colleagues packed their gear.

At this hour, Namba Heads offered limited dinner options. Hungry and tired, Ange was relieved to see Jimmy still taking orders from workers and stragglers as she drove by. Unable to focus on anything so mundane, she suggested Jimmy prepare a selection of his recommendations. She also picked up some beers and a bottle of white wine at the bottle shop. Word of the night's discovery was clearly out. Sombre looks met Ange as she went around town securing dinner.

When she got back to the cabin, her forensic colleagues had showered and were relaxing on their porch. Retrieving some plates and cutlery from their sparsely equipped kitchen, the guys laid out the food whilst Ange popped back to her own cabin to take a quick shower and change into something comfortable.

The mood lightened over the delicious food and a well-earned glass of wine. Sharing a meal has a way of doing that, breaking down barriers and stimulating conversation. One of the team said that he would stay on, having organised for his wife and two children to join him for the weekend. Hopefully, he could organise a larger cabin, but they could squeeze into their current digs if need be. His colleague would take the station wagon and its crucial evidence back to the laboratory.

Ange marvelled about the ability of her and her colleagues to compartmentalise their work and social lives—that he would be happy to spend a weekend holiday with his family, having just completed one of the most horrific tasks imaginable. Nonetheless, they were still human beings, needing to put some distance between their taxing day and the hope of a good night's sleep.

The three police officers chatted into the night, sharing war stories, and debating their different perspectives on life. One thing they had all agreed on was that the Northern Rivers region of New South Wales was one of the county's most spectacular.

Suddenly, the predicted storm swept through and sent them scurrying to their beds, upending their temporary haven, and encouraging those unsavoury thoughts from their day to creep back in.

Chapter 34

New Experiences

After her few glasses of white wine following such a stressful day, Ange had fallen asleep the moment her head hit the pillow. She even slept through the storm and heavy rain. However, as often is the case after enjoying a touch too much wine, she woke prematurely as the alcohol wore off and the rigours of the day came back to fill her thoughts.

Still dark and well before dawn, Ange lay in bed, willing herself back to sleep, vainly trying to avoid thinking about the case and her many questions and theories. She heard the soulful and melodic sound of the 'wake-up-bird', an apt nickname, calling its cousins into action well before daybreak. At the first blush of dawn, the kookaburras cackled and exploded into raucous laughter, as if daring anyone to find life more hilarious. The storm bird, after its annual coastal migration south from Papua New Guinea, bleated its soulful and pitiful mating call, the summer curse for subtropical insomniacs.

Ange lay there trying to distinguish the individual birds from the surrounding cacophony, before she suddenly and miraculously drifted back into a deep sleep. She awoke at around 7 a.m. feeling remarkably refreshed. As soon as she walked from her cabin, she could hear the rumble of a large swell pounding the coast. The air was thick with the smell of the ocean.

After some coffee and toast at the cafe, Ange drove out to Bushies Beach to check out Sliders, her first stop in a lap of the headlands, to see first-hand how the various surf spots were handling the swell. On the way, Ange swung off the bitumen and turned up the sandy trail one more time. The heavy rain from the previous evening had wiped away any wheel tracks, and Ange could see that she was the first vehicle along there today. The drying air would soon transform the wet, compacted sand back into its shifty self.

The moment Ange's car engine stopped, the tinnitus of the emerging summer enveloped her, that rhythmical mating chorus of the cicadas, summer's whining rendition of white noise. Somehow feeling that she needed to stay quiet, lest she disrupt their strident discord, Ange gently closed her car door and walked carefully over to the burial site.

Hers were the only footprints, but she gazed in awe at the patina of night-time activity, etched into the blank sandy canvas that the heavy rain had prepared. She could see the highways of industrious ants and other small insects; the larger footprints of small marsupials and how they scurried from bush to bush in their efforts to limit exposure to watchful owls and other night-time predators; bird prints as they hopped around on the ground, feasting on the insects who ventured out after the rain. On the edge of the bush, a hungry echidna had left its distinctive spoor as it devoured an ant's nest.

The footprints of a dingo or large dog were obvious, circling the gravesite before realising that any treasure had already been looted. Ange marvelled at how this frenetic activity happened every night, as it had for millennia. This put into perspective her own little chaotic corner of the world and any thoughts of her own importance. Nature had a way of doing that, putting Ange in her place amidst its wonder and complexity.

Shaking herself from this mournful trance, Ange went to check out that other force of nature—the surf. Arriving at the car park for Sliders, she found several surfers discussing the massive swell, debating which tide might yield the best waves. It looked far too powerful and intimidating for Ange, and she faced the prospect of a lazy day. As she drove back down the road, Brett Tompkins flashed his lights at her, and they both pulled over. Brett jumped from his car and came over to Ange's window as she wound it down.

'Hi, Ange, are you planning to surf today?' he asked.

'Well, I was planning to, but the swell looks far too heavy for me,' she replied, disappointment obvious in her voice.

Brett flashed a broad smile. 'I have a few errands to run, but how about I pick you up in an hour and I'll take you to a secret spot only diehard locals know about? Wear your walking shoes and pack a backpack with some water. I'll grab some pizza rolls at the bakery, and we can make a day of it.'

It sounded intriguing and exciting, so Ange readily agreed to this plan.

Brett arrived at the caravan park slightly later than expected, by which time Ange had attended to her unread emails. Showing initiative, Billy had sent one to say that he was trying to track down where the burner phone had been purchased, no doubt using fake ID, and that the first set of forensic results should be ready on Monday.

Ange decided to take a break from the case this weekend, lest she spin her wheels and waste time. She needed to see those reports from the forensic pathologist, and she had to resist making assumptions and drawing premature conclusions until these were in hand. It was the one downside of an overactive imagination. In the corners and shadows of her mind, Ange was sometimes prone to creating fanciful theories that took her away, rather than towards her quarry.

Sliding her surfboard and backpack into the back of Brett's Land Cruiser, he drove up the headland to a small car park off a backstreet. Having been forewarned, Ange was pleased that she had brought along her new midsized board—it was much easier to carry. Walking along a narrow sandy track through banksias and grass trees, they navigated towards a grove of casuarinas on a farther headland, with its secret hidden bay below. It was quite a walk, and she was pleased to have remembered her Akubra, perhaps an incongruous adornment to her surfboard, practical as it was in keeping the sun at bay.

Brett explained that this break needed a big swell and a large deposit of sand to work. 'Midway,' as its nickname suggested, was in the middle of a series of serrated headlands that made up the northern finger of Namba Heads, Sliders making up the southern finger. Apparently, quite a few locals had been monitoring the sandbanks at Midway, waiting for a swell like this. The break tucked back around under a high headland; the waves wrapped around a series of rocky outcrops before making their way into the bay, cleaned up as they turned to face the wind, and dropping in size along the way. Brett said that the spot would get better as the tide fell, so there was no hurry.

Following a steep and difficult path, they climbed down the headland onto the rocks and into a little bay. Ange could see the waves weren't as severe or unruly as she had seen at Sliders. They took their time putting on sunscreen, waxing their boards, and doing some stretching before donning their wetsuits.

Leaving the protection of their shoes, Ange followed Brett along the painful spiky rocks to a ledge about a metre and a half above the water. Timing his move, Brett ran the last couple of metres and launched himself into the water, paddling aggressively so that he could clear the rocks before the next wave. As soon as he was clear, he looked back and beckoned to Ange, who did the same thing, albeit less gracefully.

Brett was speaking to four other local surfers and introduced Ange when she paddled over. The other surfers had been in the water about thirty minutes, and the waves were good and getting better, even though infrequent. Tucked in close to the rocks, the take-off zone was tiny, meaning that the spot could comfortably handle just a small group of surfers. Brett was quick to pick up a moderately sized wave, leaving Ange to catch her breath and look around at her surroundings.

Far out to sea to the north, Ange could see a flock of seagulls and terns, feeding voraciously on a school of baitfish which had come to the surface, pursued by larger predators from beneath. This hardly seemed fair to the baitfish, attacked from below and above as they huddled together, believing that there was safety in numbers. Small bonito and northern bluefin tuna were still prevalent at this time of year, and their insatiable appetite left plenty of scraps for the scavenging birds.

Ange kept a watchful eye that none of these schools ventured too closely, as she knew that there were likely to be even larger predators than tuna in this melee. 'Just like my day job,' Ange reflected wryly to herself.

Every so often, a large mutton bird would dive-bomb into the water nearby like a crazed kamikaze pilot, seeking deeper water and larger fish. After many seconds, the bird would pop to the surface, often with a flapping fish in its beak, keeping a watchful eye on Ange as if to say, 'What are you looking at? Find your own fish.'

Brett snapped Ange from her reverie, paddling over to give her some encouragement. She responded, catching a couple of smallish waves which she surfed conservatively, helping to grow her confidence. Catching the wave required a strong paddle, leaving a relatively easy take-off, before it hit the sandbank and hollowed out through the midsection, ending on a nice shoulder section in which to execute some cutbacks or more adventurous turns.

Brett caught a cracking wave and paddled out with a huge grin on his face. 'Have you ever had a tube ride?' he asked.

Ange answered in the negative, to which Brett replied, 'Well, today is the day. The tide is perfect, and that middle section is hollowing out nicely on the sandbank. You'll need to take one of the larger set waves.'

Somewhat apprehensively, Ange tentatively agreed to this suggestion.

'OK, great. What you need to do is to hang back close to the break on the first section, staying as high on the wave as possible. Then, as you approach the midsection, tuck in close to the face as the wave steepens. After that, all that remains is to keep a straight line and head to the opening.'

'Sounds simple,' Ange replied to his helpful tips, knowing deep down that it would be anything but.

To make sure that Ange wouldn't chicken out, he yelled out to the other locals in the water, 'Ange is going to have a crack at her first ever tube,' squarely putting her on the spot. The locals then joined forces to position Ange in the right place within the take-off zone and waited for the perfect wave. Ange had absolutely no choice but to paddle into the wave that they'd selected for her.

She managed the take-off easily but then forgot to stay high on the face, failing to harness the power of the wave and maintain her speed as it hollowed out. She was caught flat-footed in front of the wave and the lip came over and pummelled her into the water, knocking the wind out of her.

Despite the natural reflex to grapple towards the surface, it is impossible to swim in aerated white water. Pushed deep underwater, rolled and rolled by the turbulence, Ange knew to stay calm. She felt the bottom, pleased that it was sand and not a razor-sharp coral reef. Her orientation restored, Ange waited until the bubbles cleared around her, then pushed to the surface and took a welcome deep breath.

Still being towed along by her board, her leg rope stretched to its limit, Ange looked up to see another wave coming and realised that she was squarely in the impact zone. With no time to retrieve her board, she dived deeply under the water to escape another pounding, all the while being pulled towards shore by her straining surfboard. Three more waves of this, and she knew there was little chance of paddling back out, so she awkwardly pulled herself onto her surfboard and belly-boarded towards the small sandy beach.

The walk back out to the jump-off spot gave her some time to catch her breath and to watch how the more experienced surfers navigated that hollow section. It was spectacular to see the surfers disappear behind a curtain of water and reappear moments later, raising their arms and whooping and yelling with excitement. Ange realised her error, knowing that she had to stay higher on the face next time.

Grinning from ear to ear, Brett said they had seen her board tombstoning and knew that she had copped a dusting. Tombstoning was yet another fresh experience for Ange, never having surfed waves this big and powerful. The analogy was clear, the nose of her quavering board signposting her watery internment, temporarily at least.

The smiling faces of the crew strengthened her resolve to show them what she was made of. On her next attempt, Ange remembered her previous error and stayed as high on the face as she could. As she lined up for the middle section, she was caught by surprise at how quickly the wave hollowed out. Failing to tuck into the wave face and keep positive pressure on the inside rail of her surfboard, Ange was flipped up and over the falls before she knew it. There was no escaping the curling wave as it wrapped Ange up with her board in a gut-wrenching wipeout.

Even though this wipeout was worse than her first, Ange knew not to panic—there was nothing that could hurt her other than panic itself. She could soon stand on the bottom and quickly extracted herself from the impact zone. A few minutes later, she was back out into the line-up, grinning and ready to take her chances again. Her toughness and determination impressed the others, and they coaxed her onto the next promising wave to line up in front of her. This time, with the benefit of her previous painful errors, Ange executed her moves perfectly.

As she lined up for the hollow section, Ange tucked in close to the face, seeing the wave magically fold over ahead of her. As the watery curtain enveloped her, Ange was stunned by the surreal and fleeting experience. It wasn't what she had expected, but there was no time to think. Her eyes remained fixated on the safety of the shoulder, subconsciously expecting to be pounded into the water at any moment, sensory overload shutting off her hearing, despite the roaring wave. Ange wasn't even sure she'd been barrelled at all.

In an instant, her watery eclipse was over. Ange shot into the sunlight and to the safety of the shoulder and the deeper water. Her hearing suddenly rebooted, and she could hear the thunder of the wave behind her. Full of adrenaline and surprise at what had just happened, she collapsed shakily on her board.

Autopilot kicked in, and she immediately paddled back out, not wanting to be caught inside by the next wave, the memories of her recent poundings still vivid. Once she was in the clear, Ange replayed the sequence in her mind, realising that she had indeed just experienced her first ever tube ride. In that instant, Ange knew that she would likely spend the rest of her life striving to repeat that experience—over and over again.

She paddled back out, shaking and elated. The guys had all been watching and, not seeing a tombstoning board, could tell that she had been barrelled. They were cheering and congratulating her. It was one of the most exhilarating moments of Ange's life.

The tide was dropping rapidly, and the middle section started to close out, the fleeting nature of what had just happened apparent. Ange and Brett retreated to the beach to have lunch and rehydrate. Despite what you might think, it is easy to get dehydrated when surfing, and Ange knew to drink plenty of water. It was a relief to remove her wetsuit and escape to the cover of a large boulder that had fallen from the cliff face. Ange had heard somewhere that sharks could sense urine in the water from a great distance. She couldn't say whether that was true; however, relieving herself in her wetsuit, although a common practice amongst surfers, was simply not her style.

With her comfort now restored, Ange rummaged around in her backpack to find a tube of sunscreen. She squeezed a dab on each arm before handing the tube to Brett, asking if he would mind rubbing some on her back and shoulders. She enjoyed the feeling of Brett's hands as they caressed her back under the pretext of sunscreen application. She shivered as he gently massaged her neck and shoulders, deftly relieving the tension of hours spent paddling. Brett lingered a touch longer than necessary, much to Ange's delight, and she imagined how many beachside dalliances had started this way. Reluctantly shaking off that thought, she reminded herself that she was ostensibly in Namba Heads on assignment, her professionalism never far beneath the surface.

Safe under the cover of SPF50+, they sat on the beach for a couple of hours, enjoying the warmth of the sun and the buzz of their morning surf session. When the tide was right, Brett suggested they paddle back out for another surf. The wind was due to shift to the east-north-east in the evening, and the heaving swell would destroy the sandbanks. While it was not as good a session as the first, they all enjoyed plenty of quality waves, albeit without barrels.

Her new dolphin friends came by to check out the fun. Then, as if to say, 'What are you doing surfing on our spot?' a trio caught one of the larger swells out wide, using the pressure wave to show their skill—jumping and diving to make the point.

On the walk home, Brett pointed out another break called 'Wobblers', so named because of a wicked cross-chop that radiated back off the rocks, quickly making a chump of even the most talented surfer. There was another break called 'Pointers', further beyond Midway on the outermost reach of the headland.

Pointers was a nice left-hander, apparently, but highly exposed and somewhat intimidating. Brett conceded he was yet to experience Pointers at its best. 'Also, the name doesn't help.' He grimaced, imagining the white-pointed predators that might lurk beneath.

Brett explained to Ange the ethereal nature of the breaks around the headlands of Namba Heads. It could take years before Midway performed again as it had today, enjoying just the right combination of wind, swell, tide, and sand deposits. The locals were on constant patrol, watching the build-up of sand as it moved in and out. Enormous clouds of sand were often held in suspension far out to sea before coming back to land and depositing themselves on the coast in a matter of days, only to disappear again overnight. Why sand was deposited in one place and moved from another was clearly a complex matter, an equilibrium easily upset.

Dropping Ange back to her cabin mid-afternoon, Brett suggested they should resume their aborted date at the Bella Vista this evening, if she was up to it. 'Sounds like an idea,' Ange replied breezily, and they agreed to meet in the beer garden at 7 p.m. Washing out her wetsuit and hanging her gear out to dry, Ange marvelled at the day she had just experienced. After a shower, a deep lethargy washed over her and she realised how fatigued she was, falling asleep as soon as she lay down on her bed.

Chapter 35

Back to Bella Vista

Ange was pleased that she'd had the foresight to set an alarm on her phone for 5:30 p.m.; otherwise, she probably would have slept through, waking at midnight, missing her date, and completely messing with her body clock for good measure. She showered and painstakingly dried her hair with the pathetic attempt at a hairdryer, the curse of hotel accommodation everywhere. These asthmatic contraptions were bordering on useless, most likely procured by male purchasin g officers, all bachelors and sporting No. 2 buzz cuts.

Her everyday makeup would not do for this evening. Ange retrieved her 'professional' cosmetic case, reserved for special occasions and filled with all manner of products that she had acquired over the years. Even someone as no-nonsense as Ange was susceptible to the marketing guile of the cosmetic industry, adroitly exploiting the rich vein of vanity as they did. Nonetheless, Ange considered that being aware and proud of one's appearance was a good thing, respectful of yourself and those around you. As she rummaged around in her tightly packed cosmetic case, she came across her emergency pack of condoms. Ange unconsciously checked the use-by date. Sadly, they had not been called into active duty for a while. 'All good. I still have another six months before my celibacy become s official,' she thought dryly.

Ange was pleased to have brought along some nice clothes this trip. She chose a simple white linen dress by a local Byron designer, which she teamed with an orange-and-yellow necklace of oversized beads by Bimba y Lola, a gift from one her more stylish male fails, and a bright red '70s-style bangle she'd just picked up from a groovy online store called Apartment 5B, topping it all with some yellow espadrilles. She looked herself up and down in the ubiquitous mirror-cum-wardrobe-door and was quietly pleased with the overall effect, finding herself imbued with confidence and anticipation of a fun night.

She arrived at the Bella Vista Hotel just before 7 p.m., deciding to toggle her phone to vibrate, lest her date night be rudely interrupted again. She was just about to deal with the mandatory Covid-19 check-in on her phone when she noticed Brett walking casually along the street. Habitually punctual herself, Ange appreciated that trait in others. Tall and handsome, with an air of confidence, he had a laconic gait that gave the impression that time was not his master, despite this punctuality. Ange saw his gaze take in her outfit, pleased that she had made such an effort.

'You look great,' he mentioned, naturally and without guile.

Accepting his compliment with a broad smile, she replied, 'You too. Let's hope we don't get interrupted this time!'

They found a quiet table away from the music. Ange offered to get the drinks and looked around the beer garden as she waited at the bar. It was almost as if she had dreamt the past seven frenetic days. Sporting the same crowd, same musician, and same relaxed vibe, it was a Bella Vista version of *Groundhog Day*. Ange realised Namba Heads was running to a different timekeeper than city life, even when compared to neighbouring places like Byron Bay. It was both comforting and unnerving at the same time, loving both nature and the bustling city life as she did.

Drinks in hand, Ange and Brett quickly picked up from their previous date, the conversation naturally starting about surfing before moving on to lifestyle and the challenges of attaining that elusive work-life balance. Over dinner, the range of topics expanded, and they discovered there was much they had in common but also much they disagreed about. The evening was proving both pleasant and stimulating, and the conversation flowed without effort, the powerful chemistry between them palpable.

As is often the case, the conversation eventually stalled, and the evening reached a transition point. Strongly attracted to Brett, Ange suggested they take a walk on the breakwater, ostensibly to check the surf. The predicted stiff breeze hadn't arrived, and the air was still and heavy with sea spray. The huge swell crashed heavily into the breakwater, reverberating through the rocks as they strained against the power of the sea. After her magnificent day, kissing Brett seemed the logical next step. The chemistry that she had imagined on the beach today was real, and a shiver raced down her spine as his arms gently wrapped around her. The feeling of his powerful hands through her soft linen dress was thrilling. They almost ran back to her cabin.

As soon as they were safely inside, Brett pushed her against the closed door, kissing Ange with a delicious sense of urgency, as if the dash back from the breakwater had been an eternity. Ange paused and stepped back. Standing confidently in front of him, she kicked off her espadrilles and slowly unbuttoned her dress. Ange clutched the dress around her for a moment, as if pondering a point of no return, before letting it gently slip to the ground. Taking time to relish the tension and suspense, she somewhat coyly removed her underwear, pleased she had chosen well in that regard.

It was such a turn-on to stand there completely naked, her bikini lines showing from her day spent in the sun with this handsome man, empowered and proud of her body. She delighted as Brett fixated on her every move, the hunger in his eyes unambiguous as she deliberately moved closer. Ange struggled with the buttons of his shirt, her eagerness causing them to turn suddenly obstinate. Sliding her hands lightly across his chest, she lingered for a moment before slipping his shirt over his shoulders. Pausing for a moment to admire his body, she wrapped her arms around his back, pressing their bodies together, her desire obvious. The feeling of his chest against hers was electric and she could feel the power in his shoulders, developed through countless hours of surfing. Abandoning all pretext of restraint, Ange became lost in this collision of mind and body.

Much to her delight, Brett was a confident and considerate lover. After such a period of unintended celibacy, Ange had almost forgotten how exciting it was to feel another body close to hers, the need for intimacy such a basic instinct, repressed as it had been. A deep sense of satisfaction gradually displaced her excitement and lust.

In the early hours of the morning, sharing a double bed proved too much for them both. Brett retreated home to the comfort of his own bed, apologising that he had a busy day ahead. Having said their goodbyes, Ange lay alone on her bed pondering her day and the possibilities for the future. 'Maybe when all this is over,' she hoped. Despite such a strenuous day and night, sleep proved a restless endeavour.

Chapter 36

Hidden Delights

Waking up to the stiff east-north-east breeze that Brett had predicted, Ange decided it was time to head back to Byron Bay. She was still buzzing from the wonderful night before and sorely needed to burn off some energy before tackling the drive north.

Ange donned her exercise gear, deciding it was time to explore the full extent of Namba Heads. A quick check on Google Maps showed a great walking loop of around ten kilometres, covering all the headlands and the beaches in between, returning via an inland track. Ange packed up and settled her bill with the manager before driving up onto the headland to park her car at the starting point she had identified.

The trail started through the scrub before picking up a coastal track that wound its way around the many headlands. The stiff onshore breeze slammed into her as soon as Ange moved beyond the protection of the thick bushland, and she sometimes had trouble keeping her balance when the wind gusted. She came to Midway, where they had surfed yesterday. It was a complete mess, a washing machine, the water milky with sand and froth.

She scanned out to sea; the wind was far too strong for birds to feed, giving some respite to the hapless baitfish. This reminded her of the saying 'It's an ill wind that blows no good'. As she gazed out onto the ocean, Ange reflected that her sea was actually a mosaic of deep greens, not the blue of storybooks. Only when the sunlight caught the seawater between the white sandy bottom did the ocean reveal its bluish tendencies.

Continuing her trek, Ange came across a deep fracture in the cliff face of the next headland. Waves were being funnelled into the crevasse, focussing their strength before they crashed loudly into the cliff face, as if determined to make the crevice ever larger. With each crashing wave, a great whoosh of spray and thick white froth shot up the cliff face, where it was smashed into pieces and scattered by the wind, sprinkling the surrounding grass and trees with these frothy confetti.

Ange came to a small protected rocky outcrop on which a large flock of terns was resting. These handsome birds were hunkered down, perfectly lined up and facing directly into the wind, seemingly comfortable and patiently waiting for the wind to drop so they could continue their assault on those baitfish. Ange heard the distinctive shriek of a sea eagle and looked up to see the caller high above, drifting back and forth across the headland as it searched for its next meal. If a great white shark was the top predator below the water, the sea eagle was its equal above, man of course besting them both.

The tide was dropping, exposing shellfish and seaweed clinging to the rocks. Ange walked over to admire the deep emerald-green seaweed that swayed in the currents, in the process disturbing some small rock crabs that scurried off into their hidey holes. Stopping to gaze into a crystal-clear bucket-sized rock pool that had been exposed with the dropping tide, Ange studied the incredible display of anemone and other sea life. Seeing the extent of life inhabiting this tiny pool, she pondered the immensity and diversity of what the ocean before her held.

There was movement, noise, and life everywhere, kept in tune by the relentless rhythm of the ocean. No wonder she found the ocean both calming and stimulating, challenging yet contemplative. No two points in time were ever the same; nature was always moving and adapting, continually offering a fresh face and a novel experience.

On the next headland, high above the ocean, Ange gazed out across the white-capped ocean, hoping that she might see a whale, or that her dolphin surfing mates might come through. On the horizon, she could see two large container ships, unmistakable with their ungainly form, like gigantic Lego blocks floating in the ocean, finding they had it to themselves now that the pandemic had firmly anchored pleasure cruising. She smiled, imagining herself as heroine Lucy, fighting crime and defending the weak in a nautical version of *The Lego Movie*. Ange's vivid and wacky imagination was never far beneath the surface.

She pondered Terry's favoured theory on shark attacks and the imagery of a great white shark following the whale migration paths, picking off the weak and the young as they circled menacingly. In a light-bulb moment, Ange suddenly deciphered the pattern in the coordinates which guided Dave's midnight missions.

Her mind now racing from her contemplative trance, Ange automatically reached into her gym pants and extracted her mobile phone, sending a text to Billy.

Billy, can you plot those coordinates we found on the burner phone and overlay the principal shipping routes off Namba Heads?

Despite today being Sunday, Billy texted straight back, his reply covertly appearing on her phone, still toggled to silent after the previous night's escapade, reminding Ange to turn the ringer back on.

On it

Ange marvelled at the power of the subconscious mind and how it could subliminally solve the most complicated of puzzles when cleared of the clutter and detritus of daily life.

Still reeling from the implications of her breakthrough moment, uncovering secret bays and rocky inlets along the way, Ange wound her way onto a long, curving beach that culminated at Sliders. Large banks of sea foam littered the beach, whipped up by the huge surf and corralled by the wind and the waves. During a cyclone last season, Ange had read warnings not to walk through the foam. Apparently, sea snakes found this foam very much to their liking, attracted by the combination of a warm woolly blanket and the protection from eagle eyes.

Ange navigated the long crescent of Bushies Beach, giving the banks of foam a wide berth as she went. She walked past Sliders and over the headland that protected her new favourite surf break, reaching the exquisitely desolate back beach. Bathed in sea mist, the wide sandy expanse stretched south from the headland and into the hazy distance before it would meet the next river and its protective headland, and so on.

She walked down the deserted beach, searching for the start of the inland trail. She came across several kangaroo footprints in the sand, and further along she saw some distinctive emu prints. They were commonly found in western NSW, where Ange had grown up, but she was unaware that emus also lived on the coast.

Finding the inland trailhead, she left the beach and the tearing wind. Ange knew from her criminology studies that persistent strong winds could have negative psychological effects and even lead to increased crime rates, so her sense of relief did not surprise her when she cleared the dunes and entered the sanctuary of the bushland.

Ange followed the trail, crossing paths with Bernadette Williams, who was admiring a small flock of yellow-tailed black cockatoos, munching away on the seedpods of some banksia trees. These large glossy black birds featured a yellow spot on each cheek to match their yellow-and-black eyes, the overall effect being somewhat comical. They rendered an ear-piercing screech as they flew from tree to tree, their flight exposing a brilliant swathe of yellow tail feathers.

'Curious birds, aren't they?' suggested Bernadette Williams, by way of a greeting.

'And noisy,' replied Ange, 'but most impressive, and a real treat to see them here in their natural habitat.'

Ange explained she had been involved in prosecuting a gang of wildlife traffickers, with parrots being highly valued. Reflecting on her rowdy alarm clocks, Ange asked rhetorically, 'Why is our birdlife so darn noisy?'

Williams appraised Ange for a moment with a sideways stare before asking if she wanted to see something special. Staying under the cover of the bush, she led Ange slowly and quietly towards a low grassy depression.

A small flock of emu congregated in the grassy hollow, out of the wind, grazing on seeds and insects. Ange whispered that she had noticed emu footprints on the beach, surprised that they lived on the coast. Williams explained that emus and kangaroos often came down onto the beach to graze on the seaweed and kelp washed in by the waves.

Williams explained to Ange that many environmentalists wanted to lock up parks and keep people out, an approach that she didn't agree with. 'I cannot see how you can expect society to protect the environment unless people get the chance to experience how special it is,' she stated forcibly, echoing Terry Scott's philosophy.

Ange agreed with this, adding, 'If only some would take more care. I'm sure ignorance is a factor.'

Seeming to reach a rapport, Ange and Bernadette said their goodbyes and continued their respective ways. It took Ange another forty-five minutes to reach her car, thinking that this had been a wonderful way to get her daily exercise.

Before facing the drive home, Ange called Darren Billings to tell him she was heading back to Byron Bay and would keep him informed of any progress.

'What a dream posting you have, looking after such a lovely town,' Ange told Billings. His noncommittal reply suggested he might not agree with her, something she found most surprising.

Chapter 37

Ships in the Night

Refreshed after her weekend, Ange was at her desk in the police station early on Monday morning. She spent the quiet time before the daily onslaught sketching out the case on a large whiteboard. Ange found the graphic representation of her case most helpful, and she realised how scant the evidence was to link the various protagonists together. The reports from the forensic pathologist due today would be crucial.

Billy arrived soon after Ange, chuffed when she congratulated him on his excellent support work and initiative. Impatient and unable to wait for the written report, Ange asked Billy for the phone number of the head pathologist, a Dr Andrew Evans, someone she had worked with before. Checking the time and seeing it was now officially business hours, Ange rang the number and introduced herself.

Dr Evans opened the conversation. 'I guess you're ringing me about the investigation in Namba Heads—I saw you were the detective.'

'Yes, I'm desperately hoping you can tell me something instructive, as I've got nothing other than dead ends at the moment,' Ange replied.

'Let's start with what we know. The blood fragments taken from the deck are human and match the DNA of the hair and skin samples found on the bench seat in the cabin. They also match the strand of hair taken from a third location, a shed where your missing teenager was living. All these samples match the DNA of the body recovered on Friday,' explained Dr Evans.

'OK, excellent,' said Ange, feeling that the investigation might finally move forward. She already had reasonable evidence to suggest that the body recovered was that of Jake Thompson, but this was now beyond doubt.

'Moving onto the post-mortem. Young male, likely in his late teens or early twenties, died from an epidural hematoma after a sharp blow to the temple. The bones surrounding the temple fractured inwards, lacerating the middle meningeal artery. In these cases, blood subsequently builds up around the brain and compresses it. He would have died in minutes, I expect.

'I checked the photos taken by the investigating team, and it's my opinion that he died after striking his temple on the corner of the bench seat, the one where the matching skin and hair samples were recovered. He would have collapsed onto the deck, probably unconscious and bleeding profusely. This would all seem consistent with the evidence collected,' Dr Evans concluded, pausing for a moment to let this sink in.

Ange realised that, despite the text exchange recovered from the burner phone, she couldn't be completely certain whether the death was an accident, manslaughter, or even murder, perhaps after a struggle or fight. Based on her investigations so far, Dave Fletcher didn't seem like the sort of guy who would murder Jake Thompson, but stranger things had happened. However, given that the two protagonists in this sorry episode were dead, it seemed a moot point and not something to focus on at this stage. Given that the trawler had been battling rough seas, an accident seemed the most likely explanation.

'That is helpful. Is there anything to link the boat and the house?' Ange inquired.

Much to Ange's dismay, Dr Evans explained, 'There was nothing concrete. However, we found traces of narcotics that match the analysis from the metal box tested earlier in the week.'

'How strong do you think this link might be?' probed Ange.

Dr Evans was confident in his reply. 'We used chromatographic analysis, which showed that the chemical signatures are a close match. Impurities and differences in production techniques allow us to distinguish between different sources.' Bursting her bubble yet again by stating the obvious, he finished with, 'Of course, that doesn't mean that we can establish any concrete link. They could have simply purchased drugs from the same local dealer, something quite probable in a small town.'

'Great.' Ange smirked. 'You guys always keep me guessing. Anyhow, thanks for jumping on this for me so quickly. Oh, by the way—were there any fingerprints taken at the site where the strand of hair was retrieved, the place where Jake

Thompson was living?'

After a pause, the pathologist reported that there were no prints noted in the report. That news didn't especially surprise her, seeing how spotlessly clean the place had seemed. They had been lucky to even find a strand of hair.

After she hung up from the call, she sat in her chair and reflected on the conversation. She needed to consider the prospect of someone else being involved, perhaps a local dealer. She would need to ask Billings about this. However, a dealer could come from anywhere. They would also need to verify dental and medical records to be certain that the body was indeed Jake, but Ange felt they had enough evidence to move forward on that assumption.

She updated the whiteboard that she had prepared earlier with the new information and then called her team together. They stood in front of the whiteboard as Ange stepped through her conclusions.

1. *Fletcher was involved in something dodgy, leading to his death. Paid around $25,000 for his trouble.*

2. *Appears Jake Thompson died on the trawler, likely on the night before Fletcher's death.*

3. *Someone, not Fletcher, moved Jake's body from the boat, cleaned up, and buried his body in bushland. Two people?*

4. *Amy Lightfoot staged death to escape her toxic relationship with Ted Kramer. Lightfoot feels Kramer is involved in something dodgy.*

5. *Lightfoot and Ted Kramer in Namba Heads because of Joe Kramer—is he involved as well?*

6. *Ted Kramer left town after the disappearance of Lightfoot, made no inquiries about his girlfriend.*

7. *Cannabis and cocaine match potentially link house and trawler.*

Ange stated her opinion that Ted Kramer was of definite interest and she needed to pursue that angle. She also gave the group a brief summation of the historic link between Joe Kramer, Namba Heads, and the Tea Trees development.

'Do you feel that we have enough evidence to secure a warrant to access the Kramers' phone records?' Ange queried her boss.

'Unlikely. You'll need something more concrete. I used up all my brownie points on that last disastrous drug bust,' Grady replied, looking pointedly at one of Ange's sheepish colleagues, his shoes suddenly of interest as he avoided any eye contact with his boss.

After the meeting, Ange sat down with Billy and they planned out their next steps. She undertook to tackle the awful task of ringing Jake's mother and telling them the tragic news. She would also ring Amy Lightfoot back and ask her about drug use, amongst other things.

Ange asked Billy to look at motor vehicle registration data covering both the Kramers' and the Society. Sitting back in her chair to think for a moment, she decided it was worth ringing Darren Billings to ask what sort of security cameras they had in the town. She also needed to check if Billings was aware of any local drug dealers.

This train of thought sparked a new idea. Remembering Jimmy's story about how he had thwarted his scammer, Ange planned to ring him and see if he still had any video footage from the period surrounding Fletcher's death. One way or another, she could hopefully secure another stack of video footage for Billy to trawl through.

Ange turned to her phone, facing up to the terrible prospect of ringing Jake's mother. Telling a parent that you're investigating the likely death of their child is simply the worst part of the job. Taking a deep breath, she rang the number on file for Jake's mother. The conversation was every bit as traumatic as she had feared. Ange choked back tears. Pulling herself together, she secured his mother's consent to access Jake's medical records so that they could establish a concrete ID, asking her to go down to the local police station to sign a consent form.

After she had hung up, Ange stared blankly into her computer screen for minutes afterwards, thinking about the tragedy of such a promising life cut short. A sense of anger and indignation at the injustice of it all came over her, arousing a fresh resolve to get on with the investigation. She asked Billy to organise securing the consent of Jake's mother and getting the medical records for the coroner as soon as possible.

She then texted the number of Amy Lightfoot, asking her to call Ange back as soon as she could. The phone rang immediately. 'Hello, Detective. It's Amy Lightfoot here. You wanted to speak with me?'

Ange noted to herself that Amy Lightfoot had offered her name, which was an encouraging sign. Knowing how nervous Amy was, Ange started by inquiring how she was doing before getting down to business. 'Can you tell me about drug usage? Did you or Ted Kramer use narcotics?'

There was a long pause before Amy answered, 'I don't want to get in trouble,' suggesting to Ange that she had used drugs.

'That's not why I'm asking,' explained Ange. 'However, I would like you to be honest with me.'

Ange heard Amy take a deep breath before replying. 'I occasionally smoked cannabis with Teddy, but nothing more than that. Teddy once suggested we try something stronger, but I didn't want to take a pill that contained who knows what.'

'Don't worry, I even tried cannabis at university,' Ange replied, hoping to put Amy further at ease.

Amy confirmed that the cannabis was Ted Kramer's, but she didn't know where or who he had gotten it from.

'Did you ever see any large quantities of cannabis or other drugs?' Ange asked hopefully.

'No, nothing like that,' Amy replied confidently.

Ange switched topic. 'Can you describe the phone you found?'

Amy's description matched the phone found on the boat, opening the possibility that someone had purchased them at the same place and time.

Finally, Ange asked for a description of their vehicle.

'We used to drive an old white four-wheel-drive Mitsubishi van that was set up for camping. We used it for tripping around and often drove down onto the beach south of Namba Heads for Ted to surf, sometimes camping on the beach overnight. I had some great times with Teddy in the van. I used to love camping on the beach. Bluey always came along with us—that's Teddy's dog. I miss Bluey,' Amy explained wistfully.

Ange thanked Amy for her honesty and finished the conversation by telling Amy that she would likely be in touch again.

Ange already had Jimmy's number saved on her phone. Looking at her watch, she realised that the lunchtime rush should be over by now. She was part way through describing herself when Jimmy cut her off. 'I know who you are, Detective Watson.'

Not at all surprised he knew her name, Ange asked how long Jimmy saved his video footage.

'After last problem, I keep it for months,' Jimmy replied. 'Cloud storage is cheap these days.'

Jimmy readily agreed to provide access, and Ange took his email address down so that she could send him the dates she was interested in. Given that Jimmy's takeaway window was right on the main drag, Ange hoped the camera had a wide-angle lens, and they could identify any vehicles driving past.

Ange's next call was to Darren Billings. She realised she should keep him somewhat informed of the latest developments, and her conviction that the body recovered was that of Jake Thompson. Billings appeared as offhand and disengaged as usual. Ange then asked if the town had any security cameras monitoring the streets. Billings was aware the council had planned to install a string of security cameras over a year ago, but a strong anti-Big Brother element in town had had the idea canned.

Billings added, 'Let me put it this way—I don't think Namba Heads will set any records for the take-up of the Covid-19 vaccine when it becomes available.'

Getting the picture, Ange went on and probed Billings to see if he was aware of any drug dealers in town.

'None that I know of. I'm sure that a bit of cannabis gets horse-traded here and there, but I've seen no evidence of large-scale dealing. As you've already found out, Namba Heads is a small community where everyone knows everything about everybody else, so I'm reasonably certain I would have heard about any permanent dealers. As I understand it, any drugs that do come into town arrive from the larger centres to the north and south. Byron Bay mostly.'

Billings' assurances didn't totally convince Ange, nor was she sure he would even notice any dealing under his nose. So, beside the entry to 'Local drug dealers' on her checklist, she wrote 'probably none?' before ending the call. She then remembered her text to Billy the previous day, so she rang him to ask if the pickup coordinates correlated with the shipping routes.

'Oh, sorry, I forgot. I finished plotting them earlier today. They match perfectly—all of them were within the shipping route that rounds Namba Heads and Byron Bay,' Billy confirmed.

He then went on, relishing some fun facts learnt during his research. 'Did you know that over one thousand, five hundred containers get lost annually at sea? In fact, forty fell overboard in May this year near Sydney, when a containership lost power in heavy seas.' Billy loved this sort of stuff.

'What happens to them?' inquired Ange, unable to resist asking despite the serious task at hand.

'Apparently, very few are recovered, with most sinking to the bottom. Those that don't sink often float just below the surface and present a major boating hazard,' Billy expounded.

'If a shipping container can get lost, then a small floating package deployed overboard would be undetectable,' Ange reasoned out loud.

By the end of the day, Ange felt they were making progress and left the station feeling somewhat buoyed. It would, however, take her some time to shake off the distress and sadness of Jake's mother.

Chapter 38

Good Fortune

When Ange arrived at the station on Tuesday morning, Billy was hard at work on his computer.

'Morning, boss. So do you want the good news or the bad news?' he asked happily.

'Why can't it be just all be good news occasionally?' she thought before requesting Billy start with the good news.

Billy looked at his notes before replying. 'I found a gold Corolla registered in the name of Joe Kramer, and a silver Holden station wagon registered with his Society. Ted Kramer sold his white Mitsubishi van three weeks ago, for the sum of six thousand dollars.'

'Can you trace the new owners? Six thousand seems cheap, given how popular vans are right now,' Ange commented.

'Already have—that's the bad news,' Billy replied. 'The number plate turned up in an accident report in Queensland. I spoke to a sergeant at the Rainbow Beach police station. Apparently, a couple of backpackers were attempting to drive the van around a notorious beach traffic hazard called Mudlo Rocks. On their way to Fraser Island, they drove along Cooloola Beach late one afternoon and got themselves bogged and stranded amongst the rocks on an incoming tide. They had to abandon the van.'

'Bloody hell,' exclaimed Ange in frustration. 'Why can't we cut a break on this case?'

'The van got smashed to pieces during the night, and a squillion litres of salt water have been through it. It happens at least twenty times a year, according to the sergeant. Mostly inexperienced or impatient drivers. The local tow truck driver dragged it out the next morning, and it's now sitting in the local wrecker's yard with a pile of other vehicles who met similar fates. Seems like a profitable business being a tow truck driver at Rainbow Beach. Apparently, the record is eighty-three vehicles caught by those rocks in one year,' Billy explained, clearly astonished with this little titbit of information.

'Billy, can you ring the wrecker's yard and tell them not to touch the vehicle just in case we needed to inspect it? Although it seems unlikely that it'll yield anything of value after all of that.'

Shaking her head and grimacing as she walked away, Ange exclaimed, 'You can't make this stuff up.'

Ange went to her desk and checked her emails to find that Jimmy had organised a Dropbox folder with the video feed from the requested days. She forwarded the email straight away to Billy and asked him to see what he could identify, fully expecting to extend her run of bad luck.

It was lunchtime, so Ange went for a walk across the railway line into town to grab some sushi, one of her favourite foods that she had missed in the past week. Nothing so cosmopolitan as a sushi restaurant had found a home in Namba Heads. She walked down to the shore to enjoy her food, looking to see if any surf was streaming into the large bay. There wasn't much to report surf-wise, but it was a postcard day at Byron Bay.

In the past few months, Main Beach had suffered massive beach erosion. Ange had read about what had happened in the news. It was a phenomenon called headland bypassing, and it seemed an appropriate event to accompany a global pandemic. Only a year ago, the beach had seemed a hundred metres wide, and it reminded her of the discussion with Brett Tompkins and her Midway experience. Where the sand went was anybody's guess.

'Maybe someone up north in Tweed Heads is sitting on our sand right now. It's like a game of musical sandcastles. It's all fun and games, running around in a circle until the music stops, and then one of us sits down and falls into a crater, all hard and rocky,' mused Ange while she savoured her sushi.

The sand would come back to Main Beach in time. Maybe Tweed Heads might give it back—if they had taken it—nobody really knew. One beach in Ireland took thirty-three years to get its sand back. Ange hoped that Byron Bay would fare better.

There were still plenty of young holidaymakers and backpackers around, compressed onto the foreshore and whatever pockets of beach they could find. Looking out over the sparkling water and up to the iconic lighthouse, Ange marvelled at how Byron Bay was indeed one of the great beaches of the world, even despite its current state.

She arrived back at the station to find a very excited Billy. 'I found the van. It was driven along the road to the marina on two occasions, around the time of Fletcher's death. The first was just before midnight, when Fletcher made his last fishing trip, returning twenty minutes later,' he explained.

Ange and Billy agreed it was unlikely that Kramer could have retrieved Jake's body and cleaned the boat within that small window of time. Perhaps Fletcher had done this himself before Kramer had driven over to the marina, but that would have been a colossal task after the night he had just endured. In any event, Fletcher had been told to dock the boat and go home. Someone else must have cleaned up the mess. This suggested that Kramer wasn't working alone, convinced as they were about his involvement and that Jake had died during Fletcher's final fishing trip.

'What about the second time? Was that during the night that Fletcher died?' Ange asked hopefully.

'No. The van doesn't show up again until six a.m. on the morning after Fletcher's death,' replied Billy.

'That's a pity,' said Ange.

She thought through the implications of this new information. Somebody had moved the body. However, they needed to consider the possibility that Ted Kramer had just been an unlucky insomniac on the night Jake died, out for a midnight drive. Further, Dave Fletcher might indeed have killed himself, and then they were back at square one. Ange knew they needed to verify the identity of other vehicles that had driven past Jimmy's restaurant on the nights of both deaths, but she wanted to focus on the Kramers for now.

'Billy, can you contact Jimmy and ask him to supply the additional video feeds for the pickup dates stored on the burner phone? Hopefully, this might show that Kramer's midnight drives correlated with those dates, thereby implicating him in those dodgy activities at the very least.'

After adding that additional task for her already busy assistant, Ange went to see her boss with the latest developments.

'Boss, from where Ted Kramer was living, there are only two ways to the marina where Dave Fletcher died. The first is down the main drag, where Jimmy's restaurant is located, and the second is through the back streets, which would take you past the police station. If you were up to anything dodgy, I can't believe that you would risk driving past the police station. You would choose the main drag every time. Jimmy doesn't advertise his camera, and it's very well hidden from view. Kramer wouldn't have suspected his movements were being captured on video.'

Grady just stood staring blankly at Ange, creating an awkward moment's silence, something Ange broke when she could endure no more.

'I think we should investigate the Kramers' phone records and credit card transactions covering the past couple of months. I'll need a warrant for that, boss. What do you reckon? Do we have enough evidence to secure one from a magistrate?' asked Ange hopefully. Knowing that Covid-19 had killed the cashless economy, she hoped to trace their movements, perhaps even the purchase of some burner phones, if they were lucky.

'Why both Kramers?' said Grady sharply. 'We're only looking at Ted Kramer and his suspicious movements relating to Fletcher and the trawler. Anyhow, shouldn't we wait until we've analysed the full extent of video footage from the Chinese restaurant?'

Ange knew that this was a weak part of her grand, unified Kramer theory. 'Even if others were doing the drug pickups, we have enough to make Ted Kramer a suspect. We have him on video footage which lines up with the deaths. He then suddenly disappears and sells his car. Plus, we found traces of narcotics in the house where he was living, as well as the stuff about his suspicious behaviour that Amy Lightfoot told us about. If Joe Kramer sent his son to Namba Heads as Lightfoot alleges, perhaps we have enough on him as well. Shouldn't we make sure that his Joe Kramer isn't behind all this and sent his son to Namba Heads for reasons other than environmental activism?'

Grady stood and looked at her impassively, assessing her weak logic and seeming to peer directly into the innermost workings of her mind. Ange really wanted to secure that warrant, as she wanted to be sure of her footing before confronting the Kramers. Given how quickly Ted Kramer had abandoned his girlfriend and their house, Ange wanted as much evidence as possible, hopefully enough to lay charges the first time they brought the pair in for questioning.

'Prepare the warrant,' Grady replied, resigned to the fact that Ange would not let this go. 'I know a friendly magistrate who might be available to sign it. It will be your funeral if this turns to shit, Detective,' he warned.

It took the rest of the day to get the warrant signed and to make the requests from the phone and credit card companies. Hopefully, they should have the information that they were seeking by tomorrow at the latest.

Chapter 39

Unusual Connections

Billy beat Ange to the station again on Wednesday morning. Looking up from his computer, he explained that Jimmy had sent through the additional video footage they had requested. He'd only just started this painstaking task, but Billy confirmed the van had driven by on the first pickup date. Ange felt sure it would be the same result for the others.

She was now almost certain that Ted Kramer was involved in Dave Fletcher's broader extracurricular activities, with a strong but still circumstantial link to narcotics trafficking. There was also a high probability that he had something to do with Dave Fletcher's death and Jake Thompson's burial. However, there were some large evidentiary gaps to her theories. A lot of work remained if Ange was to construct a watertight argument on either front. How Joe Kramer might be involved was purely hypothetical and undoubtedly a stretch of her imagination.

The call and text history from the telecom company arrived in her inbox. Given that Billy was busy, she started with Ted Kramer's call history. Starting with the most recent entries, she quickly realised that Ted Kramer had retreated and gone to ground at his father's house in Mullumbimby. Ted Kramer's texts were so minimal and trivial that Ange suspected that anything helpful would likely be associated with the yet-to-be-located burner phone, the one that Amy Lightfoot had mentioned.

Losing patience with Ted Kramer's unremarkable record, she turned her attention to his father. Ange had a strong sense that Ted Kramer was simply his father's minion in whatever was going on.

It was a tedious job. Working backwards from yesterday, she had to cross-reference each number to see if it showed up on a directory service or a Google search.

There were lots of gaps, and lots of repeated numbers. Joe Kramer was certainly active, whatever he was doing. There were many calls linked to Namba Heads so Ange focused on those first. It's amazing what shows up in a Google search when you simply enter a telephone number.

Joe and Ted Kramer had communicated often. Not unusual for father and son, and this activity had increased during the two weeks after Fletcher's death. This was nothing that Ange considered excessive. She wondered whether perhaps there might be three burner phones used for anything illicit communications; one for Ted Kramer, one for his father, and the one used by Fletcher that had been found on the boat. Her searching revealed that Joe Kramer had rung Councillor Terry Scott, which didn't surprise Ange unduly given their mutual interest in Tea Trees. She would need to discuss this with Terry.

Kramer had also rung Bernadette Williams. She was listed as the prime contact for the Namba Heads Landcare Volunteer Group, so also not surprising. Sergeant Billings' number came up as well. There were a series of calls in the past six weeks to a mobile phone located in Namba Heads. A Google search revealed this number was associated with a company called NH Projects Pty Ltd. Ange searched company registrations and was shocked to find that the sole director was Brett Tompkins. It was first registered just over two years ago.

Ange had to think about this latest revelation. Namba Heads was a small place, and coincidences happened, but this particular coincidence was confronting. Confused and concerned, Ange went for a walk along the foreshore, something that usually helped to assemble her thoughts. 'Why would Brett be in regular contact with Joe Kramer?' she thought.

Was he involved in something illegal, like drug trafficking? Was this the actual source of his apparent wealth and property development was just a cover? Had he sought her out to monitor what she was doing? If she confronted Brett, then would he alert the Kramers? Ange's imagination spiralled out of control as she realised how her dalliance with Brett had the potential to screw up the entire investigation. She needed to talk this over with her boss, as difficult as that might be.

As it turned out, she need not have worried. 'You weren't to know that Brett Tompkins might somehow be involved. Anyhow, these types of connections and insights show the importance of fieldwork. Of course, it will also lead to some difficult situations,' said Grady kindly. His pragmatic attitude also made Ange feel better about the expenses claim she would lodge at the end of the month.

The issue remained—how to deal with this fresh information without putting the Kramers on alert? The two of them brainstormed the problem, eventually concocting a plausible story that Ange was working on an unrelated matter concerning the affairs of the Byron Bay Coastal Protection Society. This should give her some cover to dig further without raising too many alarm bells.

First, she rang Terry Scott. As casually as she could and after the usual pleasantries, Ange said to Terry, 'It never rains, but it pours. I've also been looking into the affairs of the Byron Bay Coastal Protection Society after we received some complaints. A recent search of phone records shows you received several calls from Joe Kramer.'

'That bugger,' said Terry tersely. 'He must have spies in the town. Calls me whenever there's the slightest hint of work going on around Tea Trees. We can't even maintain the road without him berating me and suggesting that I'm in the pockets of developers.' This confirmed Ange's suspicions that they were indeed not friends or associates.

Comfortable with Terry's explanation, she then called Darren Billings. 'Kramer keeps me busy with some complaint or conspiracy theory whenever a building starts in town. I cannot tell you how many times he's sent me on some goose chase about illegal building works, only to find law-abiding citizens going about their business. It makes me look bad,' Billings explained in an exasperated voice.

Ange pushed on. 'Have you heard of anything suspicious about him?'

'No,' said Billings defensively. 'You might have gathered that there's a lot of division in the town over that Tea Trees development. Kramer knows how to play the game.'

Ange decided she would have to circle back on Billings. Perhaps he was running interference for the Kramers? On the other hand, Billings might feel defensive that he wasn't on top of the goings-on in his own town. Ange still didn't feel completely comfortable about Billings.

Next call was to Bernadette Williams, who explained that Kramer wanted her to spy for him and keep track of Tea Trees. 'I don't like the man or his methods,' she stated sharply. Ange knew that enough had been said.

Last, she rang Brett Tompkins. He sounded pleased that she had called. Ange tried to sound as businesslike as possible, explaining her bogus investigation and asking him why there were several calls logged between him and Joe Kramer. Ange could sense that she had struck a raw nerve, and Brett's reply sounded defensive.

'Well... The guy still wields a big stick down here. The town is still divided over Tea Trees, and edgy about any form of development. I felt I needed to keep a dialogue going. I'm a developer, and I know how much trouble that guy could cause me.'

Ange took Brett's explanation at face value, telling him she would probably need to contact him again. 'Well, that was certainly a bit of a passion killer,' thought Ange as she hung up. Given her history with Brett, perhaps she could have gotten her boss to call, but she wanted to hear his voice when she confronted him over his link to Joe Kramer. Was she jumping to rash conclusions and sub-consciously turning Brett into another 'Male Fail'? Whatever was going on, she was certainly regretting her ill-advised night of passion.

She went back to her computer, typing in the name of Brett's company. Amongst other things, it revealed that the company had lodged three develop-ment applications with the Council. 'Online tools like this must be a godsend to the likes of Joe Kramer,' she thought as she reviewed the applications.

The first two were small duplex housing developments around Namba Heads. The latest one detailed a large townhouse project called New Horizons. 'NH Projects, Namba Heads, New Horizons... cute,' thought Ange. The development application had been lodged just on three months ago, and it was still under consideration by Council.

A search of New Horizons Namba Heads revealed a professional-looking website promoting a smart centrally located 'over-50s' townhouse complex. Ange again called Terry Scott. He knew the project well, as Brett Tompkins had briefed him some time ago before lodging his development application. Terry was supportive, although his preference remained for projects that attracted young families and not over-50s. Terry said that the project was still out for public consultation and would not come before the Council for a month or more. Ange felt somewhat relieved that there appeared to be some substance to the company, although she realised that this research should have been done before she con-fronted Brett over Joe Kramer. The relationship with Brett was threatening her professionalism as a detective, so she resolved to be more considered with how she dealt with him.

Billy came over to voice his opinion that the credit card information was proving a dead end. It showed that the pair moved up and down the coast, but nothing out of the ordinary. 'Anyway, it would be risky buying burner phones with a fake ID, and then using a credit card under a completely different name to pay for them. Cash would be easier and safer,' deduced Billy.

'I agree, Billy. That makes sense. If Ted Kramer was into something dodgy and was the person who made the payments to Fletcher, then cash wouldn't have been a problem. It also possible that someone else could have purchased the burner phones,' concluded Ange. 'Let's leave the credit cards and focus on analysing the rest of Jimmy's video footage and the phone records,' concluded Ange, thinking to herself that Billy was proving to be both diligent and intelligent.

'I've already been able to track their movements via their phones,' Billy replied. 'Ted Kramer's mobile phone data confirms the video footage, putting him near the marina whenever Dave Fletcher had completed a pickup at sea.'

'Great work Billy. That's crucial information,' said Ange. In her experience, most criminals weren't the masterminds that they considered. Lucky for her, it was stupid mistakes, like carrying their mobile phones around, that often brought them undone.

'We'll need to trawl through Ted Kramer's call records, but it'll be hard knowing he likely used a second phone for anything illicit,' Ange surmised, thinking that even Ted Kramer was unlikely to make such an obvious mistake.

'Joe Kramer was nowhere near any of these events, mostly Mullumbimby and Byron Bay. He visited Namba Heads twice, and Ted Kramer went to Mullumbimby every so often. Both of Joe Kramer's visits to Namba Heads were during the day and are unrelated to any of the dates we're looking at here,' Billy explained.

'That doesn't mean he wasn't involved,' Ange replied sharply, unwilling to let Joe Kramer off the hook. She concluded it was now time to rattle the Kramers' cage.

Chapter 40

Mullumbimby Dawn

Ange spent the rest of that day documenting her case against the Kramers. She sorely wanted to press for a search warrant and to bring them into the station for questioning. She set out her logic in her ever-present notebook.

1. *Dave Fletcher found with burner phone detailing a series of pickups, with evidence that he was receiving cash payments in return.*

2. *Fletcher's deckhands confirm pickups and manner of retrieval. No evidence found on the boat of equipment used in said retrievals. Pickup coordinates all within the main shipping channel.*

3. *Cash box found in Fletcher's boat shows evidence of narcotics and cash. Same narcotics signature found in Ted Kramer's house.*

4. *Appears that Jake Thompson dies during Fletcher's last fishing trip. Suspected accident.*

5. *Fletcher dies on trawler on the night after final trip.*

6. *Video footage directly links movements of Ted Kramer with pickup dates, the night of last fishing trip, and Jake Thompson's death.*

7. *Ted Kramer skips town when girlfriend goes missing. Moves back to Joe Kramer's house in Mullumbimby.*

8. *Joe Kramer in regular contact with key local residents.*

9. Byron Bay Coastal Protection Society is under investigation because of accounting irregularities.

By the time she had finished assembling her thoughts, Jim Grady had left for the day, so she would have to dwell on this overnight and push for a search warrant tomorrow. She walked down to the foreshore and sat on a park bench, looking out to sea. The afternoon was in full swing, and her beloved Norfolk pines were casting a long shadow over the foreshore and onto the beach. The breeze was light but showing hints of the coolness that would accompany the setting sun. The foreshore was littered with people: singles, couples, families, small groups, large groups, all communing and drawn to this magnificent oceanic theatre to extract the last vestiges of the day.

The afternoon on the beach was Ange's favourite, when a soft back light painted a pastel picture, one quite distinct from the harsh early-morning perspective affronting still-sleepy eyes. A late surf was the true 'afternoon delight' in Ange's opinion, a convenient stance to take when unintentional celibacy offered no alternatives. Ange wandered back down through the town, stopping at a small Vietnamese restaurant to pick up some takeaway pho for dinner before heading home to ready herself for the day ahead.

Come Thursday morning, she was pacing anxiously around the station and immediately confronted Grady when he finally arrived. Setting out her evidence manifesto, she assailed him with her theories. Whether she had sold him her ideas or he just wanted to get this obstinate woman out of his office, she couldn't be sure. However, Ange extracted his commitment to seek out a magistrate and secure a search warrant covering Kramer's Mullumbimby address. 'Make sure you dot your i's and cross your t's on this one, Detective. You're pushing the boundaries here,' Grady warned sternly.

Ange promised to get the paperwork to him before lunch. Billy had arrived at work during her pleadings, and they set to work documenting their discoveries and setting out the rationale for their proposed search.

Jim Grady seemed pleased with their report and promised to do his part and secure the warrant. Ange outlined her plan to check their phone pings to ensure that they were at the house in Mullumbimby. She wanted to be there first thing the next day, no later than 7 a.m. Ange then requested some extra support, and

Grady agreed to allocate four other police officers to assist. Ange would organise a forensic team—she knew just the guys. They spent the rest of the day coordinating these resources and organising a briefing with the team that had been assembled. They agreed to meet at the station at 5 a.m. the next day.

That night, in anticipation of her important early assignment, a half-awake restlessness had cursed Ange. Despite a scratchy start, adrenaline and a caffeine fix at the station had her raring to go by 5 a.m. Friday morning. Billy, now her private tech consultant, had already confirmed that both the Kramers' mobile phones were currently ensconced at their Mullumbimby address. Hopefully, both Ted and Joe Kramer were still fast asleep. Their convoy departed bang on time.

Ange liked Mullumbimby and was a regular visitor with her friends to catch some music or visit the markets. The Mullumbimby markets were among the few that had resisted the avalanche of cheap mass-produced Asian imports now found all over the world. For more than a generation, the town had maintained its reputation as a hub for cruisy music, free loving and easy drugs. When drugs were abundant, there was always a seedy underbelly, and Mullumbimby was no exception. However, Ange could overlook this stuff on her days off and enjoy the refreshing change of pace and scenery that a day trip to the town offered.

Situated within a delightful hamlet in the Byron Bay hinterland, Mullumbimby was also changing, attracting those who might have saved some money from their boring office jobs in the city and yearned for an edgy rural lifestyle. The township housed an eclectic collection of hard-core old-timers and transitory green-changers. There was even a smattering of communes dotting the surrounding hills and picturesque valleys, perfect for those wishing respite from a hectic modern world. The town remained laid-back and slow-paced, but the cracks were showing. There was now a busy Woolworths supermarket, and a few brand-name chain stores were setting down roots. Ange suspected she would all too soon be called to Mullumbimby to investigate clashes between ageing hippies and rapacious developers.

The drive into Mullumbimby was quite something. The cane and cattle farms along the road revealed its rural heritage. Large camphor laurel trees offered their shady green canopy to the long, wide streets. Twin rows of tall palm trees stood as sentinels on the main street, as if holding guard over the impressive historic buildings that had served this important rural town for generations. Ange loved how these buildings were preserved, albeit in various states of repair.

The convoy arrived without fanfare at the Kramers' address just on daybreak. Ange and Billy waited as two uniformed officers attended to the formalities at the front door, whilst their two colleagues quietly jumped the fence and surveyed the back. A barking dog shattered the peace and quiet at the first knock. Ange presumed that the barking was from Bluey, Ted's dog.

A sleepy-eyed Joe Kramer answered the door before quickly finding his game face and calling on his most indignant voice, asserting police harassment and declaring loudly that the world was in the pockets of big business and developers. Kramer made sure any nosy neighbours could easily hear his protestations of victimisation, with Bluey's relentless barking adding nicely to the overall effect. Ange had to hand it to Joe Kramer—he knew how to leverage any opportunity. She, on the other hand, had heard it all before.

In the meantime, two officers came around the side of the house in the company of Ted Kramer. 'We caught him trying to scoot over the back fence,' one of them explained.

Ange thanked her colleagues before turning to the Kramers. In her best official-sounding voice, she informed them they were being taken to the Byron Bay police station for questioning in relation to a series of events at Namba Heads. Once she had dispensed with that formality, Ange left the pair in the safe hands of her uniformed colleagues.

Her forensic team sprang into action, pleased that they weren't looking over a dead body this time. Ange and Billy put on gloves and shoe covers before taking a quick look through the house. Typical of a traditional country cottage, the weatherboard house had once sat on stilts before being raised and the ground floor enclosed. Upstairs showed a small two-bedroom residence where the Kramers lived, with the offices for the Society below, connected by a central staircase. Ange and Billy couldn't see anything particularly interesting in their cursory walk-around.

Bluey was still barking. Ange checked he was securely tied to his kennel and had ample water to drink. She asked Billy to remind her they might need to enlist the help of the RSPCA, subject to how the day progressed, of course.

The pair then headed back to the station, fervently hoping that their forensics colleagues would uncover sufficient evidence to justify the Kramers' dawn awakening.

Chapter 41

Ducking and Weaving

The situation with Brett Tompkins was gnawing at Ange. Despite Billy being in the car with her, she called Brett on the drive back to the station.

'Brett Tompkins,' the voice answered, his circumspect tone echoing loudly through the speaker of Ange's car.

'It's Angela Watson here, Brett,' said Ange, choosing to remain with a more serious persona over the carefree Bella Vista version of last weekend.

'What can I do for you, Ange?' said Brett cautiously.

'I wanted to let you know that we've taken Joe and Ted Kramer into the station for questioning in relation to some serious matters,' responded Ange.

'What sort of serious matters?'

'I'm not at liberty to say,' said Ange, pausing before making a snap decision, 'but it involves matters relating to narcotics importation.'

There was a long pause before Brett replied in a serious tone, 'I'm not involved in anything illegal—if that's what you're thinking.'

'I don't know what to think, Brett, but I would appreciate you explaining your relationship with the Kramers.'

'I only know Joe Kramer. I've had nothing to do with his son,' Brett firmly replied.

'Brett, it would be good if you could come into the station and provide a statement concerning your relationship with Joe Kramer.'

'OK, when would you like me to do this?' Brett queried.

'Now, if possible,' was Ange's quick-fire reply.

Brett said that he would come up to Byron as soon as he had showered and had a cup of coffee.

As soon as Ange had hung up from the call, Billy chipped in. 'You two seemed to know each other quite well?'

'Don't go there, Billy,' replied Ange, thereby shutting down Billy's line of inquiry.

Back at the station, Joe Kramer was proving a noisy customer. Jim Grady came over to say that both men had demanded to see lawyers, and Joe Kramer was arranging for one of his many legal counsels to represent them.

Ange told Grady that Brett Tompkins was coming into the station to provide a statement. He wasn't happy that Ange had called Tompkins like that, knowing what he did about their relationship. At least Billy had been with her to witness the call on speakerphone. Grady insisted he sit in on all the interviews. Ange had no problems with this, of course, but she asked if Billy could also sit in the proceedings. She told Grady how impressed she had been with his work so far and expressed her belief that he had a bright future. Grady agreed with this suggestion and went off to schedule the interviews with the Kramers for after lunch.

Ange grabbed Billy and suggested they head downtown for some breakfast and some proper coffee. Once they had ordered and taken a seat, she asked for his opinion on where the case sat. Billy gathered his thoughts before replying. 'I don't know. Something in all of this doesn't stack up for me. Joe Kramer was angry and indignant at the intrusion. He doesn't come across as someone who's facing serious charges like narcotics importation or conspiracy to commit murder. Orrr...he could be one super-tough customer who will prove hard work for us. Ted Kramer, on the other hand, is definitely involved in something dodgy and looks to me like someone who can feel the walls closing in on him.'

'I agree, something doesn't align with these two characters,' said Ange. She was sensing the crumbling pieces of her grand, unified Kramer theory. They were enjoying their second cup of coffee when Ange got a call from the station to tell her that Brett Tompkins was waiting in reception.

Arriving back at the station, the pair collected their boss from his office, and the three police officers took Brett into a small interview room off the main foyer. Once seated, Grady looked in Ange's direction, nodding to show that she could open the batting. 'Brett, can you tell us about your involvement with Joe Kramer?'

Brett replied quickly and confidently. 'It's nothing illegal. Annoying and frus-trating, but not illegal. Soon after I had lodged my latest development application for a large townhouse project, Joe Kramer contacted me. He threatened to stall my development approval on environmental concerns. I told him that this was rubbish, and he had no right to interfere. However, a couple of days later, I received a call from one of the assessment managers, saying that they had some concerns about sustainability. Apparently, she had some new-found misgivings about the proposed density and the potential impact on the environment.'

Brett paused briefly before continuing, his annoyance clearly genuine. 'This was completely contrary to all my pre-lodgement meetings and discussions with councillors and council officers. At the very least, the hassle Kramer can cause a council officer makes them jumpy. Worse still is the thought that Kramer has people in the Council assisting him. I then received another call from Kramer, suggesting that I employ him as a consultant. He would help ensure that any concerns about environmental sustainability would be addressed. I knew it was a shakedown, but what could I do?'

'You could have reported him,' Ange countered.

'And say what? That Joe Kramer, famed environmentalist, offered a consultancy service to assist my development?' Tompkins looked pointedly at Ange. She could see how naïve her comment had been.

'In the end, I agreed to pay him six thousand dollars for a lame report to support my application. He even tried to pass it off as a donation to his blasted society, which I gather gets him neatly around any taxation implications,' stated an annoyed Tompkins, raising air quotes around the word *donation*. 'It really pisses me off, but I have a business to run, and delays will cost me ten times that.'

This all made sense to Ange, so she finished the interview by saying that they would get a statement typed up straight away. She asked Brett to stay until they completed it so that he could sign it.

'It drives me crazy how people go on about property developers. Where do they think people are going to live and work?' said an exasperated Brett Tompkins, property developer.

Ange and Billy led him back to the reception and went to prepare his statement. Once this was all sorted, Ange took the signed statement in to her boss and discussed the potential implications. She was starting to feel that perhaps Joe and Ted Kramer were dealing in different and unconnected areas. They decided they should wait for the feedback from the forensic investigators before dealing with Ted Kramer, and then leave Joe Kramer to last.

Chapter 42

The Net Widens

J ust before lunch, Ange's mobile phone buzzed. It was the lead forensic investigator. 'Fingers crossed they found something useful,' thought Ange, knowing that their job would be much easier if they could find a concrete link between the Kramers and the events at Namba Heads. She knew the guys would collect items like shoes and clothing that might help determine where the two had been. However, that type of analysis would take time.

Keeping Ange in suspense, the caller gave a brief summation of their search and the samples and items that they had collected. 'Oh,' he went on casually, pausing dramatically to fully pull Ange's chain, 'we also found a large quantity of cash hidden in Ted Kramer's room, mostly fifties and a few hundreds. I didn't count it, but I reckon there's fifteen to twenty K there.'

Ange's pulse quickened with the news she was hoping for. 'Can you focus on the money first, checking for fingerprints that match Dave Fletcher? Also, check for a chemical profile of narcotics and anything that can link the money to the cash box found on the boat. When can you get back to me?'

'I'll try for tonight, but probably mid-morning tomorrow,' came the reply.

'OK. We'll have to wing it a little, but we probably have enough to go on for the moment. Please be as quick as you can. Thanks for the call,' she said, before hanging up.

Ange went to Grady's office and told him about the cash. His response caught her by surprise.

'I've just received a call from Major Crimes in Sydney. They asked me to summarise our investigation and they want to attend the interviews. How the hell they knew what was going on is a mystery to me. Anyhow, it turns out they've been looking into a major drug importation ring operating up and down the coast, based out of small coastal towns like Namba Heads. The people behind this operation are well resourced, highly organised, and good at covering their tracks. Major Crimes consider that Ted Kramer is a person of genuine interest in their case. Their lead investigators will be here tomorrow. They expressed concern that Ted Kramer not only poses a flight risk but might be in danger himself.'

'We can't hold the Kramers overnight unless we charge them,' Ange replied, knowing that her boss knew this all too well.

'I think we have enough to charge Ted Kramer with importation of narcotics along with suspicion of being involved with the deaths of Jake Thompson and Dave Fletcher. We could throw in the disappearance of his girlfriend as well, which might catch him off guard. Perhaps you could first make sure Amy Lightfoot hasn't been in contact with Ted Kramer?' Grady concluded.

Still sitting in Grady's office, Ange rang Amy Lightfoot. She toggled her phone to speaker mode so that Grady could hear the conversation.

'Hi, Amy, It's Angela Watson here. Have you been in contact with Ted Kramer since your disappearance? Even with anyone who might know Ted. Think carefully. This is very important, Amy. You need to be completely honest with me.'

'I haven't spoken to anyone, not even my parents. I know I should ring them, but we don't speak very often, so I don't think that they'd be worried about me yet. The only person who knows where I am is my girlfriend, the person who picked me up at Namba Heads. I'm still scared, Detective,' replied Amy. She paused, as if thinking through the implications of the call. 'Has anything happened to Teddy?'

'Ted is safe. He's with us now. I'll be in contact again shortly. In the meantime, I want you to stay put. Don't go out and don't contact anyone whatsoever,' stressed Ange forcefully before hanging up.

Grady dismissed Ange, saying that he needed to think all this through. He also wanted to make a few calls to see if he could get some intel off the internal rumour mill, something that might explain why Major Crimes had inserted themselves.

The startling events of the morning had made Ange nervous. Needing to soothe her churning stomach, she went for a walk downtown to her favourite sushi takeaway, picking up some sushi rolls and eating them on the foreshore whilst she collected her thoughts. By the time she arrived back at the station for their 1 p.m. interview with Ted Kramer, the combination of her favourite food and some quiet time had settled her nerves and she was raring to go.

Billy and Ange met with their boss just before 1 p.m. to work out how they would approach the interview. Given the developments with Major Crimes, they needed to ensure Ted Kramer remained in police custody until tomorrow at the latest. The trio agreed Ange would lead the interrogation and Grady would back her up if needed; Billy was there strictly as an observer. At 1 p.m., the three of them walked to the interview room where Ted Kramer and his lawyer were waiting.

Byron Bay had its own district court, and the police and the town's lawyers interacted often. Their relationship ranged from excellent to downright mutual distrust, and everything in between. She had not dealt with the lawyer before but recognised her face. Ange introduced herself and her colleagues before they sat down and dealt with the interview formalities.

'Ted Kramer, we have evidence to suggest that you are involved with the trafficking and importation of narcotics, the events surrounding the deaths of Jake Thompson and David Graham Fletcher, as well as the circumstances around the disappearance of Amy Lightfoot,' said Ange brusquely, not wishing to beat around the bush.

If Ted Kramer looked crestfallen and potentially scared, his lawyer seemed genuinely horrified. Before she could speak, Kramer retorted, 'I had nothing to do with Amy's disappearance.' His silence on the other charges was telling.

Recovering her composure, Ted's lawyer quickly cut him off by saying, 'I need to speak with my client alone.'

The three police officers left the room. Closing the door behind them, Ange said, 'Well, that wasn't necessarily the shortest interview I have ever had, but it's up there!'

They waited patiently for over ten minutes while Kramer and his lawyer consulted.

Finally, Kramer's lawyer came out to speak with the three police officers. 'I have suggested to Mr Kramer that he should seek alternate legal representation, and I have given him some suggestions on who may be appropriate. I'm a planning and environment lawyer who handles the occasional civil libertarian matter, for goodness' sake. This is Byron Bay after all. I was doing Joe Kramer a favour, given how much work he's sent my way over the years, but I'm certainly not a criminal lawyer.'

'Are you representing Joe Kramer as well?' Ange queried the lawyer.

'I was planning to, but I'm not so sure if I can after the bombshell you just dropped,' the lawyer replied.

Ange glanced at Grady before replying. 'I have a feeling that the next interview is more likely in line with your specialty. If you could come back in an hour, we'll be ready for you and Joe Kramer.'

After she left, the three agreed Ange had made a wise decision to keep this lawyer in the picture. She was less likely to take an overly aggressive stance representing Joe Kramer, given what she now knew about his son.

Chapter 43

A Slippery Customer

Ange and Billy followed their boss back into his office to prepare for their interview with Joe Kramer. Ange and Billy stepped through the scant evidence they had collected, and it was clearly obvious to all three that they had nothing to link Joe Kramer with the more serious charges levelled at his son.

'I haven't been able to glean even a skerrick of information from my service colleagues. Major Crimes is a black hole about this, so it's clearly a serious and highly confidential investigation. What is your sense of where we are, Ange?' Grady asked.

'It goes against the grain of my initial conclusions, but I think that Joe Kramer has a neat shakedown going against property developers. At worst, he might be guilty of bribing council officers and corruption on some level. There's nothing to suggest he's involved in murder or narcotics trafficking.'

Ange paused for a moment before changing gear. 'However, I strongly suspect that Ted Kramer had gotten himself into this mess on his own. I also think that Joe Kramer will be far too cunning and wily to allow any criminal case to be made over his developer shakedown. He'll be able to pass these off as legitimate activities relating to his role as head of the Byron Bay Coastal Protection Society, even though we suspect that the reality is quite different. The tax office might have a different view, but that won't help us.'

'OK,' said Grady. 'We need to get as much information as we can, but his lawyer will have already briefed him on the charges being laid against his son. Perhaps we take a cautious and conciliatory tone initially with Joe Kramer. I can step in and turn on some heat if needed.'

Having agreed to their plan of attack, each went to their desks to check emails and attend to any other pressing matters. Ange took a call from the forensic lab, who said that they had found traces of human blood wedged in the sole of a Dunlop Volley canvas sand shoe found in Ted Kramer's bedroom. They hoped there were sufficient blood fragments for a worthwhile DNA test, but it would be touch and go. Ange marvelled that Dunlop Volleys, once reserved for old tennis players and roofers, were now cool again. Cool enough that Ted Kramer didn't want to dispose of them when he should have.

At 3 p.m., the three police officers assembled once again outside the interview room, before opening the door and filing in. Ange had barely discharged the introduction and formalities before Joe Kramer piped up.

'I remember now—we have met before, Detective. You attended one of our events a few years back.'

Kramer was clearly trying to unsettle her and gain some high ground, but Ange ignored his brazen interruption. She also refused to acknowledge the sharp glances from her colleagues.

'Mr Kramer, by now you would know that we have detained your son, Ted, to answer some very serious allegations.' She guessed this conversation would have started differently without the likely counsel of his lawyer. Ange knew enough about Kramer to know that he was no shrinking violet and would likely have immediately gone on the offensive, citing police harassment and his many conspiracy theories. This time around, Joe Kramer appeared to be on his best behaviour, despite his earlier ploy.

'Could you please explain your knowledge of and involvement in any of the charges against your son?' continued Ange.

'I have nothing to do with any of those matters. I sent Ted to Namba Heads to move him away. He would be safe in that backwater, I thought. Ted was associating with a bad element which had moved into Mullumbimby, and I was concerned,' said Kramer before looking Ange directly in the eye. 'I know that lots of people don't like me in this area, Detective, but I'm not involved in anything illegal.'

Unable to help herself, the situation between Kramer and Brett Tompkins being a sore point, Ange quickly countered. 'What about your shakedown tactics with property developers?'

Pausing briefly before smiling, sensing that he was in more familiar territory, Kramer replied assuredly. 'I'm providing a valuable service for the development industry, Detective. It's far better to deal with environmental sustainability in the planning stage, as opposed to fighting an expensive legal battle in the Planning and Environment Court in Sydney. I'm assisting several clients.'

His lawyer looked Ange confidently in the eye, her mojo restored in the comfort of her specialty, confirming that they felt on stronger ground.

Ange knew she had nowhere to go. They had no hard evidence connecting Joe Kramer with narcotics trafficking, or either of the deaths, the only link being his son. They were also light-years away from laying any charges against Kramer concerning official corruption. The three officers quickly wrapped up the interview before letting Joe Kramer leave the station, suggesting that they would undoubtedly need to speak with him again and not to leave town.

'I have no intention of going anywhere but home, Detective,' said Kramer, giving Ange his most ingratiating smile.

As he walked out the door, Ange turned to her colleagues, not wanting to wait for their inevitable question. 'I just went along to one of his events as a guest of my friend Kerrie. Kramer blew me off as soon as he learned I was a police officer.' Not waiting for their reply, she marched back to her desk.

It had been a long day, but it still wasn't even 4 p.m., and Ange saw a busy weekend ahead of her. Feeling like she needed to clear her mind, she decided to escape into the comfort of the ocean and a quick surf. She dashed home to get changed and retrieve her surfboard from the flat, strolling down through the town to Main Beach, board tucked under her arm, towel wrapped over her shoulders, the flip-flop of her Havaianas in tune with the scores of others meandering through the streets.

Ange walked along the beach until she found something resembling a surfable wave. Summer would soon be in full swing, so she chose her springsuit, the first time since last summer. The still-cool water caused a sharp catch of breath as the first wave washed over her. As she sat out beyond the break, bobbing up and down with the rhythm of the waves, her subconscious processed and packaged the events of the day, almost unbidden. Immersed in her reflective daydream, Ange didn't know how many waves she had actually caught before riding her last onto the beach. Cleansed by the ocean, she towelled off, satisfied with where her case was positioned. Tomorrow would be another challenging day, but Ange was excited about the prospect of working with Major Crimes.

Who would have thought that this sleepy part of the country would be the focus of such a major investigation? The next twenty-four hours would provide a novel experience for Ange, and she hoped to learn a lot from her more experienced colleagues.

Chapter 44

Carcharias

Rain had arrived overnight, and the temperature had dropped markedly with the cooler southerly winds, reminding Ange that summer was still some weeks away. A long day beckoned, so she stopped off for breakfast along the way before walking to work, wrestling her umbrella in the stiff breeze. The dreary morning did nothing to dampen her spirits, and she arrived at the station buzzing with caffeine and anticipation.

Even though it was Saturday, Ange first cleared her desk of any daily tasks that might clutter her thoughts. Ted Kramer's new lawyer arrived soon enough, asking to speak with his client and looking decidedly unhappy about needing to work on a Saturday. Ange well knew the reputation of Simon Phillips, a tough and accomplished lawyer who wasn't prone to missteps. He would be a formidable ally for his client. She led Mr Phillips to a small interview room, retrieved Ted Kramer from his cell, and left the two of them to go about their business. They had a lot to talk about, reasoned Ange.

She had just sat back down at her desk when the two detectives from Major Crimes arrived. Jim Grady went out to greet the well-dressed visitors, a male and female duo of serious demeanour. Ange hadn't really known what to expect, but it surprised her to find that they weren't really all that much older than her. Grady took the visitors into his office, where they spoke for about twenty minutes. He then led the two officers from Major Crimes to a larger meeting room, asking Ange and Billy to join them as he walked by. Billy positively beamed that Grady had included him in such a high-level discussion.

As Ange and Billy entered the office, the female detective stood and introduced herself, immediately stamping her authority. 'Detective Watson, I'm Senior

Detective Sally Anders from Major Crimes in Sydney, and this is my colleague Detective Henry Ng from the Queensland Police Service. This has all been great work.'

Ange sensed that Sally Anders didn't grant many concessions. Ange then introduced Billy as her colleague in the investigation, elevating his sense of worth to new heights.

Anders clearly had no time for small talk and was straight down to business. 'In the course of the past six months, we have been investigating a major drug importation syndicate operating from several small coastal towns up and down the coast. We started hearing about the syndicate after the Covid-19 pandemic had disrupted the movement of freight through the ports and across the borders. Initially, we figured it was temporary and the syndicate would retreat to the major ports once freight movements normalised, but it hasn't played out that way. An interstate task force was set up with the New South Wales and Queensland police forces, called Operation Carcharias. The syndicate is well financed, well organised and highly secretive. This is the first potential crack in their defences.'

'It's a scientific word associated with shark,' explained Henry Ng wearily, seeing the confusion on the faces opposite. Clearly, he was tired of explaining what had seemed a clever choice of code name at the time.

'Cool name. It's also the Greek word for shark,' Ange commented, having learnt this from a Greek girlfriend one night at the pub. 'Much better than something boring like Stingray or Flathead.' Ange smiled as her wicked imagination ran off with all manner of silliness.

Anders did not seem similarly amused, annoyed at her control of the floor having been disrupted. 'Moving on... how about you tell us what you've discovered, Detective?' asked Anders.

Quickly regaining her composure, Ange took a deep breath, nervous that her work was about to be critiqued by more experienced colleagues. She then headed into the fray, setting out what she had learned in her investigations and the conclusions that she had reached to this point.

'I think Ted Kramer became involved with a bad element in Mullumbimby relating to drugs. Whether he was a user, a dealer, or simply fell in with the wrong crowd, I'm not sure. His father moved him to Namba Heads with his girlfriend, Amy Lightfoot. His father, Joe Kramer, is an environmental activist who once won a major case centred in Namba Heads, so he figured it was a sleepy backwater where his son might be safe. Whether it was Ted Kramer who sought out his unsavoury friends or the other way around, I can't say. What his motivation was, I also can't say, but there are substantial sums of money involved. My theory is that Ted Kramer was asked to procure the services of a willing trawler to pick up packages that were dropped out at sea on the shipping route. They needed a boat that went in and out regularly, would not draw any attention, and was large enough to travel out wide in all but the worst weather.'

Henry Ng interjected, 'What evidence have you found to support this, Detective Watson?'

'First, we retrieved a burner phone from the trawler after the apparent suicide of Dave Fletcher. His wife found it after commissioning a survey of the trawler prior to sale. The texts retrieved from the phone set out a series of coordinates outlining pickups, which correlate with fishing trips made by Fletcher. We plotted these coordinates and realised that they were all in the major shipping routes offshore from Namba Heads. The phone records also contain evidence to suggest Fletcher was being well paid for his services.'

Both visiting detectives asked how Fletcher completed the pickups, almost in unison, as if this had been puzzling them.

'My belief is that they used a VHF radio beacon. Whilst this is not as accurate as other methods, it has the added advantage of being cheap and readily available. More importantly, you must be close to the transmitter for the receiver to home in on the signal and locate the package. Remember, this is a small object bobbing up and down in the waves at sea level. Using this method, you need to know its location with reasonable accuracy in the first place before you have any ability to home in and locate it. I learned this from a whale researcher who uses the same technology. However, we didn't recover any equipment to this effect from the boat or in the possession of Fletcher or Kramer. The other permanent deckhands support this theory. They've given an accurate description of how they managed the pickups,' answered Ange with confidence.

Anders and Ng looked at each other with raised eyebrows, suggesting to Ange that her explanation was not conclusive from their standpoint. Anders asked Ange to continue.

'Second, we have video footage that shows Ted Kramer had driven towards the marina each night, immediately following the return of Fletcher's trawler. Kramer would have been unaware that he was being caught on video, and the only other way to access the bridge was to drive past the local police station. We believe Kramer retrieved the packages picked up by Fletcher, although we cannot be entirely sure of that. The movements of Kramer line up perfectly with the pickup dates on the burner phone.'

Seeing no obvious red flags, Ange pushed on. 'Third, we located a hidden metal cash box on the trawler. Forensics show that it had contained cash and showed traces of narcotics. A former rental property in Namba Heads where Kramer and his girlfriend lived contained traces of narcotics with the same chemical signature. Finally, a search of the Kramers' property, held yesterday morning in Mullumbimby, uncovered a large amount of cash. I expect the forensics report before lunch, but my hunch is that we'll be able to establish a firm link regarding the cash.'

'What were you doing in Namba Heads in the first place?' asked Anders.

'I was investigating a missing person, a young male. He was a promising semi-pro surfer who was last seen in Namba Heads. My investigations showed he worked on Dave Fletcher's boat as a part-time deckhand. Texts from the burner phone place him on board the boat during Fletcher's last trip out to sea,' Ange explained. She took a sip of water before continuing.

'The evidence suggests that there was some sort of accident on board that resulted in the death of Jake Thompson. The weather had turned, and the sea was up. Fletcher appears to have panicked after the death of Thompson and sent a text to his handlers stating that he wanted to end their arrangement. The reply text told Fletcher to exit the boat and to act normally. We believe that either Ted Kramer or someone else moved Jake Thompson's body during the early morning and buried it in bushland. A walker discovered the body by accident. I hope forensics will show that Kramer was on the boat following Jake Thompson's death. It seems unlikely that Kramer would have had time to bury the body before driving back, which opens the possibility that others are involved. During my investigation, Sharon Fletcher, the wife of the trawlerman, approached me and explained that she had concerns that her husband had not committed suicide. These suspicions were amplified after she discovered he'd received a large amount of cash that was unaccounted for. Male suicide rates are always three to four times those of females and have increased yet again through Covid, so it would seem a good way to disguise a murder. We know the Fletchers were under financial pressure, but we currently don't have any hard evidence to prove that Dave

Fletcher's death is anything other than suicide.'

Ng interjected. 'Do you have anything to connect the texts with Ted Kramer?'

'No, except for the coincidental car movements that correlate with the pick-ups,' replied Ange. 'Our analysis of both Ted and Joe Kramer's personal phone records yielded nothing useful. We suspect that he may have had a burner phone, but we haven't yet found it.'

Ange suddenly remembered her conversation with Amy Lightfoot. 'Ted Kramer's girlfriend found an unusual phone in his pants when she was cleaning up one day. Her description of that phone matches the one we retrieved from Dave Fletcher's boat. We feel that the two phones were most likely purchased at the same time, but that's just an unsubstantiated theory at this stage. We stopped work on tracing the origin of the phones and focussed on the video evidence. We know someone, presumably Ted Kramer, had organised to meet Fletcher on his boat at midnight on the night of his death, but we don't have video footage that places Kramer near the boat when Fletcher would have died. Kramer's vehicle didn't appear again until the next morning after daybreak. He may have driven another way, or another unidentified vehicle may have been involved. It's also possible that Dave Fletcher simply killed himself out of remorse following the accident with Jake Thompson. We cannot be sure of these points yet. By the way, Ted Kramer sold his vehicle in the weeks after Fletcher's death. This also seems suspicious, but unfortunately it was subsequently destroyed in a freak accident. We don't expect it will yield any further evidence.'

Ange checked her colleagues were keeping up with her information dump. Receiving no questions, she went on. 'The case then took an unusual twist when Ted Kramer's girlfriend went missing while taking a late-afternoon swim. An extensive search failed to locate the woman. However, she subsequently called the missing person's hotline, and we confirmed her identity and that she was safe. She had staged her disappearance to escape an allegedly toxic relationship, stating that Kramer had become increasingly erratic and violent in the weeks leading to her disappearance. We've kept her reappearance secret, and Ted Kramer is unlikely to know that she is alive. He left town in a hurry and retreated to Mullumbimby, where he seems to have been holed up with his father, Joe Kramer, ever since. We're now sufficiently convinced that Joe Kramer isn't involved in narcotics trafficking, but he has a nice little unrelated shakedown running, involving property developers and development approvals.'

The two detectives seemed to share a knowing glance. Anders then thanked Ange and asked to use the meeting room to make some calls. She also asked Ange to let her know when the latest batch of forensics was at hand. They all concluded that it would be best to delay their interview with Ted Kramer and his lawyer until after lunch, settling on 2 p.m.

Chapter 45

Slipping Away

As she walked back to her desk, Ange paused at the kitchen, deep in thought. More out of reflex than a need for caffeine, she poured herself some coffee. The challenge of the past hour offered ample stimulation, and this poor public service excuse for a drink was still sitting on her desk, lukewarm and abandoned, when Simon Phillips asked to see her. Ange asked Billy to take Kramer back to his holding cell whilst she dealt with his waiting lawyer.

He was calm and assured, as if his plan of attack was well fixed. He asked Ange when he should come back for their interview. Ange explained that there were some other detectives from Sydney who would join them, and he should come back at 2 p.m. He raised his eyebrow at that news, which Ange interpreted as anticipation at the prospect of locking horns with Sydney detectives. Certainly, his confident smile showed no sign of concern or discomfort. Ange knew Phillips would be no pushover.

Accompanied by pangs of uncertainty and insecurity, Ange retreated once more to her desk. The suspense was killing her, so she rang forensics. The lead forensic investigator answered promptly. Ange had now gotten to know him well—they were 'besties', in fact, after their evening of Jimmy's takeaway and a few drinks.

'I was going to ring you after lunch. It's been rather hectic here today. I haven't got time to type anything up just now, but we've made some interesting discoveries from yesterday's haul,' he said, much to Ange's relief.

'First, the narcotics profile from the cash matches the samples from the metal cash box and the house in Namba Heads that Ted Kramer rented. As I said earlier, I cannot say that this is concrete proof that the same cash was once in all three locations.' He paused briefly before delivering the news Ange craved. 'However, we found Dave Fletcher's fingerprints on the cash.'

'How sure are you about the fingerprints?' Ange quicky inquired.

'Quite sure. We found some good prints on the cash, and we had plenty of good reference samples from Fletcher's boat and the burner phone,' he replied.

'Anything else to help me out?'

'I hope so. We have a partial DNA match for Jake Thompson from the fragments of dried blood found in Ted Kramer's sneakers.'

Anticipating Ange's next question, he went on. 'The match isn't perfect, as the fragments were old and the sample we extracted from between the tread was poor. I would put it at a seventy-five percent certainty. If he hadn't been wearing relatively new Dunlop Volleys with their thick rubber zigzag tread, I don't think we would have recovered anything of value at all.'

Ange thanked him before hanging up, saying that she looked forward to seeing the final report. Armed with this new information and the confidence that it well supported her theories, Ange walked around to the conference room. She saw that the two detectives were on the phone and in earnest conversation. She waved through the glass partition and successfully attracted their attention, and Senior Detective Anders held up her hand, motioning for Ange to wait until they had finished their call.

This took longer than Ange expected, and she was about to abandon her vigil and head back to her desk, evoking memories of standing outside the head-teacher's office awaiting sentencing over some misdeed or another. She had just turned to leave when the door open behind her and Anders asked her to come in, apologising for the delay. Ange sat down and gave them a summary of the forensic results just in. Anders and Ng looked at each other before nodding, whereupon Anders asked Ange if she could grab her boss. They needed to chat.

He was also on the phone, so it took Ange another ten minutes before the two of them walked back into the conference room and sat down opposite Anders and Ng.

Sally Anders got straight to the point. 'If needed, we have authority from the DPP to offer a plea bargain with your suspect to secure his assistance with our investigations. This assumes that he has some worthwhile information and will cooperate fully.'

Seeing Ange bristle, she quickly clarified herself. 'That is assuming he isn't guilty of murder, which would complicate matters somewhat. However, I think your evidentiary gaps would suggest that there's a strong possibility that he may not have murdered Fletcher. That, of course, assumes Fletcher's death wasn't suicide as you propose.'

Injured by this bombshell, Ange and Grady retreated to his office, collecting Billy on the way. A heated 'discussion' ensued. Ange was upset that Major Crimes wanted to take the investigation off her hands before she'd completed the job. Grady tried vainly to convince her about the politics at play. Billy just sat there wide-eyed, listing to the debate.

Exasperated, Ange finally turned to Billy. 'What do you think of all this, Billy?' She was confident of his support to see his first big case through to completion.

Billy took a moment before replying. 'I haven't been a police officer for very long, but I do see the terrible damage and consequences of drugs. I think we need to consider the bigger picture here. Nothing we can do will bring Fletcher or Thompson back to life, but I think we should do everything we can to catch these sharks circling in our community and stop the drugs.'

Billy's reply caught Ange and their boss by surprise with its maturity and pragmatism. Now completely outflanked, she reluctantly agreed with Billy's conclusion, convincing herself that the likely murderers were circling inside the narcotics syndicate.

Ange and Billy left their boss's office somewhat dejected, feeling that their first big case had slipped through their fingers.

Chapter 46

Jigsaw Puzzle

Time dragged interminably. Ange glanced constantly at her watch, willing 2 p.m. to arrive. If she was going to lose control of the case, as least she needed to complete the remaining pieces of this jigsaw puzzle that had been consuming her. Ange fretted that Kramer's lawyer would stonewall them and leave her unsatisfied and annoyed, her case left in limbo.

Fifteen minutes before her deadline, Anders and Ng came by Ange's desk and asked her to join them in Grady's office. The four settled their plan of attack for the impending interview. Ange would attend to the formalities before handing over to Anders and Ng. Ange would provide background and context, but the clear aim was to secure Kramer's cooperation in their wider investigation. They asked if Ange had experience with Kramer's lawyer and she offered her opinion that he would be formidable.

Their two adversaries were already seated in the interview room by the time Ange, Anders and Ng arrived. Introductions and formalities complete, the three detectives readied themselves for battle. They needn't have been so anxious.

Cutting straight to the point, Simon Phillips spoke first. 'My client is not guilty of the two deaths, or the disappearance of his girlfriend. He will cooperate regarding the narcotics charges on the proviso that he is granted immunity from prosecution and provided witness protection if necessary. My client is concerned for his safety and scared of the likely consequences his cooperation might summon.'

The detectives looked at each other, pleased that the interview had gone this way and the power dynamic was on their side. Anders opened the batting for their side. 'We have authority to grant your request, but we need some details filled in.'

She paused for effect. 'If we suspect your client is guilty of murder, then all deals are off.'

Simon Phillips readily agreed to her proviso, appearing confident that his client might be stupid, but he wasn't a murderer.

Focussing on the gaps in their knowledge, Anders asked Kramer how he came to be living in Namba Heads and how he had become involved with narcotics. Over the next thirty minutes, the officers sat back while Kramer provided the background to his involvement.

Confirming what his father had told them, Kramer explained he had dabbled in selling small amounts of cannabis when living in Mullumbimby to make some pocket money and provide some independence from his father. Being well connected in the town, his father got wind of his activities and his nefarious associations, forcing Kramer to move to Namba Heads.

Kramer explained he was quite happy for a couple of months, exploring the surf breaks, making the odd token effort to spy on the Council and their plans for Tea Trees. However, realising that there were no dealers in town, he reached out to his former associates and secured some regular supply. Kramer insisted that his only objective had been to make a bit of cash to provide some independence from his dad.

His associates weren't interested in such trivialities but suggested a more profitable idea. Kramer explained his task had been to obtain the services of a large boat, preferably a trawler, to facilitate the retrieval of packages dropped at sea. Ange suddenly understood that the syndicate would need the services of multiple boats in multiple locations to accommodate the unpredictability of the sea and the weather.

'Once I had Fletcher hooked, my associates provided me with a series of dates and coordinates. My job was to confirm whether Fletcher was likely to be fishing and available to make a pickup. I had given Fletcher a burner phone, and I had a similar one myself that we used to communicate,' Kramer explained. 'Once a package had been successfully collected at sea, I would retrieve it from the boat and make the payments to Fletcher. I then delivered the package to an agreed location in the bushland. We had a series of drop sites organised around Namba Heads, and they would leave the cash—enough for me and the next job.'

Ng asked if Kramer still possessed his burner phone.

'I was supposed to destroy it, but I hid it in case I needed some leverage down the track. It's been turned off ever since,' Kramer replied.

This revealed to the three officers that he was not completely stupid and might have inherited some of his old man's cunning. Anders took the lead again. 'How much did you pay Fletcher for his pickups?'

'The going rate was five K, but I offered him an extra two K for that last trip. My associates seemed anxious over that one,' answered Kramer.

Ange stepped in, unable to help herself. 'How did you get Fletcher involved in the first place?'

'I made a point of running into him in the surf and having a chat while we sat out the back. When he told me about his financial troubles, my associates suggested I offer him five K upfront as a sign-on bonus, on top of the usual five K per pickup. It was a lot easier to get him involved than I thought it would be,' answered Kramer.

This level of payments suggested that the parcels likely contained a significant haul of drugs and that the investigators were on the right trail. Anders pushed on with her interrogation. 'OK, tell us about that last trip.'

'I received a message from Fletcher when he was about to come back into the marina, saying that there had been an accident and his deckie was dead. I told him to dock as normal and go home. The weather was pretty bad by this point, so I immediately went over to the boat to collect the package. When I arrived, I found the deckie in the cabin and there was a lot of blood. I didn't recognise him, but I now realise that it was Jake Thompson, a surfer I'd seen around.'

Ange was now bursting at the seams, desperate to hear the explanation for some gaps in her investigation. She couldn't help herself. 'How did Thompson get from the boat to the bushland where his body was buried?' she asked.

'I don't know. I updated my associates on the situation, but I never knew what happened to him as I never went back on the boat,' explained Kramer.

'Who are these associates of yours?' asked Ange.

'I don't know. We only ever communicated by text message.'

Anders was getting testy about Ange's interjections and shot her a stern look. Ange pretended not to notice. She bit her lip as Anders asked about how Fletcher managed the pickups. Kramer perfectly described Ange's theory on the receiving device and how the system worked.

'Fletcher had no troubles until that last night, so it must be fairly straightforward. I'm certain it's the same setup marine researchers use. I met one of those guys out on the rock wall one day when he was searching for a lost whale tag,' Kramer explained.

'Is it possible that the researcher was involved?' asked Ng.

'Unlikely. I heard he coaxed one of the charter boats to take him out to sea and they did ultimately locate his missing tag,' replied Kramer.

'Tell us what you know about the death of Dave Fletcher,' probed Ng—the very question that Ange was desperate to have answered.

'I have absolutely no idea. All I did was organise for him to be on his boat at midnight. I only found that he was dead the next morning when I drove by to check out the surf. Fletcher wanted out, and I assumed my associates would simply secure his silence and quickly wrap up any other loose ends. They had the death of Jake Thompson to hold over his head, so I figured that the meeting would be about that.'

'In hindsight, do you think Dave Fletcher committed suicide, Mr Kramer?' asked Anders.

There was a guilty pause before Kramer replied. 'No, I think they killed him. There were too many loose ends.'

'Why did you leave town?' continued Anders.

Kramer's face darkened. 'When Amy went missing, I panicked. She was an excellent swimmer, so I knew she was unlikely to have drowned, and the chances of a shark attack were extremely slim. I think the gang I was involved with silenced her to scare me and secure my silence. Perhaps they thought Amy was another loose end that needed to be dealt with. Amy knew nothing about it. I really liked her and I feel terrible about what may have happened.'

Clearly Ted Kramer had no clue that Amy Lightfoot was safe and sound, which was part of the reason Kramer was sitting there now, confessing. He was plainly worried about becoming the next casualty in this sorry set of events.

Risking the ire of her colleagues, Ange jumped in one last time, still not totally convinced that he was an innocent bystander during those last two fateful evenings. 'Why did you get rid of your vehicle?'

Kramer seemed confident with his reply. 'Amy and I had some great times in that van, camping on the beach and travelling to surf spots. After she went missing, the van was a painful reminder of our times together and what may have happened to her. So, I stuck a for sale sign on the window and parked it on the main street. Vans are hot property right now, particularly a 4WD one like mine.

It sold in no time to a couple who were drifting north.'

It had the ring of truth and correlated with their investigations. Looking at her colleagues, Ange realised that this now was as far as she would go in this investigation.

Sensing a pause in proceedings, Simon Phillips took over, clearly having studied the body language of his adversaries. 'My client has recounted the events that occurred in Namba Heads, and I'm sure you realise that his testimony rings true. Before he helps you any further with your narcotics investigation, we need to settle our plea bargain.'

The two Sydney detectives looked at each other, nodded, and then Anders turned to Ange. 'Thanks for your help, Detective. We'll take this matter from here,' she said, dismissing Ange with a perfunctory smile.

The others stayed in the room for hours, finally emerging in the early evening. Jim Grady came over to Ange and Billy, telling him that the case now officially sat with Major Crimes and the task force. Ted Kramer was being transferred immediately to a secure location for further questioning.

The pair would need to assemble all the evidence and pass it over to Major Crimes. Ange was to tie up any local loose ends, but other than that, the case was over as far as the Byron Bay police station was concerned. It was a bitter pill to swallow, but she knew deep down that they would not bring a major narcotics operation down with the limited resources of a provincial police station.

Chapter 47

Loose Ends

The events of the previous day had left Ange feeling unsatisfied. On one hand, she now understood what had happened in Namba Heads over the course of those fateful weeks. On the other, she was left with that terrible unsettling sensation of unfinished business, like forgetting to clean one's teeth before going to bed. The terrible tragedies had been explained, but the actual source of those events remained a mystery. More disturbing was the prospect that the perpetrators still lurked close by. Ange knew she had to put this behind her and get on with her own job, leaving the case to Anders and Ng and the superior resources of the Carcharias task force.

Ange awoke very early Sunday morning, now convinced the Namba Heads chorus had become a subliminal echo that conspired against her sleeping habits. The early-morning surf before the wind freshened helped settle her angst. Even though it was Sunday, Ange knew that the case was causing many people to toss and turn at night. She didn't feel this fair to those affected.

At around 10 a.m., Ange went to the station, ready to tie up the loose ends. First up, she rang Jake Thompson's mother.

'Hello, Mrs Thompson, it's Angela Watson here.'

'Do you have any news about Jake?' came the ever-hopeful reply, as if perhaps the news of his death had been a terrible mistake.

'Our investigation has confirmed that Jake's death was an accident, Mrs Thompson. He appears to have suffered a fatal fall whilst on the trawler, hitting his head in bad weather. I'm truly sorry for your loss,' Ange explained.

'How did his body get from the boat to the bush, and who buried him?' said Mrs Thompson, asking the obvious.

'There's an ongoing investigation as to the death of Dave Fletcher, which I cannot go into. However, we believe that the relocation and burial of Jake's body is connected to the death of Fletcher. I can confirm that Jake has nothing to do with the focus of that investigation and that his death was simply an unfortunate accident.'

Jake's mother paused for a moment, digesting this news before gathering herself to respond. 'I knew Jake was dead, but I somehow hoped for a miracle.'

Ange contemplated their conversation for some time, still upset about this pointless tragedy. Being able to blame someone would have been nice. Even better if they were in police custody. This lack of closure left Ange feeling empty to her core.

Taking another deep breath, she rang Sharon Fletcher. This would be a tricky call, as it posed many more questions, most of which Ange would be unable to answer. As the phone rang, Ange imagined Sharon working away in her little office at the co-op. Once Sharon was on the other end of the call, Ange explained she was now confident that Dave had not committed suicide and had been murdered.

'Why would anyone murder Dave?' Sharon asked, her desperate tone betraying the angst and hurt she felt. Ange knew that this news would be no comfort to Sharon Fletcher, replacing one set of demons with another.

'We believe your husband had become involved with some dangerous people and their illegal activities. I can't go into the specifics of those activities, as they remain part of an ongoing investigation. We hope that the investigation will determine who killed your husband, but I'm now no longer part of those efforts,' explained Ange.

'I presume that this is all linked to the cash Dave used to fix the boat?' asked Sharon.

'It seems as if Dave's financial pressures caused him to become involved with some bad people, Mrs Fletcher, and he paid a terrible price.'

Sharon Fletcher burst into tears, sobbing in waves between her words of reply. 'Things were tough, but we weren't really that badly off. If only he had come to me and discussed his worries, we could have sorted it all out and he would still be here.'

There was nothing Ange could do but say sorry. However, before ending the call, hoping it might provide some cold comfort, Ange told the grieving widow she would be happy to provide a statement confirming that Dave had not committed suicide. Hopefully Sharon and her family might then be eligible for an insurance payout. 'It won't bring back your husband, but the money might help build a new life for you and your family,' Ange said before promising to be in touch should there be any further developments and ending the call.

Amy Lightfoot was her next call, with Ange filling her in on the situation regarding Ted Kramer. Ange felt that Amy at least deserved to know how deep a hole her boyfriend had dug for himself. 'Ted has agreed to cooperate with our investigations. He was involved with some bad people, Amy. The case is now being handled by a Major Crimes unit in Sydney.'

There was a long pause as Amy digested this information. 'Does Teddy know I'm OK?'

'No, Amy, he does not, and it must stay that way. You may even need protection yourself if the case drags on, but you will need to stay low for the foreseeable future. It is essential that Ted thinks you are still missing. I will give your number to Senior Detective Sally Anders, and she will ring you shortly. You need to take her call and follow her instructions. In the meantime, stay out of sight.'

Amy finished by saying, 'Ted isn't a bad guy, which is why I didn't want to report him for domestic violence. He's a bit of a lost soul, living in the shadow of his father without ever having the courage to make his own way in life. At least I have some explanation for his erratic behaviour over the past six months, especially his recent violence and bad temper.'

'Your disappearance, whilst not necessarily the right thing to do, has turned out to be the best thing for your own safety, and probably the investigation as well,' said Ange before hanging up.

The three toughest calls now behind her, she called Terry Scott and filled him in as best she could. Terry pressed her about the details of the ongoing investigation, but Ange ducked and weaved as best she could before going out on a limb and assuring him that Namba Heads was no longer a focus.

'What about the missing woman? If we don't clear up her disappearance, people will think that Namba Heads has been the scene of another shark attack,' demanded Scott.

Ange replied, 'I see no evidence of that, and it seems to have gone through to the keeper. You need to leave this alone, Terry. It's very important that you do as I ask.' Both knew that Terry was not good at leaving things alone, but Ange was satisfied with Terry's begrudging agreement.

Billings was his usual disingenuous and offhanded self. Ange still had misgivings about Sergeant Darren Billings. Whether he was just lazy and disinterested, or antagonistic towards Ange for working his beat, or perhaps he was being cagey and knew more about the events surrounding Namba Heads than he let on—Ange couldn't be sure about any of that.

The ineffectual sergeant would now have to deal with Senior Detective Sally Anders. She was one formidable woman indeed, and Ange secretly dared Billings to check Sally Anders up and down at their first meeting. She smiled at the thought of that prospect.

The last name that Ange needed to cross off her list was Gus Bell. Gus was pleased to hear from her, and grateful to understand what had transpired to take Jake's promising young life. He asked Ange for the contact details of Jake's mother, as he wanted to speak with her personally and tell them how impressed he had been with Jake during their all-too-short relationship.

Ange looked over her desk, suddenly exhausted. She and Billy could start getting the evidence together for Anders and Ng on Monday. All her energy evaporated, and she felt flattened out. Not only was her case in the hands of someone else, but these insidious criminals had poisoned Namba Heads. Two normal everyday people were dead, one was in hiding, and even more had had their lives upended. It was depressing. A nice slow walk and a swim were in order.

As she picked her way along the eroded beach, her towel draped over her shoulder, looking for a safe place to swim, the analogy of her case and what had happened to the beach struck home. Namba Heads was now safe, for the moment at least, but the drugs would find their way somewhere else. Perhaps another small village nearby would soon find itself ripped apart. Ange might have helped stem the flow of drugs in one direction, but like the sand, it would all inevitably turn up elsewhere. This was an even more depressing thought, one that even a swim in her beloved ocean failed to wash away.

Chapter 48

Goodbyes

The Byron Bay juggernaut marched on. Ange was soon immersed in several cases, mostly minor and certainly nothing so all-consuming. Almost three weeks had passed since Major Crimes had breezed into town and she was struggling to remain motivated.

It had shocked Ange how narcotics traffickers could so easily upset the balance of such an idyllic coastal village like Namba Heads. Despite this tragic backdrop, being involved in such a complex case had proven far more intoxicating than she could even have imagined, providing confidence that she was capable of solving complex, high-stakes cases. The syndicate behind the Namba Heads' operation was a formidable adversary, and Ange wasn't sure she would ever be happy with her regular mundane caseload. In short, she was in a funk.

The Joe Kramer Show kept on playing. He wasted no time in convening a town-hall meeting focussed on the negative community impacts of development. Covid-19 had presented a boon for regional housing, but equally so for sensationalism and peddlers of conspiracy theories. He was proving to be a remarkable survivor and the fact that his son was in custody had seemingly not dampened his activist spirit.

Brett Tompkins hadn't bothered to call her. Ange was no shrinking violet, but she wasn't about to pick up the phone and ask him out on a date, especially after she had all but called him a criminal.

One morning, Jake Thompson's mother rang, asking for her help. 'When will you release Jake's body? I'm eager to give my son a proper burial, surrounded by his family and friends. It's terrible that we haven't been able to properly say goodbye.'

This revelation blew away Ange. 'Leave it with me, Mrs Thompson.,' she said sharply.

Ange immediately went to see Jim Grady. 'Boss. I just had a call from Jake Thompson's mother. We still haven't released his body. What the heck? That's just plain cruel. Someone needs to sort this out. How well do you know Senior Detective Anders?' she demanded.

'Reasonably well,' said Grady ambiguously. 'Leave it with me.'

He came back to Ange before the end of the day. 'Tell Jake's mother that someone will contact her shortly and arrange for the release of her son's body. Like you, I simply cannot believe this sort of thing happens. The boy was only ever an innocent bystander and Major Crimes had no reason to act like that,' raged Grady. 'I convinced them to contribute towards his funeral expenses.'

'Thank you, boss. I'm very grateful for your help,' Ange replied.

Jake's mother was also truly grateful. Ange knew Jake's funeral would be a great outpouring of grief, an important marker for family and friends.

One day, out of the blue, Ange took a call from Gus Bell. 'Hello, Detective, I hope that you're well. I'm having a small function at our shop in Byron Bay that I would like you to attend. Friday week at six p.m. I really hope you can make it.'

'Sure. Sounds interesting. It will give me an excuse to drool over some of your boards,' replied Ange enthusiastically, relishing the prospect of some release from her long stretch in the doldrums.

'I understand from Jake's mother that you helped with Jake's funeral. She really appreciated your help. That was good of you.'

'It was the least I could do under the circumstances. It was cruel not being able to properly say goodbye to her son. I sometimes think my big-city colleagues think everyone outside Sydney is a second-class citizen,' replied Ange, still smarting over the way Major Crimes had commandeered Jake and her case.

'OK, then,' said Gus, seeming unsure of where to go with that last comment. 'I guess that's even more reason for you to attend our function,' he concluded, leaving Ange with no option but to accept, intrigued by what he had meant by that last statement. She neglected to tell Gus Bell that she had been worried he might have been grooming Jake Thompson, figuring that thought was best kept a secret.

Lacking motivation at work, Ange decided to visit Namba Heads over the coming weekend. She desperately needed to get out of town and take a break from her uninspiring cases. She called Terry Scott to check that all was well in Namba Heads ahead of her visit.

'Why don't you pop down and catch up for dinner sometime?' asked Terry

'Sounds great, Terry. I'm making a weekend of it. How does next Saturday work for you?'

Terry was true to form and his decisive best. 'Done. I'll let Jenny know. See you at seven p.m. unless we speak beforehand.'

She left Byron at first light on Saturday morning and drove directly to the car park at Bushies Beach. As she drove through Namba Heads, images of her investigation came flooding into her consciousness.

She passed by Jimmy's Chinese takeaway, which had proven so crucial in breaking the case. She then drove over the bridge and imagined the two thugs on their way to murder Dave Fletcher. She swung by the marina, the scene of Fletcher's murder. Then came the fisheries co-op, where Ange pictured a still-grieving Sharon Fletcher toiling away to prepare for the Saturday crowds. The road to Bushies Beach took her past the location where Jake Thompson's body had been crudely buried, ruthlessly cast away and hidden amongst the thick coastal scrub. By the time she had arrived at Bushies Beach car park, her brain was in a state of fibrillation. So many of the questions that accompanied these thoughts remained unanswered.

On autopilot, Ange stuffed her gear into a backpack and carried her surfboard down onto the beach, her midsize board, the one she found best suited Sliders. The day before her was sparkling and nature had turned on its very best. The sea was the deepest of greens, and a light south-westerly breeze was moving over the ocean, rippled in places and glassed off in others. In the distance, over towards Sliders, Ange could see a pod of dolphins wallowing around, playing, or feeding, or both perhaps.

As she paddled out at Sliders, she scanned the crew in the water, looking for Brett Tompkins. She still felt uneasy about how their interview at the station had left things between them. Sliders was where they had first properly connected, precipitating their dalliance, or romance, or whatever it was they had experienced. One thing was certain: there had been some powerful chemistry between them. He was nowhere to be seen.

With all this going on, it was no wonder her surf was more one of reflection than one of epic rides. As always, the ocean and the waves helped bring rhythm and order to these swirling emotions.

After her surf, Ange drove back across the river to check in at her favourite caravan park. She prepared to have a cruisy day, breakfast at her favourite coffee shop, a walk through the Saturday markets, perhaps pick up some prawns from the fisheries co-op to be enjoyed on the riverbank under the majestic Norfolk pines. A recuperative afternoon nap to prepare for dinner with Terry and Jenny Scott was a must.

The manager greeted her warmly and told Ange that he had upgraded her to one of the waterfront cabins.

'Have you seen Brett Tompkins around?' she asked, as casually as she could.

The manager looked at her sideways. 'No, I haven't seen him around for a while. But I am curious that you ask. Brett seems lucky with attractive women.'

'What do you mean by that?' Ange countered sharply, thinking the manager was referring to her thrilling late-night liaison. She was still smarting about how she had potentially compromised her investigation.

'Well, Brett rented a cabin for a while when he first came to town. He occasionally took one from time to time after he moved into his own place, apparently for visiting family and friends, since he didn't have enough room in his apartment. I caught him with that woman who went missing some time back. I reckon they were having a fling,' the manager explained.

He saw a look flash across Ange's face. 'I guess I should have mentioned that fact earlier. It only just occurred to me,' he quickly elaborated. 'What happened to her, anyway?'

Trying vainly to keep an air of ambivalence and distance herself from this conversation, Ange replied as casually as she could. 'Not sure. It's not my problem anymore.' Her indignant tone was a telling insight that this news was a weekend spoiler.

Chapter 49

A Foundation

Ange fumed over Brett Tompkins for days, his apparent duplicity preventing her from completely letting go of him or the case. This wasn't so much about his alleged affair with Amy Lightfoot, but more that he had failed to even mention that he knew her, despite being aware of Ange's investigations. This intimated that he might somehow be involved with the criminal network, and even his involvement with Joe Kramer now seemed less innocuous.

Unable to let sleeping dogs lie, Ange had searched on the council website to find that they had approved his development application, also finding that NH Projects Pty Ltd had been sold, along with the project. It seemed as if Brett had simply pulled up stumps and vanished.

'What is it with me and men?' she thought. Ange constantly asked herself whether it was her job that kept getting in the way? Was it just a run of bad luck, or was she just a total basket case and a terrible judge of character? She wasn't naïve—her dalliance with Brett was just a one-night affair after all, not the first for Ange. However, her few days with him had promised something more, at least in her eyes. Ange didn't like the feeling of being duped, disappointed at her inability to see beyond his facade. 'At least the sex was good,' she reasoned, trying to find a silver lining amongst her latest failure.

It was easy to blame the job, but she knew this was something she would need to work out. Ange didn't want to end up a bitter old woman with no one around to love and be loved by. She saw lots of people in Byron Bay who were fresh from their first, second, or even third divorce. It seemed like a tough way to live, constantly chasing that first blush of love but never finding the fulfillment and happiness of a true lifelong companion.

'It's lucky that I have my friends and surfing to keep me sane,' Ange concluded as she lay awake at night. She was constantly tormented by the doubts and fears that lay beneath the stimulations of her day, pondering the rollercoaster that was her life. Communing with nature to surf somehow seemed to smooth out some bumps and lumps, although she knew deep down that she was always taking in this arrangement. Humankind had made this habitual, always taking from Mother Nature, even when she was exhausted and spent.

Whilst Ange's tossing and turning refused to provide any worthwhile answers, she realised that tending to those valued relationships must remain her responsibility, ensuring their equilibrium endured. This was something easier said than done. In the end, whether human or not, life was all about one's relationships, the strength of which carried you through the highs and lows, their balance requiring constant care and attention.

Anyhow, life goes on, and there was always plenty of work to keep her occupied, as unfulfilling as this was in her current frame of mind. It hadn't helped her depressive state to learn that Walton had deftly sidestepped the case of the woman and her bitchy lawn, and that the matter had landed back on her plate again. It proved to be a more troublesome case than first thought, as the woman had cultivated an extensive list of suspects. Ange finally exposed the criminal mastermind to be a neighbouring boy who the woman had berated mercilessly for years. The woman wanted to press charges but reluctantly backed down when Ange suggested the boy had a strong case for pressing harassment charges. It hadn't stopped her whining to Ange about 'what the world is coming to', 'lax sentencing rules', and 'ineffective police', to name but a few of her observations on life. In the end, Ange figured the boy had spelt her middle name perfectly.

It was hardly a case of life and death.

She was late arriving at the Bell Surfboards function, something she hated doing. By the time she entered, the Friday night crowd was noisy, the shop full of people talking and enjoying themselves. Spring was in full flight, and Byron was bursting at the seams with people eager to flee the cities and their eight months' worth of lockdowns and restrictions. Ange saw Joy Thompson off to the side. Never knowing quite how to handle these situations, having been the bearer of such tragic news, Ange was pleased when she came over to say hello. Joy introduced Ange to the Andersons. 'Jake's number one surfing buddy, Henry, and his father, David.'

'We really appreciated your efforts in finding out what had happened,' said David Anderson.

'We all miss Jake,' added Henry, still clearly hurting after losing his best mate.

Gus Bell had seen Ange walk in and gave her a warm welcome. He had a knowing smile on his face, pleased about some secret or another.

'Oh, and by the way, thanks for convincing us to stock those longboard wheels. I understand you pestered the guys at the counter to source a couple for you. They've been flying out the door since your friend Kerrie posted a picture of herself with one strapped to a Bell surfboard. On top of this Covid-induced surfing revival, we can't keep up with orders,' said Gus with the satisfied smile of a happy business owner.

'I'm pleased,' replied Ange. She had given a set of the wheels as a present to Kerrie, who of course had two Bell surfboards. Kerrie had a knack for riding the wave of popularity, so Ange was not at all surprised that she had caught this one.

'Let's catch up for coffee soon,' Gus said before he walked away to attend to his other guests. Ange was definitely up for coffee with Gus Bell, one where she wasn't worried that he was a molester of young boys.

Ange had invited Billy to accompany her, and she was sure he would already be there. Since the case in Namba Heads, they had established a terrific working relationship. Ange liked Billy and found him good company. She delighted in his ability to find wonder and humour in everyday events. She figured they would develop into a formidable team.

As she scanned the crowd looking for Billy, she could see that the room was filled with Byron Bay glitterati. Actors, artists, sportspeople, surfers, business and community leaders. Everyone who was anyone in Byron Bay was there, such was the pull of the iconic Bell brand. She spied her friend Kerrie in the thick of the action and squarely in her element. The room buzzed with energy.

Gus needed to work hard to quieten the room, finally gaining everyone's attention. 'Thanks everyone for coming to our small ceremony. We are here to honour the all-too-short life of a most talented surfer, Jake Thompson.' He beckoned to Jake's mother to join him.

'Jake was one of the most startling surfing talents I had ever come across. It was just blind luck that I ever got to witness his brilliance. Not only does his family feel his loss, but we all lost a talented and promising surfer from our fold. My dad and I decided to do something positive to support gifted young regional surfers like Jake. So, we partnered with some local artists and combined with the art of my dad, Bobby Bell, I am pleased to unveil our latest surfboard, the JayTee, based on Jake's favourite design.'

With that, Gus pulled down a veil to reveal four magnificent surfboards, each a work of art from every perspective.

'Tonight, we have four very special JayTee design surfboards to share with you. Bobby Bell has shaped and signed each board, and each mural is an original work by one of the local artists here tonight. We're going to auction these unique surfboards later in the evening once you've all admired them sufficiently. All funds raised tonight will support the Bell JayTee Foundation.

'For those of you who cannot afford a new board but would still like to help the foundation, we've produced some limited-edition tee shirts based on the surfboard designs. You'll also notice that the tee shirts reintroduce the original Bell logo from the 1970s. Everything old is cool again, and we may bring back the logo permanently subject to what you guys think. Personally, I think it's beyond cool, but then I'm biased. Anyhow, by supporting us tonight, you'll not only help develop new regional surfing stars, but you will also support our talented local artists.'

With that, Gus handed over to his father, who mesmerised the audience with his surf stories and memories of a life spent in the ocean. Jake's mother was positively beaming, seeing their son honoured in this way. David Anderson purchased one of the limited JayTee boards, which seemed a lovely way to remember Jake. This proved a very emotional moment for Joy Thompson, realising the depth of affection that the Andersons held for her son.

Ange was the first to buy one of the tee shirts and prevailed upon Bobby Bell to sign hers. She loved the retro Bell logo and insisted that Bobby sign underneath the motif. The auction was a massive success. At the end of the proceedings, Gus proudly announced that they had raised over twenty-two thousand dollars for the JayTee Foundation.

Looking around her, feeling the buzz and sense of hope in the room, Ange reflected it was indeed 'an ill wind that blows no good'.

Content with her own role, she finally weaved her way over to a somewhat star-struck Billy, looking forward to the rest of the evening.

Chapter 50

A Surprise Visit

Rising early on her Saturday morning off, Ange found the surf wasn't happening, which was a disappointing follow-up to such a wonderful evening of surfboards, surf stories, and anticipation of surf experiences to come.

It was still early when she drove up to Bangalow, intending to wander around the farmers' market and purchase her weekly fresh produce needs. Also, Kerrie's birthday was coming up and the markets would be a good place to pick up a small gift, although finding something unique for Kerrie was a total nightmare.

A vibrant market circuit operated around Byron Bay, where the different markets would rotate around the various coastal and hinterland towns. Lisa, a close friend of hers, had a superb cake stall and relied on the markets to sell her delicious wares. Hers was the type of stall that made coming to the markets worthwhile, since her amazing creations were unavailable in normal bakeries or shops.

Lisa's stand was always busy, and Ange looked forward to stopping off and giving Lisa a 'coffee and comfort break', a 'loo and latte layover'—one easily gets the drift of where these little word games strayed, not above toilet humour as they both were.

Ange was buying some plump red tomatoes at one of the many fruit and vegetable stands when she glimpsed Darren Billings in the distance. He was lurking in the service alley between the stalls and speaking with two heavily built and intimidating characters. Their conversation didn't appear to be focussed on the quality of the lychees; they were clearly engaged in a heated disagreement.

As soon as she made a move to amble discreetly in their direction, a firm hand grabbed her arm from behind.

'I think you had best come with me, Detective,' said the deep confident voice.

The man deftly revealed his police badge before leading Ange away from Billings and his dangerous-looking mates. They turned into a little alley between stalls to find a waiting Senior Detective Sally Anders.

'Hello, Detective Watson,' said a smiling Sally Anders. 'Fancy seeing you here. Business or pleasure?'

'Definitely pleasure, my weekly grocery shop—plus to help my friend out on her cake stand and give her a break,' Ange replied, somewhat warily.

'That's good, then,' replied Anders.

'What is going on here?' Ange asked pointedly, never one to be backward in coming forward.

Anders pondered this question for a moment before explaining. 'I must insist on your confidentiality on this, Detective Watson. We are now quite sure that those two thugs you saw speaking to Sergeant Billings killed Dave Fletcher and buried Jake Thompson's body in the bush. We have them on video footage taken from the Chinese takeaway.'

'Do you have Billings working for you?' exclaimed an incredulous Ange, her disappointment obvious that Billings might have been chosen over her to progress the case.

'God, no!' replied Anders smartly. 'That man is a moron. Believe me, I know, having been subjected to transcripts of his texts and phone conversations. Billings has been on the take—basically turning a blind eye and running interference. He also had a hand in ensuring Dave Fletcher's death was recorded as a suicide. It's not surprising that he was no fan of yours, prodding and poking around in his patch as you did.'

'I can assure you that the feeling is mutual,' interrupted Ange, accentuating her general distaste of the man. Secretly pleased that her misgivings about Billings had been well founded, she mused that Flathead might well have been a preferred name over Operation Carcharias, knowing that the likes of Billings were involved.

Anders explained the source of their case against Billings. 'A sports betting agency reported Billings. Otherwise, he might well have gotten away with his involvement. He has a gambling problem, and they're obliged to report anyone engaged in gambling activity that seems at odds with their occupation and source of cash. His name came our way because he was logged against the case file. We're also suspicious that there are people in the gambling agencies who feed the names of any police officers and other officials who suffer big losses to organised crime—but that's another matter.'

'We believe Billings was recruited to monitor things in Namba Heads. Some-one cleared a substantial gambling debt that he had accumulated, and he also appears to have been paid a regular trickle of cash, a retainer of sorts. Based on his gambling activities, this flow of cash seems to have increased markedly once you turned up. The investigation is still underway, and we will not let these characters out of our sight now. Hopefully, they will lead us further up the chain of command before we need to bring them in. We really want to turn the tap off at the source and not be tempted by the drips and dribbles—like these guys.'

Anders let this sink in, hopeful that her summary would provide some closure. 'You need to leave this with us, Detective,' she stated firmly, making her best efforts to stare down any potential resistance from Ange. 'I am sorry about that mess with Jake Thompson's body and his mother. My colleagues can be insensitive at times.'

This admission failed to mollify Ange. 'Did you know that Brett Tompkins and Amy Lightfoot were having an affair?' she asked defiantly, as if hoping that superior intel might cut her into the inner circle.

'You don't need to worry about that, or Brett Tompkins for that matter, Detective,' Anders quickly remonstrated before softening her gaze to explain. 'Brett Tompkins is not a criminal and is definitely not involved in anything illegal. I cannot say anything more, but there is nothing you should be concerned about there.'

Holding firm with Ange's perplexed gaze, Anders sought to conclude their discussion. 'Are we good, Detective?'

Ange paused, giving as good as she was taking in the staring department, thinking through the implications of what Anders had told her, mindful of her identical request of Terry Scott to respect her own assurances.

Before she could reply, Anders showed a rare glimpse of the person beneath. 'We're all very impressed with the work you did on this case, Detective. I cannot tell you how valuable your efforts have proven to be.'

Sizing up Anders one last time, as susceptible to flattery as the next person, Ange replied, 'Yes, we're good. Maybe we'll meet again sometime, but I'll leave this to you guys.'

Ange would never have made any glib commitment like that had she known what was about to happen.

Read GlitterStrip – Book Two
of The Saltwater Crimes Trilogy

Follow Ange as she picks up the trail and pursues the criminal syndicate behind the tragedies in Namba Heads.

Scan or click here to purchase Glitterstrip through Amazon:
https://www.pg-robertson.com/glitterstrip

Scan or click here to join the author's mailing list and stay alert to new releases and hear the latest news:
www.pg-robertson.com

facebook.com/profile.php?id=61570934517294

instagram.com/petergrobertson/

amazon.com/stores/P-G-Robertson/author/B0BY4B55VP?ref=ap_rdr&store_re f=ap_rdr&isDramIntegrated=true&shoppingPortalEnabled=true

Now read the beginning of GlitterStrip...

It was a beautiful place—if that was your thing. The dusty crushed-granite road wound its way between large eucalypt trees that stretched across the road. It was approaching midday, and the shadows cast by the trees made it difficult to spot the worst of the relentless corrugations. The car vainly ducked and weaved before it shuddered to a sudden stop.

The two men had driven from Sydney and it was almost disturbing, the quiet that greeted them as they exited their car—depressing, even. As soon as the dust settled, a squadron of flies descended, seemingly onto them in an instant, vying to enter every available orifice. A more desperate and godforsaken place the men had never visited.

One of the men looked down at his phone before speaking. 'This is the spot—according to the GPS coordinates we've been given. I wish we knew what we're looking for.' The loose plan, it seemed, going by the hand gestures, was best summarised as 'you look over that way and I'll look over this way'. This was a solid plan, considering the broad nature of the job they were tasked with.

Less than ten minutes had passed before one of them shouted out that he had found something. 'Bring the shovel,' he yelled to his mate, signalling that digging was involved, although who would do the digging was not clear. The tone of the man doing the yelling inferred that this would not be him, seeing as he'd done the finding.

It wasn't as big a job as feared. The digging man didn't want to get all sweaty. It was hot, being the middle of the day, even though summer was some way away. There had been no rain for months now and the soil was dry and dusty. He only needed to make a few digs before he hit something solid. 'It could be anything,' said the man holding the shovel before he carefully scraped away some of the loosely packed soil. Finding some purchase, he pressed down on the handle and levered up what he'd found.

It's quite a good preserver; dry, dusty soil in the bush. The tattooed arm that emerged from the ground was in remarkably good shape, all things considered. Male, most likely. The two men looked at each other, not particularly surprised by this development. This was part of the job, after all.

The man with the shovel scraped back the disturbed soil and returned the ground to normal—if by normal you meant ground that had an unnamed body buried in it. The man not wielding a shovel pulled out his mobile phone, pleased to find that he had mobile reception. There weren't many places so godforsaken that one couldn't make a phone call.

'It's me. It's a body. Looks male to me. You'd better get a team out to do it properly.'

Which was a rather offhanded way of saying that this was now a murder site.

 If you would like to continue reading Glitterstrip, scan the QR code or visit □

www.pg-robertson.com/glitterstrip

Author's Note

The characters in this book are entirely fictional. I have created them from good friends, acquaintances, strangers I've encountered, some people that I've met in the surf, and others that are purely imaginary. Even though the storyline is purely fictional, personal experiences and events have influenced many of the situations and ideas that support the plot. Likewise, except for any household names, the companies and enterprises that underpin the plot are figments of my imagination and similarly fictitious.

My heroine, Detective Ange Watson, is a mixture of friends, some who surf and some who do not. I hope you like Ange as much as I like my friends.

Namba Heads is an imaginary town that is based on the many small coastal villages of the Northern Rivers region in New South Wales, Australia. The major towns and centres referred to in the book are real, however, and my story contains surf spots that are both real and imagined. I hope my writing does justice to this spectacular part of Australia.

The story is set on the traditional lands of the Bundjalung people, which extend from Yamba in northern New South Wales up into southern Queensland, a region much loved by most Australians. I acknowledge the Bundjalung people, who are the traditional custodians of this magnificent place, and pay respects to the Elders, past, present and emerging of the Bundjalung Nation.

So Many To Thank

Firstly, let me thank you, the reader, for making it this far. That you have persevered to read my book is incredibly gratifying. I trust you enjoyed yourself.

Of utmost importance, is the need to thank all those who have helped me get to this point with my writing. Your generosity in investing precious time to read my early stumbling, error-ridden drafts is humbling, and your honest feedback has been invaluable. Even though you may not have realised it, you gifted me the confidence to push on and put myself out there. I probably should list you all individually, but the list is long and I risk missing someone important! Hopefully, I have already told you in person how much your input has meant to me. I cannot thank you all enough.

The Island Book Club deserves a special mention. I will forever remember the scene of our inaugural book club meeting, sitting on the beach in our camp chairs one glorious afternoon, champagne in hand and laughter in our hearts.

I am also grateful for my 'media team', Annabel Robertson, Sophie Robertson, and Ben Hall, whose skills and comfort with new media amaze me. I must also thank my editor, Eliza Dee, and my cover designer, Karri Klawiter, for their dedication and forbearance in enduring my many rookie errors.

Finally, if you have a spare minute, I would appreciate you posting a review of Tombstoning on Amazon, either by scanning this QR Code or via your purchase history.

Surfing Terminology

A brief description of some of the surfing terminology that I have used throughout The Saltwater Crimes series follows:

'**Tombstoning**' occurs when a surfer is held under the water by a wave following a heavy wipeout. Whilst the surfer is being dragged deep beneath the water, their surfboard is straining on the surface, connected as they are by a fully stretched leg rope. An obvious metaphor for a perilous situation, tombstoning is never a good sign and rarely fun for the surfer, although bystanders or fellow surfers will invariably find it all most amusing after the fact.

A '**left-hander**' is a wave that breaks to the surfer's left. That is, as the surfer catches the wave, he or she will turn to the left. Obviously, a '**right-hander**' breaks to the surfer's right.

A '**goofy-footer**' is someone who surfs with the right foot forward, and a '**natural**' is someone who leads with their left foot. The decision to choose one side or another is instinctual and set for life.

Surfing '**forehand**' indicates that a surfer is facing the wave face, '**backhand**' is the reverse. Most surfers find surfing forehand easier, particularly in steep demanding waves. Hence, a 'right-hander' favours a 'natural', and a 'left-hander' best suits their 'goofy-footed' cousins.

The '**line-up**' is the term used for the queuing area where the waves start breaking.

The '**peak**' of a wave is a term commonly used for beach breaks. It defines the apex of the wave face. Once perfectly positioned at the 'peak' of a wave, a surfer can choose to go left or right. The other descriptor for perfect beach breaks is 'A-frames', but these dreamy situations are disappointingly rare.

A '**rip**' is where seawater, carried in by the crashing waves, combines into a channel and rushes back out to sea. Dangerous for swimmers, they can be a godsend for surfers to help ease a long and tiring paddle.

Being '**inside**' means the surfer is the one closest to the breaking point of the wave, which is the surfer who is farthest inside on the line-up. On a headland or reef break, this would be closest to the rocks or reef, and inevitably the most ambitious take-off point. The surfer sitting farthest 'inside' technically has a right of way, a case of fortune favouring the brave. It does not always work that way, wi th **'drop-ins'** being the scourge of surfers around the world, usually spoiling the wave and often dangerous to all concerned.

Jostling for the premier position at the take-off zone is part strategy, part bravado, and part aggression. Called **'hassling'**, this can easily spiral out of control, and fights in and out of the surf are not uncommon in crowded surf breaks, and where localism is rife. **'Dropping in'** on an aggressive local will usually end badly. The old way to surf was to take turns. As the 'inside' surfer departed on their wave, the next would slide across and assume the vacated spot in the line-up, gaining rights to the next wave, and so on. This type of surf etiquette is now relegated to isolated or sparsely populated breaks.

A **'grommet'** is surfer slang for a young school-aged surfer, a term usually reserved for those with talent, their lightness, speed, and flexibility sometimes grating on the older surfers around them.

The **'rail'** on a surfboard is the outside edge, the shape and taper of which are critical in how a board performs.

The **'rocker'** of a surfboard describes how the nose turns up. Boards made with a pronounced rocker are more forgiving when tackling powerful, steep waves. Boards fashioned with minimal rocker make catching smaller and fuller waves easier, but are prone to nosedives during steep or late take-offs—but this might be my age talking.

'Longboards' and **'shortboards'** create quite different surfing styles and favour different wave formations. Longboards typically range from eight to eleven feet, or 2.5 to 3.3 metres. Shortboards are under seven feet, or 2.1 metres. The weight of a surfer will often dictate the type of board they choose, and the division between a longboard and a shortboard has blurred over time.

The number of fins on a board varies depending on the style of board. **'Single fins'** are mostly reserved for longboards or surfers wanting a traditional style. The original surfboards were all single fins. **'Twin fins'** are highly manoeuvrable, usually earmarked for small wave boards. A **'thruster'** sports three fins and is the most popular and versatile configuration for shortboards. **'Quads'** have four fins and sit somewhere between a twin fin and a thruster in terms of functionality.

A **'quiver'** is simply a collection of surfboards used by a surfer, as in a 'quiver of arrows' used by an archer.

Finally, a **'tube ride'** is when the surfer positions themselves within the curl of the wave, precariously covered over by the breaking lip, but remaining relatively untouched within the eye of the storm—so to speak. It's the most exhilarating of all surf manoeuvres, and waves that are 'tubing' are highly prized, yet relatively rare. Surf spots that regularly produce tube rides are usually very popular, difficult to travel to, or jealously guarded secrets.

Australian-isms

For the benefit of non-Australian readers, below is a short explanation of some idioms that I have used on occasion.

'Back of Woop Woop'. Far away from everywhere and anywhere. Beyond the black stump is another synonym.

'Bad egg'. Someone who is rotten to the core.

'Berko'. Going crazy mad, angry and out of control. The Tasmanian devil goes berko if cornered while eating their dinner.

'Buggered, stuffed, screwed, rooted'—you get the drift.

'Bushie'. Someone who lives in the country, most commonly on a rural farm/property/station, and well away from any major towns or cities. In general terms, one's degree of 'bushie-ness' is also directly proportional to the distance one lives from the coast.

'Curly request or question'. Refers to a difficult request or loaded question.

'Deckie'. A shortened name given to the deckhand working on a fishing trawler.

'Feeling crook'. Feeling sick or unwell.

'Firey'. Slang for firefighter.

'Larrikin'. Part rogue, part joker. The sort of person to enjoy a beer at the pub with, but not someone to risk with the family jewels. Larrikin is often used to describe the affable kookaburra, one of the coolest and most personable birds in Australia, also a ruthless killer of small birds and animals.

'Nong'. An idiot or fool, a term used endearingly and in jest toward a friend or loved one.

'A park'. A park can refer to either a park with grass and trees, or a single parking place for a car. Go figure!

'Roached'. Has its roots from the word cockroach. Being roached normally refers to the situation where someone has scuttled behind your back to do no good.

'Rort'. Another word for scam or con.

'Seachange & Greenchange'. Seachangers leave their lives in the city and move to the coast. Greenchangers move to the country.

'Spit the dummy'. A dummy, in Australian vernacular, is also known as a pacifier. When a baby is about to throw a tantrum, their face with turn sour, before they spit out their dummy and go berko. It's a wonderfully descriptive phrase—part facial expression, part change of mood, part warning for the carnage about to be unleashed.

'Stunned mullet'. Refers to someone who is in a form of temporary shock. An actual stunned mullet will be floating helplessly on the surface and unable to swim away.